On St. Nick's Trail

The Talking Dog Detective Agency

M K Scott

Cozy Mysteries by M K Scott

The Talking Dog Detective Agency
Canine Cozy Mysteries

A Bark in the Night

Requiem for a Rescue Dog Queen

Bark Twice for Danger

The Ghostly Howl

Dog Park Romeo

On St. Nick's Trail

The Painted Lady Inn Mysteries Series
Culinary Cozy Mysteries

Murder Mansion

Drop Dead Handsome

Killer Review

Christmas Calamity

Death Pledges a Sorority

Caribbean Catastrophe

Weddings Can be Murder

The Skeleton Wore Diamonds

Death of a Honeymoon

Cakewalk to Murder

Sailor Take Warning

The Way Over the Hill Gang Series
Senior Sleuths Cozy Mysteries

Late for Dinner

Late for Bingo

Late for Shuffleboard

Late for Square Dancing

Late for Love 12/20

On St. Nick's Trail

M K Scott

Copyright © 2020

Print Edition

All characters in this book are fictional and figments of
the author's imagination.

Author Notes

Even though **On St. Nick's Trail** is a fictional book, its setting, Santa Claus, Indiana, is a real place. I chose Santa Claus because of many happy memories of childhood vacations in this area. The charming stores, restaurants, post office, and campground are real. I did take some liberties with people, places, and names. Feel free to check it out on santaclaus.org.

Make sure to check out the recipes at the end if the story, too.

I hope reading **On St. Nick's Trail** creates happy memories for you.

If you enjoy this series, make sure to sign up for the newsletter at morgankwyatt.com to find out about upcoming contests, new releases, and early read opportunities.

M K Scott

Chapter One

C OOL AIR STREAMED into the car from the small opening at the top of the window. Nala regretted not putting on a jacket before she left to meet her friend, Karly, at a nearby outdoor restaurant. Normally, she'd prefer to eat inside, but Max, her oversized, black German Shepherd mix, often made dining and travel problematic. An outside table was the only way the three of them could meet. Maybe she didn't have to take her dog everywhere, but she did anyway. It felt right, especially because he was her business partner, too.

The cactus-shaped restaurant sign sprouted from the ground like an overgrown weed. She turned on her blinker and slowed for the turn. Her dog shot her a look, saying, "Hope they have cheese-burgers."

She sighed. With Max, it was always about food, preferably cheeseburgers. She read something about German Shepherds having sensitive stomachs. Despite that tendency, her dog pretty much ate everything and suffered the side effects. While most people would be shocked by their pooch vocalizing in English, after about a month of Max nattering on about just everything, she accepted it, along with his story that he'd been enchanted by the girlfriend of his original owner. It must have been like those drive-in movies where a spell goes wrong. This time no zombies were storming the mall. Instead, there was a talking dog which, unfortunately, most humans didn't relish. Thank goodness, Karly, who worked at the shelter, picked her out for Max. It might have been helpful if her friend had mentioned Max could talk, but she figured it out once she quit doubting her sanity.

The car bumped into the half-filled parking lot, making it easy to spot Karly's vintage station wagon covered with pawprint stickers and reminders to spay and neuter your pet. No one would guess she was a shelter employee.

Once she switched the engine off, Max gave her an inquiring look. Right. She never answered his question. Elephants were reported as never forgetting, but she'd put Max up against them anytime. "It's a Mexican food restaurant. I did notice they have cheeseburgers on the children's menu."

"Sounds small," Max complained and contorted his face into a pleading expression, complete with liquid brown eyes.

"Stop that. I'll get you two."

"Still sounds small."

"Keep that up and you'll get nothing. You know cash is tight. I can't be buying you endless cheeseburgers with neither of us working right now. We can only live on the previous cases for so long. We're here because Karly has potential work for us."

Max's ears perked up as his tongue lolled out in a doggy grin. "She'll buy me another of those extra small cheeseburgers. You'd think she could have told you about the case on the phone."

He was right. You'd think someone who worked with animals every day would be onto their various manipulations, but Karly turned to putty when it came to the cats and dogs. It made her passionate to get them all placed in good homes. Max did have a point about the possible case. It meant it was unusual. Hopefully, it wouldn't involve hunting down a miscreant who was stealing cats.

"Let's go see."

She swung open the driver door, still amazed how heavy and large it was. Her ancient Volkswagen Beetle had been replaced by her parents' not-so-old Crown Victoria, which happened to be outfitted with a police scanner and a two-way radio due to her father being a police captain.

"Nala! Max! Over here." Karly waved from underneath a black table umbrella imprinted with the name of a popular tequila.

Nala held the car door wide for Max to exit before closing and locking it. They strolled to where the iron fence surrounded a couple of tables and let themselves in. Max immediately went to the water bowl filled with water. After lapping up a little water and splashing out much more, he settled underneath the table. Typical.

"What's up?" Nala slid into the wrought iron chair and picked up a menu, scanning it for the cheapest item.

"Glad you asked." Karly gave a short nod, causing her wayward curls to bounce. "I got a call from my Great Aunt Selma."

"Oh." Nala felt one word was a safe comment since she didn't know Aunt Selma. What she did know was Karly had a truckload of relatives, and, from the various stories her friend spun, they probably had their photo in the dictionary next to the *quirky* definition.

A waitress attired in a polyester peasant blouse and colorful skirt exited the building carrying salsa and chips. She placed them on the table and asked, "What can I get you?"

"Water is fine for me," Nala assured her, while mentally doing the math and including a tip. "I'll have the three-taco special plus two cheeseburger kid meals."

The waitress arched her eyebrows while penciling the order on her pad. Karly cleared her throat and pointed to herself. "Give me the bill. I'd like the enchilada platter and an iced tea."

"You got it." The server turned and left without another word.

Before she could inquire about the nature of the case, Max spoke. "Did you see that? She didn't even look at me. Didn't say a word about what a handsome dog or what can I get your dog. Nothing. She probably didn't even know I was here."

"It might be better that way," Nala reminded her pooch and nudged him with the tip of her shoe. "As hard as it may be to believe, not everyone is cool with dogs hanging out at restaurants. Keep it low key." She turned her attention to her smirking friend. "Does your Aunt Selma have a new beau she needs to check on?"

Most of her private eye practice had devolved to date checks, which she could usually do from the comfort of her office. It was boring. Not exactly what she expected to be doing when she chose to become a private eye. Her sometime partner and office mate, Sawyer, would throw some insurance work her way, but since he'd left for another mysterious trip, even that had dried up. She could use another quick hundred fifty bucks, although Selma might expect a friends and family discount, which would knock off twenty-five.

"No," Karly tittered and reached for the chip basket. Chip in hand, she dipped it into the salsa and held it at chin level as she replied. "Great Uncle Bob wouldn't look kindly on that. Her town is in trouble, and only you can save it."

Saving a town sounded important. Would she and Max be able

to do it? "I can use that for my resume. Town saver." The idea made her smirk, then sigh. "Right now, I need a good reason to stay a private eye. It hasn't been exactly what I'd thought it would be. There have been a few moments that've sent my heart into triple time and other times I felt I really helped, but most of the time it's been an exercise in tedium, which includes trying to catch folks on disability jumping on trampolines or dancing on tables via social media."

It hadn't given her the best impression of humankind, along with her date check service, which usually revealed secretive men who insisted on meeting in out-of-the-way places who were almost always married or in a relationship. It made her hate to take the date-check clients' money. In truth, the only reason they contacted Nala's agency was they had a hunch anyhow. All she did was confirm it. Because eating and paying her bills was a necessity, she took the money. In her own way, she was making the world safer for singles.

The thought cheered her, but she needed something more to brighten her outlook. "Tell me something good."

"Ah." Karly hesitated as she wrinkled her nose. "Are you talking about the case?"

"Could be." Nala was hesitant to go into her need to hear something positive for a change. By the time she crunched into a tortilla chip, Max had his head in her lap demanding his share. It was no wonder he balked at eating his dog food. A few chips found their way to the ground where they vanished under Max's ministrations.

"Santa is missing." Karly uttered the words with a straight face.

Had this entire trip been a setup just to get her out of the office where she waited desperately for the phone to ring? She decided to play along. "It isn't his busy time. I'm sure he's on a Caribbean island enjoying the sun."

"No, you don't understand." She gave her head a hard shake. "Maybe you don't remember, I used to live in the town of Santa Claus, Indiana."

That *did* ring a bell. Nala and Karly had been friends forever. A school report came to mind about towns with odd names. Her friend mentioned then that she had been born in Santa Claus. At least it wasn't as bad as Gnaw Bone or Toad Hop.

"I kinda remember that. Are you saying Santa left a town that was named after him?"

"Not left. Vanished. He normally has coffee with Uncle Bob every morning. They've been good friends forever. Then he heads to Santa's Candy Castle…"

Nala held up one finger. "Lemme guess. Peppermint sticks."

"Maybe. Heard he has a fondness for caramels and toffee. Anyhow, no one has seen him for two days."

An adult, even if he bore a strong resemblance to the merry old elf, should be able to have some private time. "This is a big deal why?"

Due to having stuffed a couple of chips in her mouth at once, Karly settled for her eyes and eyebrows expressing her emotions. Her eyes grew wide while her eyebrows went up and down several times. Whatever she meant, there was some strong feeling associated with it.

"Ah, I know I'm guessing here. Does it have anything to do with eyebrows? Groucho Marx?"

"Who?" Karly spat out the word along with a few chip crumbs.

"He was the Marx Brother with the bushy eyebrows. Never

6

mind. Explain it to me. Why can't an adult, especially a senior adult, do whatever he pleases? Maybe he went to the North Pole to check on the toy production."

"Be serious." Karly leaned across the table and settled an irritated look on Nala. "The entire town is depending on you. Without St. Nick, they have nothing. The town didn't even rate a post office until they changed their name to Santa Claus. People come to Santa Claus often to pose by the Christmas themed places but mainly for an opportunity to see the *real* Santa. In the process, they load up on sweets, candles, anything with the name Santa Claus emblazoned on it."

Either she or Karly was starting to spin off into the Twilight Zone. Nala didn't think it was her, but she did have a talking dog. "Right. The *real* Santa is missing."

The server returned with the iced tea and water. "There you go. Your meal will be here soon." A sparkle of mischief appeared in the woman's eyes. "I guarantee it will be here before Christmas."

Kinda funny, but neither Karly nor Nala laughed. Probably realizing she had an unreceptive audience, the server drifted off to greet new customers walking in from the parking lot.

Karly gave the server a glance and continued speaking fast and intensely. "He's as close to the real Santa as I've ever seen. Real beard. He's on the short side. Jolly. Has a way with children. He even knows sign language. He's been at the theme park as long as I can remember. Children want to tell him their list while older teens and adults come back for nostalgia purposes. The park used to be called Santa Claus Land. Without him, it's just another theme park and plenty of those have gone belly up. Most of the town works there."

Okay, she could see the problem. Santa needed to be found. "It's

September. Isn't the park closed now?"

"They're open for Halloween weekend."

"What's Halloween without the jolly old elf?" she teased, not believing Santa had a significant part to play with children suited up in their best princess or superhero costumes.

"Exactly. It's bad enough that my old home town has to compete with a new park across the state line, but there has been some vandalism in town and now this."

Vandalism really wasn't her thing. It was hard to pinpoint folks who show up in the night, do their thing, then vanish, although security cameras were always a big help. The thing was, if they had those, they wouldn't need her. "How are the two tied together?"

Karly boosted herself a little more. She was practically lying across the table to whisper the words. "The vandal signed his name."

"That should make things easy. His name?"

Karly's prone position on the table was starting to attract attention. "Jack Frost." She hissed the name and shimmied back to her seat, knocking off the chip basket in the process.

Always quick to spot an eating opportunity, Max gobbled up the wayward chips before Nala could pick up the basket. She could do without the server joking about them more. She did wonder if this whole tale was a prank. "Do you think this whole thing is a huge publicity scam? Come on, Jack Frost? He might as well have signed the North Wind."

"Go ahead and make fun, but the victims of the vandalism quickly painted over the words to prevent anyone from seeing it."

"That's not exactly helpful." At this point, she wasn't exactly sure what the town wanted her to do. It would be hard to do much if people spent their waking, free hours damaging or hiding evidence.

Many a good citizen unintentionally marred a crime scene by trying to be helpful.

"Well, yeah, I can see your point." Karly blew out an audible breath. "Consider that the town may lose its place in the hearts of children if you don't locate our Santa. Plenty of letters, often written in pencil and crayons, find their way to the small post office of Santa Claus. Many people send their Christmas cards to be stamped with the famous Reindeer and Santa postmark. The postmark tends to change annually, but Santa's always on it. The folks who come to the park might decide to opt for that renegade Mouse land instead. All the stores, campgrounds, even the golf course depend on people vacationing in Santa Claus."

"It sounds serious." Nala shook her head. "I'm not sure there's a great deal I can do."

Karly folded her arms and sniffed. "After I found you a premier crime-solving dog."

Premier might be an over-exaggeration, but Max did help. He picked up on clues humans missed. She almost felt she'd have to do it to not disappoint her friend. Then again, a big-money client could come in while she was questioning folks in the Christmassy town.

A different server arrived with their food and delivered it with a single comment, "Disfrute de su comida."

Nala covertly delivered the small cheeseburgers to the waiting Max who swallowed each one without even chewing. Good thing she didn't have her hand too close to his mouth, or she might be missing a few fingers. Might as well give him some fries, too. Not too many, though. The last thing she wanted was a gassy canine in the car.

Another sniff sounded as Karly picked up her fork, ready to attack her meal. "I'll have to call Great Aunt Selma and tell her all the work she did was all in vain. She asked me if five thousand was a fair retainer."

Nala's fork paused on the way to her mouth. "Five thousand?" That would certainly help. Maybe she could work out the mystery of the vanishing Santa. The man probably went to Vegas or something. Even Kris Kringle needed some downtime.

From underneath the table, Max mused on the case. "Think how many cheeseburgers that would buy."

"Yeah," Karly agreed as she cut into her enchilada. "When you find Santa and deliver him safely home, there will be a bonus, too."

Well, it looked like she and Max had a job. "Tell Aunt Selma we are on St. Nick's trail."

"I think he prefers *Santa*, but I'll tell her."

Chapter Two

"**R**OAD TRIP," MAX announced while watching Nala wrestle an oversized bag of kibble into the car trunk. "No need for that. There's got to be plenty of fast-food places along the way."

"Not helping," Nala grunted the words and pushed the fifty-pound bag into the space beside her box of sleuthing equipment. Her *kit* included a device that resembled a 1920s version of a movie ray gun but allowed her to eavesdrop on folks.

Fully packed, she slammed the trunk. "When I talked to Karly's Great Aunt Selma on the phone, she warned me that there were stretches of I-69 where there was nothing. She told me to make sure to gas up. Elvin Snopes, our ever-handy techie genius, is going to help us."

"Great!" Max barked twice and twirled in a circle. "Jerky treats for me! Woohoo!"

It was always food with him. She probably should toss in a few snacks for both of them or she'd hear about it all the way there. "Ah, he's not riding with us. He'll be doing his magic in his own home and will call me with the results."

"Ah…" Max plopped down and hung his head. "I'll miss him. He says the funniest things."

While her high school friend Elvin might think he was funny, he really wasn't. Maybe the movie lines and bad impersonations were amusing at first. Wait, no, not even at first. They were lame and probably only appealed to preteen males and obviously enchanted dogs.

"Yeah, right. We also need to stop by my parents' house on the way out of town. I need Dad to keep an eye on the office, especially since Sawyer is off on another mysterious trip."

Max gave a playful growl, arched his eyebrows, and added, "Maybe he's a spy."

As outrageous as the possibility sounded coming from Max, it was something she had considered. The man was gone more than he was there. At least he paid his half of the rent, wherever he was, which was the only reason she could keep her private eye career choice. "Don't be ridiculous. Remember, while we're at my parents' place, no talking."

"Ah, come on." Max lurched to his feet and bumped against Nala. "It will be fun. They keep asking me questions and laughing."

Just the memory of the awkward lunch with her sometime love interest, Tyler Goodnight, her parents, and her talking dog made her grimace. He accidentally reacted to a remark while resting under the table, and she spent the rest of the meal pretending she was throwing her voice. Even that was dicey. She never knew what he might say. Her initial apprehension turned out to be well-founded.

"With any luck, they won't be there. I'll just drop off the key and run."

The slam of a nearby screen door meant one of her neighbors was out and about. Several small dogs charged into her yard, barking as they circled Max. They might be greeting him or banding together to take on the much larger dog. Max must have thought the latter. He stood and kept turning to keep his focus on the little yappers. It must be that next-door neighbor, the one who not only monitored her activities but felt the need to comment on them, too. Lucky her.

"Yoo-hoo, Nala!" It *was* her, attired in her bathrobe and slippers. Her brilliant red hair showed signs of escaping the messy bun she must have created to step outside and visit.

No way she could ignore the woman, but any discussion would cut into her time table. Since her sleuthing policy emphasized discretion, she never mentioned she was a private eye, especially to nosy neighbors. She raised her hand in acknowledgment and scoured her mind for the right name. "Um, hi, neighbor."

"It's Gloria." She bobbed her head, then reached inside her robe and pulled out cigarettes and a lighter. "I told you my name when you moved in. I see you are packing up. Off on some exotic trip with your latest love interest?"

Her first instinct was to deny the ridiculous possibility, but for a moment, she considered it. A tropical vacation with nothing to do but have attractive males in Hawaiian shirts bringing her frozen tropical drinks with whimsical names like the Slippery Mermaid or the Drunken Sailor sounded great. It would involve a flight, too.

"Oh my!" Nala held her hands to her face, pretending surprise but probably looking more like that kid who got left behind in that old Christmas movie. "How did you guess? I have a flight to catch. You know how security is. No time to waste."

Her neighbor blinked hard. The nonsense about the romantic escape was possibly meant only as a conversation opener. Her neighbor's sudden muteness, while convenient, was hardly flattering. Best to get going before Gloria thought of something else to say.

A snap of her fingers should have gotten Max's attention. Not so with Max. He, too, regarded her with a puzzled demeanor. Not getting the proper reaction, she slapped her thigh. "Let's go."

He touched noses with his tiny friends, then slowly moseyed to the car as if he had all the time in the world. It took everything in her not to sigh, but such a reaction might result in his moving even slower, if that was a possibility. Her father had spent long hours training Max for detective work but was insistent that you didn't bribe a dog to do what it should do. That might work for un-enchanted dogs. Nala whispered the word *cheeseburger*, barely moving her lips. Her canine slowpoke leaped into the car.

"See ya!" Nala called out to the neighbor, hoping that would be hint enough for her to gather up her darlings before she backed up. A sharp whistle rode the air and all the tiny dogs returned to their owner. It must be nice to have pets who obeyed.

"You're so lucky!" Gloria put her hands around her mouth to yell the comment. "You live such an exciting life."

Not knowing how to answer that one, she settled for waving. If by exciting she meant dodging bullets, that *had* happened. On the other hand, it was more likely her neighbor imagined sunset boat rides and romantic meals on the beach. This second scenario hadn't happened yet.

They were turning out of the neighborhood when Max spoke. "I thought we were on a case. Not that I'd mind a vacation. Where are we going again?"

Since most of her cases were either insurance fraud, adultery, fraud, extortion, and on a few occasions, murder, she suspected Max didn't have the best view of humans. It might not help to admit lying to her neighbor. "We're going to Santa Claus, Indiana. Lots of folks vacation there."

"You lied?" Max used his upper-crust British accent that he'd obtained from watching a great deal of Masterpiece Theatre. It should be super weird coming from a dog, but it just sounded judgy in her opinion.

"You know Gloria…" she started and noticed the whine in her voice. "Not only will the woman talk your ear off but she gossips, too. No reason for everyone in the neighborhood to know our business. I've already told Selma we'd be there by two. I'm not sure where the place is, and we'll need to stop for lunch and potty breaks."

Listen to her. She was trying to justify her actions.

Normally Max was quick to comment, but he remained silent as if mulling over the conversation or possibly disappointed in his human. Geesh, she had never fallen short in an animal's opinion before. Maybe she had, but none of the other animals could tell her, which may have been just as well.

A forced cough sounded, causing Nala to cut her eyes to her dog. While animals could get respiratory infections, she soon picked up that the cough was Max's way of getting attention. It may have been something he picked up from television. "Go ahead."

"All right." He nodded his shaggy head. "You didn't say any-thing about our newest job because Gloria gossips."

Now his silence made sense. He was pondering the situation. "Yes, that's right."

"Okay." There was another lull. Max twisted in the seat to watch Nala. "Is it better she gossips about you taking off with your latest romantic interest?"

She hadn't considered the consequences when she glibly agreed with the suggestion. On occasion, a few of her neighbors already gave her odd looks, probably due to Max's behavior or her father sending squad cars by just to ensure her safety. Depending on how many folks Gloria talked to, she'd be the envy of the female population. Her shoulders went up in a shrug. "I'm not worried. What could possibly happen?"

Chapter Three

THE NOONDAY SUN heated the car, resulting in Nala opening all four windows a couple of inches. Most people would have taken advantage of the air conditioner, but her fellow passenger preferred to smell where they were headed. Who knows? He might pick up a clue such as the scent of a candy cane or Christmas cookies. More likely, Max would be able to tell her how far they were from the closest fast-food restaurant. So far, they'd passed numerous empty fields that had been shorn of whatever crop had filled the area. Only one still had corn standing, and there had been the rumble of a tractor in the distance.

Not many cars on this stretch of highway, she couldn't help noticing. If she counted the abandoned pickup truck on the side of the road, it brought the total up to three. Anyone who was the spitting image of the jolly old elf would be noticed. That was the premise she was going on. It would make tracking the man easier unless this section of the Midwest was filled with bearded old men with a significant belly who enjoyed ending every sentence with *ho, ho, ho.*

Road noise made it difficult to listen to the radio, but she could hear the phone ringing. Handless phone calls were another plus to owning her father's old car. Because of his days as a patrol cop, comfort was a plus in any vehicle he bought. The roomy interior and plush upholstery initially had made her feel thirty years older than her actual age. In the end, the vehicle's ability to zoom away from danger, along with its roomy trunk, won her over. Even though her father made it sound like she had to take the car to make their garage a little roomier, she knew better. As an only child, her parents were always trying to help.

It was probably her dad calling her now. The sunlight made it hard to see the caller ID. A button on the steering wheel accepted the call. "Hello? Hello!"

Nala yelled, trying to be heard over the road noise. Oh yeah, she could roll up the window. All four windows closed, which caused Max to object. "Hey."

Elvin's voice flowed out of the speakers. "You had me at *hello*."

A movie quote, which she should have suspected. "What do you have for me?'

"Not a whole lot. Our boy is named Chris. How fitting."

This was starting to sound like one of those cheesy holiday movies Karly loved with all the predictable situations. Always snow and huge outdoor trees festooned in lights with one grinch in the group who is transformed by the end of the show.

"Lemme guess. His last name is Kringle."

Elvin's laughter filled the car. "That would be rich. Oh, no, his last name is Natale. I think it's Italian for Christmas."

"Okay, what else did you find out?" Often the smallest thing could turn into a clue.

"Like I said, not a whole lot. Chris has played the part of St. Nick for the last thirty-five years. Despite hacking into his personnel file, there's little to go on. His emergency contact number goes to the Rudolph campgrounds. He works at the theme park about seven months out of the year. The month of December during the off hours at the park, he makes visits to schools, children's hospitals, and even nursing homes. He's featured a great deal in the local newspaper, and he takes a great photo."

Not helpful. "Please Elvin, tell me you found something else."

A gasping noise had her glancing sideways to where Max feigned choking and pawed at the window. No help for it. She'd have to roll down the window. Nala turned up the mobile sound first before lowering the window to an appreciative doggie *sigh*.

"No reason to huff about it. Talk about unappreciative. I found out Chris is a decent golfer. He manages to get in eighteen holes at least once a week at the Christmas Lake Golf course. There are a few shots of him with a Mrs. Claus, but it isn't the same woman over the years. On his application, he marked single, but that could have changed multiple times."

"That's it?" She tried not to sound too disappointed. No reason to get Elvin riled by a lack of gratitude, especially considering how many times he had helped her on various cases. "I mean, that's good. No arrests?"

"None."

"I expected as much. Thanks for your hard work. Invoice me." Even mentioning billing made her wince. Anything would be too much for her budget. Maybe the town of Santa Claus would pay her even if she didn't find Chris. It would be a miracle. A Christmas Miracle. Maybe she *was* in a cheesy holiday movie.

"Nala, I can't, in good conscience, charge you for zilch."

It was a Christmas miracle.

A FEW BILLBOARDS touted the nearby Monkey Hollow Winery, and another insisted she should visit Lincoln's boyhood home. They both sounded promising in her opinion. Another one reminded her she was almost at Santa Claus, which meant she should call up Selma and give her a heads up. Knowing that Selma would be her contact person and apparently held the purse strings, too, Nala had programmed the number into her phone. Technically, she was supposed to speak the number, and it would be dialed. That hadn't really worked very well. Instead, she scrolled the screen until she found Selma's number and double-tapped.

A peppy song about *the dogs being let out* stopped and gave over to the phone ringing. Max made a derisive snort. "What happened to the music?"

"Quiet. Business call."

"Hello?" a deep voice answered.

Had she dialed the wrong number? This hands-free calling wasn't much good if she couldn't get the right person. "I'm sorry. I was trying to reach Selma."

"You got her."

Karly hadn't mentioned anything about her aunt's voice. It must be a cold. "Oh, hello. It's Nala Bonne. I'm just coming into town, and I wanted to know where we could…"

Before she could finish, Selma interrupted. "Did anyone see you?"

Nala considered the almost empty highway and the fields of nothingness. "I can safely say no."

"Did you stop for food or gas in Santa Claus?"

Her eyes drifted down to her gas gauge, which was drifting toward *E*. Her stomach was in a similar state. As for Max, he could always eat. "We're not in Santa Claus yet, although the idea of food and gas does appeal."

"Don't go anywhere. Don't talk to anyone. No one needs to know Santa is missing." She enunciated the words slowly. "*It...will...start...a...panic.* Come on down the main drag. You'll see the Kringle Place Shopping Center. Next to the grocery is a shop that has brown paper over the windows. Drive around to the back. I'll let you in."

"Okay." It sounded rather cloak and dagger, but she'd play along. "See you soon."

The phone went dead, and the music returned. Nala couldn't be sure if the woman hung up or they were disconnected. Either way it was odd.

Max sent her an inquiring look, or she assumed it was, wondering about the nature of their mission. Then he spoke, "I don't see any burger places anywhere. What horrible place have you brought me to?"

How could a place not have a burger joint? Her eyes scanned the buildings that were popping up beside the road. A large sign told her where to turn to visit the theme park and campgrounds. Unlike the last couple of hours, she'd spent on the highway, there was a spattering of cars and people. Most of the buildings had wooden façades that displayed Christmas scenes and usually an image of Santa, and a long, rambling strip mall perched a little farther up.

"Looks like we found Kringle Place." She pointed in the direction of a sandwich shop. "There you go. Food. However, we can't stop now. I need to find out the protocol first."

Nala flipped on her signal, slowed, and turned into the center. Her goal was not to be noticed, but it might be hard with a population of roughly three thousand, or at least that was the information online. Every new face, car, or dog would be obvious. Maybe Selma had a plan.

As she crept behind the grocery store, maneuvering her way between a delivery truck and a full dumpster, an open door caught her eye. A middle-aged woman stepped into the opening and waved at Nala. It had to be Selma. No one else was expecting them behind the grocery store.

Just to be sure, she drove closer and put her window down. "Selma?"

"Yes," the woman hissed. As she motioned for them to come in, she growled, "Hurry!" while glancing at the grocery delivery truck before disappearing back into the open door.

All righty then. She'd park the car and go see what was up. Max had to come also. He'd been in the car forever. Nala opened the door, grabbed her purse, and slid out. Since this would be the first time, she met these folks, she wanted to look her best. Her hands smoothed over her clothes as Max shot out the door.

"Woo boy! Am I ever glad to be out of that car." He walked over to a cardboard box left out and promptly claimed it as territory of Max.

A minute later, Selma stepped out of the shop and snagged Nala's arm. "No time for primping. We have a disaster of epic proportions to prevent."

It was hard for Nala to know if she should jerk her arm back to show she was no pushover or trot along since she *did* want to get paid. Before she could decide, Max barreled between the two of them, breaking Selma's grip.

The woman glared at the dog, then addressed Nala. "Yours, I assume?"

"In a way." The concept of pet ownership upset Max. He referred to it as slavery.

They entered a short hallway that led into a room without windows and a table with four chairs around it. A bald man leaned forward on the table, peering at a map, and mumbling to himself. "He could be anywhere. Without a phone, it's impossible to reach him. Chris might even be hurt."

A dry, stale smell permeated the room. It was hard to say what the place had been before, but it was obvious it hadn't been anything for a long, long time. Nala decided she needed to control the conversation or there was a good chance of Selma dragging her around the entire time.

"All right." She took a seat and pulled a tablet and pen from her purse. "Tell me what you know, then direct me to someplace I can eat and stay."

The man glanced up, tried for a smile, and failed. He held out his hand for a handshake, which Nala made sure to give back with a firm grip. People tended to judge you by those things. "Nala Bonne, Private Eye."

"Bob Jensen, owner of the campgrounds, and I figured I was Chris's best friend. Not so sure now." He released a heavy sigh. "I should have known something was up."

Selma shot Bob an irritated look. "Enough. Your moping is not helping. We have a crisis on our hands. It's much more serious than you not having a golf buddy."

Wow! Karly's aunt was a hard case. "Let's start from the beginning. When did you notice Chris was missing?"

Selma took a seat and elbowed Bob. At least she spread her acerbic charm around. "Buck up, sweetie. Give her the details."

"I will." He pressed his hands on the table and inhaled deeply. "On the offseason, Chris and I would meet for coffee at ten, usually at his home. During the full season, we have to meet at eight to give him enough time to suit up and get to the park."

A man who was as predictable as his namesake should be easy to track. "Has he never missed a day?"

"Um, let me think." His eyes rolled upward. "About five, no, maybe six years ago, Chris got the flu pretty bad. I'm surprised it doesn't happen more often with all the children sitting in his lap. Even then, I went to his house, taking him the soup Selma made. Therefore, it's so weird we can't find him anywhere."

Nala knew she should be writing something down, so she wrote *predictable*. "Anything else?"

"*No one* has seen him," Selma emphasized the first two words. "He's a fixture in this town. After coffee with my husband, he's off to the Candy Castle to load up his pockets with treats for the children. He eats a good portion of them, too. The important thing is Chris draws families to the park. Parents who remember him from when they were kids bring their own children here because of happy memories. The park employs over two thousand people. Without Chris, we'd be just like any other park." Selma slumped in her chair and gazed down at her hands.

This was a much bigger deal than Nala had expected. Her training and previous experience had nothing to do with maintaining local economies, but she could find people, especially with Max's help. "I'll start at Chris's house. Max will need something of his to smell."

On cue, Max strolled over to the table, sat, and gave two barks as if adding his two cents. With any luck, they'd locate the missing man within twenty-four hours.

Chapter Four

INSTEAD OF HEADING to Chris's home, which would have made the most sense, Selma decided they needed to establish a cover for Nala. Just being a tourist was too ordinary. Besides, tourists showed up in the summer, not the fall. A local man attired in the Kringle Foods red and green vest and elf hat grinned while she hefted up the oversized camera that was part of her cover for her arrival in the small burg. She pretended to take his picture, even though she doubted there was any film in the camera. Where did people even get film developed anymore?

With the question in her head, Nala squeezed one eye shut and used the other to focus on the image. The grocery employee leaned on the line of carts and mugged. "I hear you're going to put this in a book. Who knows? This could be my big break."

Her finger pressed the shutter button, and then she lowered the camera to address her subject. "Are you hoping to be in the movies or modeling?"

The middle-aged man pursed his lips, then scratched his head. "Never considered either. I always wanted to be a racecar driver."

"It's never too late," Nala offered cheerfully. It wasn't as if she were an expert on racing cars, despite living somewhat near to the

Indianapolis Speedway where the iconic five-hundred-mile car race ran every year. It would be the same as thinking she could count cards by living in Vegas. No reason to stomp on anyone's dreams. "Let me write your name down. I want to get it right."

Normally, there would be a lull of months or even years between the creation of a book and its actual publication. Plenty of time for people to forget, but it didn't make it any better. Pretending to be someone else still felt dastardly, rather like smearing sidewalk chalk masterpieces. The private eye business included plenty of deceptions.

There was her pregnancy stomach she'd donned to solve a few cases after she'd read that people, especially men, tend to ignore pregnant women. Of course, none of those people were invested in her cover, unlike the folks here in this burg. There would be one or two who waited patiently to see their picture in *Midwest Marvels*. They might even go so far as to tell their friends or comment on social media. Could be a savvy publisher might even jump on the idea and make such a book. It wasn't her idea. Selma came up with the name of the book, along with the plan.

"Wally." Her photo subject volunteered his name with enthusiasm. He paused, furrowed his brow, and cleared his throat. "Better make it Wallace. Sounds better. Wallace Simmons." He gestured to Max, who sat in front of the nearby Brick Oven Pizza Parlor, drooling. "Why did you bring your dog along?"

One of the first rules of sleuthing was to try to stay as close to the truth as possible. That way you were less likely to be caught up in a lie. "I didn't have anyone to watch him."

"Makes sense." Wally leaned forward on a grocery cart and kicked one heel up. "How about this? It shows my playful side."

No choice but to heft up the heavy camera and take another snapshot. How would she be able to search for Chris when every resident would want to be featured in the non-existent book?

Wally returned both feet to the ground and gave the carts a push. "I thought you'd be like Chris, our own St. Nick."

Whoa! There might be a clue here. "How so? How am I like Chris?"

"You and your dog." He nodded in Max's direction. "Chris always has little Dasher with him wherever he goes."

"Dasher, huh?" Nala tried for a smile, but wasn't totally sure she achieved it. Maybe she might make a stab at humor "I figured it would be Rudolph."

Both of his feet were solidly planted on the ground as he leaned into the carts to get them to move. His face took on a somber mien as he announced, "Rudolph passed on years ago. I think Dasher was maybe one of Rudolph's pups, though. Yeah, he loves that dog. Takes it everywhere. Even when he's at work, Dasher is close by."

Dasher could be the clue she needed. If Chris took off on his own, then he certainly would have taken his dog. "What kind of dog is Dasher?"

"Oh, you know, a little bit of this and a little bit of that. Definitely not a purebred anything."

That was no help—he might as well say the dog had four legs and a tail. "He sounds like a great dog. Is there a photo somewhere of Chris and Dasher? I think it would be great to have some pics of local dogs."

The grocery carts groaned as Wally wrestled them into a turn. He paused for a moment and heaved a sigh. "You never miss the stock boys until they don't show up." He wiped his sweaty brow with his hand. "I bet The Candy Cane Courier has plenty of photos of Chris and Dasher. If something is happening in town, you can bet Chris and Dasher will be there." He paused as his eyes rolled upward. "I imagine you'd get better if you take your own photos of Chris and Dasher."

Her lips tugged up in a forced smile as she tried to convey joy at the intended flattery. It was hard to know if she was successful. Her mother had always been quick to tell her she was no actress. It could explain why she was always cast as a townsperson with no speaking lines in school plays. Still, her skills had to have improved some- what. What about the blind date she went on when she informed the man at the end of the date that it wasn't him, but it was her, when it was definitely him, as far as no dates in the future? Every now and then, the man would try to contact her until she blocked him. It had to mean her acting wasn't convincing, or the guy was just a creep.

"You're so right. I'll make sure to do that." She gave the man a thumbs up and a wave. "Appreciate your help, Wally." People responded better when you used their name as much as possible. That tidbit didn't come from private eye school, but from her mother, who ran an upscale furniture and design studio. By using their names, it tended to make people think you were interested in them and had their best interest at heart. Successful salespeople relied on the technique.

Selma and Bob sat in their car, watching from the parking lot. That should raise suspicions the two were having a spat and unwilling to leave their vehicle until finished. Here they were worried about her appearance raising eyebrows while their own had to cause some gossip, which could be their intention.

Don't look in their direction. Nala headed toward Max before he did something typical such as running into the pizza restaurant and begging for scraps. Most of the time she tried to keep a leash on him, but it wasn't possible while in her role as a girl photographer. Meanwhile, her dog had resorted to leaning against the restaurant door to get closer to the delicious aroma. Such behavior had trapped patrons inside who were ready to leave, but were too nice to shove the dog out of the way.

Nala grabbed his collar. "Back up."

"I'm hungry," Max whined.

The couple trapped behind the door stepped out and shot baffled glances at Max and Nala. As they strolled past, the woman gave them a second look and asked, "Is that a real dog?"

"Yes, yes, he is very real," Nala answered. Sometimes a trifle too real and very demanding.

The woman's avid expression drooped a little as she shot a hand through her silvery hair. "Too bad. I swore I heard him talk. I thought maybe he was a stuffed animal I could pick up at Santa's Toys. My grandson would have adored him if he were a toy. He's allergic to dogs."

"So sorry," Nala offered while wondering how she should handle Max blurting out things. "He whines a lot. Some people say it sounds like talking."

"Oh, really?" The woman stepped closer. "Could you make him say something?" She motioned to her companion. "Todd, come here. The dog is going to talk just like on that video."

Great. Nala did her best not to roll her eyes but managed to nudge Max, hoping he could read into her instructions and not elaborate too much. Once the man arrived, Nala knelt beside her dog and whispered, "Say *I love you.*"

Light bounced off Max's dark eyes, making it hard to read his expression. He started with nonsensical whining, and then managed, "Why wuv wu wary wuch."

The woman clapped her hands together. "That's wonderful!" Her hands went up to her cheeks. "I should have recorded it. Our grandson would have loved it! Could you do it again?"

TWO HOURS LATER, Bob unlocked the door to their lodgings for the night. "Here you go. You're in luck. It's one of our Christmas cabins. We've decided to decorate them so you can celebrate Christmas no matter what time of year it is. These go pretty fast, but we hit a bit of a lull during the week. Your cabin is the pet-friendly one. Normally, we charge an extra fifty dollars for the pet." Bob nodded in Max's direction. "I'm sure you'll keep him under control. I would be glad to get some feedback on the decorations before you leave."

"Sure." Nala hadn't come as a travel consultant, but she could give her opinion.

Bob gave her a friendly pat on the shoulder. "Good, good. I knew any friend of Karly's would be A-Okay. Selma thought it might be best if you keep to yourself. She stocked the fridge and even included a pan of her famous lasagna and an icebox cake." He rubbed his stomach. "What a treat. Here's the key."

Nala accepted a key attached to a sizable plastic reindeer. It would be hard to slip that into your pocket. Her host held up a finger and winked as he reached inside the cabin to flip the light switch.

Multi-colored lights flickered on, and music started with high-pitched voices singing about Christmas hurrying fast and hula hoops as presents. Twinkling fairy lights encircled the room. It may have been her imagination, but it smelled like sugar cookies. Max gave her a doubtful look as if questioning the wisdom of entering.

"Ah," Nala started, "It looks very festive. I'm sure I'll enjoy my stay."

Once inside, she closed the door, leaned against it, and sighed. One of the reasons she went into the sleuthing business was she didn't play well with others, or maybe others didn't play well with her.

As always, Max sniffed through each room before returning and looking up at her expectantly.

"What?" She knew her dog had some burning questions he needed to ask.

"Okay." He angled his head to the large tree in the main area beautifully decorated with ornaments, lights, and garlands. "There's a Christmas tree."

"I see it." It would be rather hard to miss. "What about it?"

"Notice anything odd about it?"

She hated these games, even though Max loved them. In many ways, it showed his intelligence, which should be a good thing. Now, she was tired, hungry, and frustrated. The lasagna sounded pretty good along with the cake. Her stomach steered her in the direction of the fridge where she checked out the goodies Selma thought were basic for her stay. She opened the freezer and found frozen hamburger patties. Max had followed her and bumped against her leg.

"You didn't answer me."

Patience. Max had to be as tired as she was, although he rather cherished the attention. "It's a lovely tree. It even has a star on the top. What could be wrong with it?"

"There's no presents. A tree ought to have presents under it."

Somehow, she had missed the obvious. "I'm sure they rent these cabins around the holidays and people bring gifts with them to tuck under the tree."

Max did a doubletake. "What about Santa? He brings presents."

Not a discussion she was getting into now. It was always a little hard to tell when Max was being serious or clowning around. "There are burgers in the freezer. I could make you one. Who knows? Maybe there's some cheese in the fridge, too."

A series of barks filled the cabin, making Nala smile. That was a definite *yes*. It always surprised her when Max resorted to his first language. He seldom kept to it, though.

"I think a burger is the least you can do after making me say *wy wuv wu* about a hundred times. Talk about degrading."

"Who knew you'd be such a hit?" She shrugged her shoulders, pretending she hadn't known how upset Max was at acting like a regular dog and performing on command. "Did you pick up any good stuff while I was being girl photographer?"

One ear tented forward to listen as she spoke. "Depends on what you consider *good*," he answered.

Nala lifted the lasagna out of the fridge and did her best not to drool. It was rather sad when she and Max were starting to emulate each other or maybe it was only her. That was even sadder. "Tell me what you heard, and I'll decide."

Max sat and cleared his throat. "There's thirty-three flavors of hot cocoa at Santa's Candy Castle."

"Tempting," Nala remarked as she cut herself a big slice of lasagna. "I'll look into that once I find Chris. What else?"

"I heard someone mention you may be a spy."

"First Sawyer, then me. You must have spies on the brain."

She located a fork and chowed down on the lasagna, unwilling to make an effort to heat it. Max cleared his throat.

"I know, I know. I'll start on your burger right away. Just needed a nibble to keep up my strength. Why would I be a spy? What would I be spying on?"

"That's the good stuff." Max nodded his sleek head. "Apparently, you're part of the competition."

Competition? While most folks accepted it was parents and grandparents who bought the majority of Christmas presents, they were still willing to let the jolly guy in the red suit take the credit. She wasn't sure how Santa could have competition. "What are you talking about? No one gives out gifts to all the children. How can Santa have competition?"

"He does, and he doesn't. It's hard to explain." He panted a little, and then allowed his front feet to slowly slide out until he was belly down on the floor. "So weak."

Even though she suspected her pooch was engaged in overacting at its worst, she still thawed a burger in the microwave in preparation for frying. "Hang on, noble companion." She spoke with a dramatic flair, playing along with her pet. "Your sustenance will be ready in a few moments. In the meantime, why don't I try to guess."

A low moan sounded that would have been more appropriate for a haunted house. She'd take that as a *yes*. Max had his head on the floor by then and had shut both eyes. If he would respond to commands on cue, he could have a career in the movies. "You said it had something to do with Santa and also, *not* with Santa."

One of Max's eyelids popped open, revealing a brown eye

brimming with intelligence and guile. Nala couldn't say what that meant, but at least he was listening. "Since Chris is missing, I will assume it has to do with one particular Santa."

Max opened the other eye and whispered something.

Nala kneeled beside her dog, concerned that the day's activities had exhausted him. "What did you say, sweetie?"

"Food," Max pushed out the word in a husky timbre.

Played. She should have known. Here she'd had Max for almost a year, and the dog was still playing her. If she wanted to know any of the gossipy details of her alleged spy activities, she might as well get his burger finished. With a grunt of disgust, she pushed to her feet and returned to fixing his burger.

The phone chime sounded. Possibly Karly checking on her, but it was more likely Selma, who'd demand to know what progress she had made in the ten minutes since they last spoke. Should she go with she had promising information, or should she just ignore the text and claim she had the sound on her phone off? Still, she should see who it was at least.

She turned the phone over and turned it on with her fingerprint. An image of Max wearing a police cap shimmered into view. Her father took that one. She figured if he couldn't get her to apply for the police academy, her dog was the next best bet. A slight tap displayed her latest message: *Get out of town. Your kind isn't wanted here.*

Her kind? What was that supposed to mean? Non-locals? Photographers writing a book? Maybe someone figured out she wasn't who she said she was, or maybe they didn't care for folks who traveled with a dog. Well, the message answered one question: Chris didn't leave voluntarily. A second look at her cell told her what she suspected—it came from a blocked number.

Chapter Five

AFTER CLEANING UP the kitchen, Nala sat in the glow of the festive tree, skimming a book about the history of Santa Claus, Indiana. Apparently, the town hadn't always been named after the jolly old elf. It used to be called *Santa Fe*, which sounded wrong. Tumbleweeds and silhouettes of adobe houses fitted Santa Fe better. While folks could call their town whatever they pleased, trouble arrived when they applied for a post office and discovered another town had already nailed down the Santa Fe name. Maybe they didn't want to change the town sign too much, so they had to find something that started with Santa, and thus the town became Santa Claus and was forever associated with Christmas. What a difference a name change made.

With that bit of information rumbling about in her mind, she fell asleep on the couch, nestled under a hand-stitched cover depicting Santa and his nine reindeer. Elves populated her dreams, motioning for her to follow but vanishing before she could catch up. If only she could catch up to one of those pointy-eared helpers who grinned at her before ducking behind an oversized present or holiday cut-out. One of them was singing something about bad boys. *Weird*. The song kept repeating. Not very Christmassy was all she could say. Even worse, it wouldn't stop.

Something cold and damp touched her hand as the annoying song continued. Nala's eyelids fluttered open only to be met by Max's steady gaze. The song came again. It wasn't a dream but her phone playing her father's ring tone. He was such an avid fan of the reality show that featured cops going about their duty, that his ring tone was its theme song. If her father was calling it was probably important. Nala blinked twice and pushed up into a sitting position, disturbing a family of fabric elves that were resting on the back of the couch.

"Snickerdoodles!" She resorted to one of her faux curses that her father had encouraged her to use in her preteen years. Ironically, shouting out cookie names did help decrease her anger. The habit stuck, giving the impression that she was very excitable when it came to sweets.

A large wooden Santa glared at her from across the room. Whoever made him must have been in a bad mood. For a moment, she studied the room since the phone had gone silent. It wouldn't be long before it rang again. Her father was not a fan of voice mail. As she expected, the song started again, and Nala located her phone before it got to the second *bad boys.*

She managed to croak out a greeting. "Hello, Father."

"Is it a *good* morning?" her father offered in an odd tone.

All her life she had dealt with her father making cryptic remarks, and she was supposed to use her observational skills and wits to analyze them. Not her favorite thing to do before her first shot of caffeine. "I'm not sure yet. I was sleeping until you called. Yesterday exhausted me."

Throat clearing rumbled into her ear. "I know. Gwen, your

mother…"

"I know who Gwen is," Nala offered while wondering if the conversation was this peculiar or if it sounded that way because she was still half-asleep.

"Anyhow," her father continued, "she wanted you to feel like you could tell us anything, and we wouldn't judge you."

Oh, they judged her all right, but maybe not as much as some other parents. "Yes, I know. I do tell you things." Of course, not everything. That would just be creepy.

"Why did you feel you had to lie to us? Worse yet, I had Tyler Goodnight mention it was nice you were taking a vacation to a tropical island. He didn't mention who you were traveling with, but from his behavior, I would say it was another man. Are you and Tyler no longer dating? And who is this other man whisking you away somewhere? I haven't even run a background check on him."

She had to be the only girl in high school who had background checks run on her handful of dates. Even better was when her father followed them in his squad car or just happened to show up in uniform wherever they were. Even knowing her father's habit of being overprotective, his remarks still baffled her. "Ah, wait a minute, I need some caffeine. Let me check and see what Selma put in the fridge."

"Who's Selma?"

She made her way to the fridge, yawning as she did so. Normally she tried to keep her father out of her business, part of being discreet. Other times, she needed his advice on things. "The woman who hired me to find Santa Claus."

Her father's voice turned gentle. "Sweetie, did you hit your head? Do you need help? Is someone listening to your conversation? If so, go ho, ho, ho."

Nala rolled her eyes. For Pete's sake, her father thought she was in a hostage situation or suffering from a head injury. "Dad, I'm okay. I left you a note and my office key. You knew I was going out of town for business. It was in the note." She swung open the fridge door and peered at the contents. There were a half-dozen plastic dishes with paper labels taped to them identifying their contents. Those she'd explore later. A two-liter bottle of Faygo cola, along with a six-pack of Ventnor's ginger ale, held her interest. Cola had caffeine, which made her choice a no brainer. A twist of the top released a carbonated hiss before she took a swig. She felt a little guilty drinking directly from the bottle and glanced around to see if anyone could possibly be filming her. No one, but she had her doubts about the wooden Santa. She reached for a cup from the cupboard and poured the cola into that.

After another long drink, she asked, "What are you talking about? I'm in Indiana, not a tropical island. A vacation would be nice. I wouldn't mind basking in the sun while being waited on hand and foot." The cola must be working because suddenly the wheels in her brain were spinning. "Oh, fudge!"

"Watch your language!"

"You taught me."

"So, I did."

Her earlier conversation with her noisy neighbor came to mind. "Do you think Tyler stopped by my house?"

"I know he did. He mentioned it when he asked about the vacation. Personally, I think he was asking if you were seeing someone else."

The one time she had to try and inject some playfulness into her life, and it went and bit her in the butt. She blew out a long breath. It figures Tyler would come by. Gloria probably popped out of her house like a Jack-in-the-box when she spotted the handsome officer. Who knows what she said? Something to underline the fact that Nala was away with someone else while Gloria always appreciated a man in uniform.

"I bet I know what happened. My neighbor was slowing me down as I was trying to leave. You know my policy about not talking about my cases or my clients."

"Solid policy," her father stated.

"Anyhow, Gloria was teasing me about going on an exotic vacation with my latest lover. Instead of dissuading her, I let her think it was true, especially since she acted like the possibility was so far-fetched. Besides, I was running behind, and I'd already told her I had to catch a plane as an excuse to get away from her."

"Remember! Lies need to skirt the truth but have a kernel of reality within."

That was another one of her father's rules for working under-cover. "I was running behind. Anyhow, it wouldn't hurt Tyler to call before showing up. It's a simple thing."

"Ah, about that."

She could imagine her father rubbing his neck and his mouth twisting to the side the way it did when he addressed a topic he'd rather avoid. "What is it?"

"Since you aren't dancing in the waves with another man, could you give Tyler a call?"

What must it be like to have a relationship where your parents weren't an integral part of it? Tyler, the former veteran turned cop, did make her heart race and even better, he got along with Max and her father. It was no secret her father would love to welcome him into the family. "If I did that, he'd know I talked to you."

"No worries. I mentioned I might give you a ring to see how you were." A forced laugh followed the remark.

"You didn't!" If she were a cartoon character, steam would be coming out of her ears. Her fingers touched her ears, which did feel a trifle warm. A heavy sigh escaped her lips. "Dad, I know you're trying to help, but I am an adult and would like to handle my own relationships."

"Ahem." A derisive snort sounded. "Tyler said the same thing but was much more polite about it. I guess I'll leave you kids to it. At your age, I was married, and we already had you."

That sounded like something her mother might say. Gwen Bonne had decided rather recently she wanted to be a Glama, a glamorous grandmother, who took her adorable grandchildren to the zoo or shopping in Chicago. "Tell Mom she is welcome to take Max to the various events everyone else is taking their grandchildren to. He's probably better behaved than most of the other pint-sized guests."

Max, who followed her into the kitchen with high hopes, sat and gave her a wide, doggy grin. "You got that right."

"Who was that?" her father asked with obvious suspicion in his voice. "I thought you were working and not on vacation?"

"I *am* working, and that's Max."

"You still doing that kooky ventriloquist act?"

"Yes, Dad." It was easier to go along with what he believed than to try to explain her dog's ability to converse in English."

Someone shouted her father's name in the background. "Got to go, sweetheart. You might want to give that throwing your voice thing a rest. It's not nearly as funny as you think it is. Bye."

The call disconnected, leaving Nala glaring at it. Not funny? As she recalled, her father was the one who egged it on. Now she'd have to decide if she should call Tyler or not. It would feel like her father put her up to it. What she needed was a legitimate excuse. Something about police procedure. Her lips twisted to one side as she considered most procedure questions could be answered easily by her father. Nala exhaled long as a spritely knock sounded on her front door. It couldn't be Selma. She would have pounded hard, then probably said something, giving a warning before opening the door with her passkey.

Whoever it was would have to take her as they found her. She shot her hands through her hair, hoping it wasn't too frightening. On the way to the door, she tugged down her shirt in an effort to make it look less wrinkled. Maybe the cola had toned down her morning breath a little. No peephole on the door, which was unfortunate, but then most campers were probably not screening their visitors.

She opened the door a crack just in case she needed to slam it closed. There was a unicorn on her porch. With no reason she could imagine a unicorn would be on the steps, she patted her leg. "Max, come here. There's something weird outside you need to see."

Because she wanted him to come, the shepherd moved about as slow as he could. "While I need to go outside, I don't want to if there's a frightening creature out there."

Nala gave herself an all-over shake, shook her head just to be sure she wasn't dreaming, and then pushed the door wide. The pastel colored unicorn bobbed and weaved, and then spoke.

"Morning, friend. Thought you'd like to get a photo of a Spencer

County unicorn. You never know where we will turn up."

Ah yeah, photos. That was her cover. Nala held up one finger, "Just a minute. Let me get my camera."

If she were an actual photographer, the camera would be as precious to her as her phone, and she'd know exactly where it was. Where could that heavy prop be hiding? When Nala entered the cabin, she'd pretty much dropped everything and headed for the fridge. In a vacation cabin, something the size of a five-pound bag of sugar should be a no brainer to locate. Somehow, all the red and green decorations served as camouflage. Her foot encountered her duffle bag, causing her to almost fall, and in doing so, she caught sight of the camera on the floor. No legitimate photographer would deposit their camera in such a manner. She scooped it up and brandished it. "Found it! Let me step outside so I can get a picture in natural surroundings. The tree will provide a nice contrast."

Max had slipped outside but gave the costumed individual a wide berth. It could be that the sound of the dual blowers providing air to keep the unicorn nicely rounded spooked him a tad.

The unicorn nodded, causing the gold horn to bobble. "You're so right."

Really? Nala had no photography experience. She was making it up as she went. While her father taught her police procedure and observational skills, her mother taught her how to bluff. All she had to do was act like she knew what she was doing. If someone acted confident, most people were willing to believe the projected image, which explained the success of scam artists.

The shutter clicked as Nala took a series of photos. She half-hoped there was film in the camera. These would be unbelievably cute, and Karly would love to see them. "Ah, that was great. I imagine they'll be a real big hit with the kids. Should I include your name?"

The unicorn pawed the air and shook its head. "Oh, no. I'm not even supposed to talk. Don't mention the talking. I just show up and bring joy wherever I am."

Nala lowered her camera and gestured zipping her lips with her free hand.

The gesture was wasted on the unicorn, who asked, "What?"

There didn't seem to be a natural conclusion to the conversation. She might as well resort to one of her tried and true methods of dealing with Max—distraction. "Kids behind you bursting out of a camper. I think they're coming to check out the unicorn spotting."

"Thanks." The unicorn skipped off in the direction of the children.

Max came out from behind the trees and plopped down beside Nala. "Wow! Creepy."

"Oh, I think the unicorn is fun and whimsical. Let's head inside and get breakfast." While Nala spoke, she nodded to an elderly, female camper slowly walking the path but paying a bit too much attention to Nala.

"My dog. I'm talking to my dog," she hurried to explain.

"Makes sense." The woman bobbed her silvery head. "I talk to my Charlie all the time." The woman came to a stop.

Even though it was a bit awkward conversing across the several feet that separated them, Nala wasn't moving any closer, not wanting to engage in a longer discourse. "Charlie must be your dog."

"Oh, no." The woman managed a grin and shook her head. "He's my dead husband. At least I get a word in now." She cackled, waved, and resumed her walk.

Not knowing how to reply, Nala returned the wave, then jogged back to the cabin, knowing Max would follow. Her foot was on the step when she noticed the door was ajar. Had she left it open when she stepped outside? Everything had happened so fast she couldn't remember. Must have been her. Her dog was already outside.

They both walked inside and closed the door. Visions of lasagna accompanied by a slice of icebox cake filled Nala's head while Max chattered on.

"This is one crazy place. What was that creature?"

"It was a unicorn."

Max gave an all-over shake. "Scary."

Sometimes, she kept forgetting a dog saw the world differently. What was fun and whimsical to her was strange and frightening to him. "No worries. It was all in fun."

A thump and shatter of glass sounded above their heads. Someone was upstairs in the loft, the area Nala had been too tired to investigate last night. Had they been there all night, or did they just enter? Better yet, why were they in her cabin? She snapped her fingers to get Max's attention, then pointed to the narrow stairway. Max shook his head. As a private eye, she'd have to investigate and convince her reluctant pooch to accompany her.

Chapter Six

NALA HELD HER breath as she strained her ears for another sound from her uninvited visitor. Childish shouts and laughter filtered into the cabin from the outside. Obviously, the children had discovered the unicorn. Her eyes narrowed as she thought about her exit out of the cabin to snap a photo of the costumed individual. Her breath rushed out in a noisy exhale when she could hold it no longer. Although she was the one who suggested an outdoor photo, what if the unicorn's intention had been to lure her from the cabin?

Leaning against her leg, Max asked in a whisper, "What are you going to do? Should we call the police? Maybe Selma. I bet she'd chase off any freeloaders."

He was probably right about the last part, and she would not bring in the police. It could turn out to be something stupid and get back to her father. Nothing compared to the police officer gossip hotline. She was fairly sure her father had it staffed twenty-four seven. Private eye work wasn't just following paper trails. Both she and Max had been trained by her father to take down bad guys. It was time to step up to the plate. She wiped her clammy hands on her pants.

While Max could be difficult, Officer Max, as her father addressed the shepherd mix, was always ready to serve. "Officer Max. Report for duty."

Her dog went from cowering against her to sitting upright, his ears tented forward, and his eyes alert. "Ready."

"All right." Nala leaned toward her dog and lowered her voice. "We're going in low. Don't know if there will be much upstairs to give us cover, but we will have to use what we can find. The element of surprise isn't on our side, but we have to be as quiet as we can. Let me get my gun first."

Even though her father made a big show of giving her a special holster for her Glock, she didn't have it on. It was too uncomfortable for driving and not for sleeping. Besides, in a quiet little town like Santa Claus, she'd been certain she'd never need a weapon. Nala tiptoed over to her purse and removed the pistol. Using her thumb, she pushed off the safety. She motioned with her hand that Max should go first. Officer Max gave a short nod and crept forward, keeping his body low to the floor. A canine officer usually had the element of surprise. Most people would direct their gaze to the height where a person would be. In general, they weren't looking around at their knees. There was also the element of unpredictability with a dog. With any luck, they should get the drop on their trespasser before he got off a shot. That should prove to Selma she was an experienced professional.

Max was halfway up the steps with Nala crouched behind him when something else fell in the room above them. Whoever it was didn't care if they were heard. Could be they felt overconfident thinking a woman and a dog would be a pushover. Nala sucked in her lips as she considered the possibility that the culprit planned on shooting them anyhow, so why bother with stealth? Her eyes moved to her dog, who had stopped on the stairs while shooting an inquiring look over his shoulder.

Maybe he considered the same scenario, too. For a second, she considered abandoning their attack plan and slipping out of the cabin to call for the cavalry. Inhaling deeply, she stiffened her spine as much as she could in her crouched position, reminded of all those times she'd searched social media on a disability fraud case and wished she had a more hands-on case. Now she was. She'd lifted her hand to motion Max forward when she swore, she heard a noise downstairs, but stairwells could play tricks by drawing the sound into the narrow passage and bouncing it around.

Max's head cleared the landing and his muscular body readied itself for the charge. As he lunged forward, Nala scampered up the last three steps, brandishing her weapon. "Freeze!"

Max confronted their unwanted visitors with frenzied barking. Dark, merciless, beady eyes stared back at her. Squirrels! The pair of rodents dashed about the room with Max in pursuit. Great! Her heart had a cardiac workout for this. The curtains were askew, the bedspread mussed, and some knick-knack lay broken on the floor along with an open book. That explained the sound. With any luck, Officer Max would chase the furry critters out of the cabin.

"Officer Max! Apprehend!"

Her dog stopped his pursuit, sat, and regarded her with a disbelieving stare. "Yuck! I'm not putting *my* mouth on them."

It looked like her normal dog was back, and the police dog was gone. "Okay. They're probably germy anyway. Let's chase them out of the place."

Despite the loft not being super big, she and Max made several laps before they were able to herd the squirrels down the stairs. With the front door shut, the creatures naturally sought out the safety of the Christmas tree, inserting themselves among the tinsel and ornaments.

"Fudge!" Nala stomped her foot when she realized her predicament. She'd have to undecorate the tree, which she didn't have time for. The first forty-eight hours were the most important for picking up a trail or tailing a killer. Who knows how long Chris had been gone?

Her dog came to stand beside her and cocked his head to stare up at her. "We could ask them to leave."

That was the type of remark she had come to expect from Max, but it didn't mean it wouldn't work. Nala walked to the front door and opened it. "Beautiful day outside." She cupped her hand around her ear as if listening to something. "What's that? A bushel basket of pecans left unguarded on a picnic table."

Nothing. It could be they weren't going anywhere if she and Max were watching. She whistled for her dog and gestured to the door. They both walked outside and moved into the shadow of a large maple tree.

Max milled a little, butting his large head against Nala's leg. "I'm hungry. I was hungry before, but with all that running around, now I'm starving."

"Shush. We'll eat when they're gone."

Max sat, then lay down with a heavy sigh, letting Nala know how he felt about waiting on an empty stomach. She might even break down and make him another burger. It depended on how long it took to de-squirrel the place. A squirrel head peeked out the open door, then it vanished back inside. A burst of high-pitched chatter accompanied them as both squirrels strolled outside. Just when Max would have lunged upward, Nala placed a restraining hand on him. They had to let the squirrels get far enough from the cabin before they slid into action. Too quick a move would send their furry visitors right back inside.

A mockingbird above them broke into its repertoire as the indecisive squirrels finally made their decision to move down the steps. That took forever. A slight pat informed Max they were headed back to the cabin. Nala wouldn't mind coffee, a shower, and breakfast. Max trotted beside her with his tail up, most likely anticipating something to eat. Once inside the cabin, she closed the door and locked it.

"Okay, let's get back to our regular schedule before any nosy phone calls, unicorns, or squirrels interrupt it."

"Amen to that, sister," Max replied. She shot him a surprised look to which he replied, "*Sister Act.*"

It was hard to know if he meant he watched the movie or he was just copying something Elvin said. It could have been either. She surveyed the room, making sure there were no more squirrels lurking anywhere. Nothing so far, which was a bonus.

Lasagna was calling her name, but it would be too spicy for her canine's delicate stomach and she didn't want to take the time to thaw and cook a patty. The expensive kibble she brought should serve, but Max would want a little something extra to convince him to choke it down. Sometimes, she doctored it with gravy. Other times, she crumbled up jerky treats and hid them in the food. In the kitchen, even though she cleaned up last night, there was something on the counter and the bag of jerky treats was knocked over.

"Max…" An accusatory tone entered her voice.

"Hey, I'm innocent," he protested and lifted an eyebrow. "What did I do?"

She moved closer to inspect the tumbled bag and the various treats spread over the counter. They were in a pattern or words, all the letters in a squarish shape, because the treats were long slender jerky ropes. It wasn't Jack Frost since the culprit didn't sign his name or didn't have enough dog treats to do it.

Nala read the message aloud. "Leave now."

"That's a little harsh," Max complained.

"Not you."

Someone had been in the cabin while they were upstairs. The hairs rose on the back of her neck. It had to be someone who didn't want her to find Chris. Fortunately, they left her evidence in the form of fingerprints. The jerky treats were too small to get a full print off, but the bag would work. At last, a break, which was exactly what she needed. They might be headed home by tonight.

"I'll be right back. I need to get my crime-solving kit out of the trunk."

Nala dashed out to her car and opened the trunk. Most of the time, she packed her supplies—that her father often referred to as her *girl detective kit*—and never used them. Usually, her brain, the Internet, doorbell cameras, Elvin, and gossipy neighbors provided the info she needed. Still, every now and then, she did need to use them and was grateful she had packed them.

All she'd need was the baby powder, cellophane tape, and latex gloves. She plucked the items from the box. Once she donned the gloves, dusted the bag with powder, and lifted the prints, she'd get them to Elvin for analysis. He had a way of slipping them into forensic labs ahead of other requests and getting the needed identification pronto. Of course, if the treat arranger had never been fingerprinted, it would be a wasted effort.

There was a spring in her step as she hurried into the cabin. No Max in the main room. That must mean he was guarding the evidence. In the kitchen, Max had his paws on the counter and had the treat bag in his mouth. As for the *Leave Now* message, it had disappeared into her dog's stomach.

"Max!" She clapped her hands together, causing him to drop the bag and drop back down to all four paws.

"I was hungry," he whined.

"That was evidence!" Her initial joy over what she thought was a case-breaking clue vanished. How could he? Yes, he was hungry. It was an animal's natural drive to seek out food, especially a dog who had been a stray like Max.

"You never told me." Max flung back the remark, acting more defensive than guilty.

Once she realized someone had been in the cabin arranging dog treats into a threatening message, she'd raced outside without considering what her pooch might do. Using the heel of her hand, she bumped her forehead. What had she been thinking?

A mental image of her father conducting one of his many lessons on keeping alert and calm when in a stressful situation materialized. Decked out in his IPD blues, he put up one finger as he spoke. "Emotions cloud the mind. Any emotion. Fear, anger, and even excitement is enough to make you miss vital information or forget proper procedure."

She had done just that. Inhaling deeply, she squeezed her eyes shut for a moment. She made a mistake, but needed to move forward. Although it was hard to maintain the icy demeanor her father insisted all law enforcement officers should have. There'd been plenty of times her Dad wasn't all that calm, either.

"Max. It's my fault I forgot to tell you not to eat the treats. It would have been nice if you hadn't chewed up the bag, though."

"My bad," he said, but didn't look the least bit repentant. "Still hungry, by the way."

"Of course, you are." She moved around the kitchen, trying to decide if her intruder had touched anything. "We'll get some breakfast. We'll need to talk to someone who might have noticed someone sneaking into our cabin. Campers notice that type of thing. First, we need to dust for prints if there are any. What else could our intruder have touched?"

"The doorknob," Max volunteered. He gave a spritely wag of his tail, demonstrating his pleasure in being the first to latch onto a possible clue.

"That's right. Good thinking."

Nala reached for the baby powder, certain there would be a decent set of prints. Halfway across the room, she stopped. The decent prints would be under her own prints. Possibly smeared. All the same, she had to try. She applied a light dusting to the knob, then applied the tape and peeled it off slowly. Whorls indicative of a print showed faintly. Most were partials, though. The hard part was keeping the tape intact and not messing it up before it got to Elvin and the lab. Nala ended up creating a paper box to safeguard the prints, and then carefully taped them into a candy box she'd emptied, still with the rich, heavy scent of chocolate in it.

"I'll call Elvin on our way to Chris's house and let him know the prints are coming. First, we need to eat."

Chapter Seven

AFTER BREAKFAST AND a shower, Nala dressed carefully, trying to get a feel for what a photographer would wear. She was clueless. Her private eye wardrobe consisted of a lot of gray, navy, khaki, with an occasional plaid pattern. Nothing to catch the eye or cause her to be remembered. However, being in a town the size of Santa Claus, she'd be memorable anyway by not having lived there all her life. Not much she could do about that. She slipped her shoulder holster on over her navy T-shirt. She planned to wear her oversized chambray shirt open to hide the weapon and give her the ability to reach for it when needed.

Max, who had stretched out on the bed, perked up when she checked her weapon to make sure it was fully loaded. He called out, "Danger, danger, Will Robinson!"

Plenty of people talked around Max, but it seemed he was only interested in repeating movie and television quotes that Elvin worked into conversations. Rather than tell Max to stop it, which would probably exacerbate the situation, she played along. "It could be dangerous. We do have someone threatening us. You need to be aware of your surroundings at all times."

A derisive snort sounded as Max moved into a sitting position and regarded her with an aggrieved air. "I'm always aware. I'm a canine. Enough said."

Sometimes she forgot how easily offended her dog could be. Still, his skills needed to be on the right things. "Your nose is remarkable at picking up the scent of fast food from a mile away. Your hearing is outstanding, too. I can open a bag of chips in a closed room, and you're right there scratching at the door."

Max's lips lifted into a wide, goofy grin. "I *am* good."

"Yes," she agreed, parceling out her words carefully since she didn't want to deal with a pouty dog all day. "I need you to apply those excellent skills to sniffing out Chris and Dasher. If we find Dasher, maybe you could talk to him."

"Not that again. Most dogs don't speak English. When they do speak in *bark*, it's more about feelings." Max gave his head a toss and mimicked. "I'm hungry. I'm scared. I'm tired of waiting to hear who's a good boy."

Her hand went up to stop the complaints. Nala needed to stay hopeful. "We'll go to Chris's house and see what we can find. I'll have to ask Bob for the address and see if he has an extra key, which will be helpful because I'm not looking forward to breaking in. We might find Chris in the basement playing old LPs, and he somehow lost track of the time."

"LPs?" Max asked.

"Never mind." Nala slipped on her chambray shirt and debated about a jacket. In the shadows, there was a nip in the air, but a jacket would be restrictive. If nothing else, she could put the heat on in her car if it turned too cool. "Let's go."

On her way out, she picked up her purse and, on second thought, the camera. No matter where she ended up, she could always claim to be taking photos. It might serve as a disguise for future assignments, too. Even though she knew she'd get a reaction, she pulled a leash from her purse. Even before she snapped it to his collar, Max coughed and feigned choking.

"Stop that. If you walk properly, there shouldn't be any tugging or chafing. Think of it as your disguise. You're undercover."

The choking stopped immediately. "Undercover, eh? Guess that makes me a spy."

"No, you're not a…" Nala didn't finish her statement. If being a spy made Max walk on a leash, then he was a spy. "First rule as a spy, you can't tell anyone you're a spy."

He winked. "Got it."

They proceeded out of the cabin, stopping outside to make a point of locking it. With any luck, it would remain locked while they were gone, not that there was anything to find. There was no documentation of why they were there. Any information on the case was stored in her purse. On the way to the main office, which was attached to Bob and Selma's house, Nala waved at several campers who initially waved at her. She had to stop a few times for children who rushed up to see the doggy. Max took their petting and complimentary remarks as his due.

The long flat office and residence were only a few steps away when she remembered she hadn't called Elvin. Slipping her hand into her purse, she withdrew her cell and called her friend.

He picked up on the first ring, "It's Buddy, the elf. What's your favorite color?"

"Anyone else would have hung up on you."

He chuckled. "Maybe, but I also have caller ID. Besides, most people don't have this number. Consider yourself privileged. What can I do for you?"

"To say we have been welcomed here with open arms would be a lie. Last night, I received an anonymous text telling me to leave. While I was upstairs chasing squirrels, someone snuck into the kitchen and spelled *Leave Now* with dog treats."

"Dog treats, huh? Diabolical. I bet Max didn't like that."

She sighed. "No, he ate the message. I may have pulled off some prints from the doorknob. I was going to mail them to you."

"You haven't mailed them, have you?"

"No. Why?" She figured she could pick them up after she picked up the address and key.

"It could take forever for me to get them, and the prints could degrade in the process. I better come and get them. I've always wanted to visit Santa Claus, Indiana."

"All right," she conceded, wondering how much Elvin's jaunt to the southern part of the state would cost her. "Is this going to be on my bill?"

"Geez, Louise, don't be such a cheapskate. Since I'm feeling magnanimous. I will only charge you for the gas."

"Thanks."

A screen door slammed, and Bob popped out of the office.

"I need to go. See ya soon." She waited for Elvin's bye before disconnecting.

Bob gave her a hearty wave. "Hello! I was just about to head your way."

"Guess it's good I saved you the steps." Nala moved closer, leading Max. She had to be extra careful no one heard. Obviously, someone knew why she was here and didn't like it a bit.

Once she and Bob were close enough to knock heads, she asked,

"Chris's address?"

"That's why I was headed your way. I figure I should come along. I know that man about as well as I know myself. If something isn't right, I'll notice it. Figured I kind of owe it to him. We've been friends forever."

"Okay." Working with others wasn't her favorite choice, but Bob didn't seem that bad. "I'll go get my car."

Nala had already turned when Bob said, "No need. We'll just take the golf cart. The house is close. When my knees are feeling good, I usually walk. Today, I'm feeling my arthritis. You don't mind humoring an old man, do ya?"

"Of course not," she assured him. "But Max…"

Her voice trailed off, leaving the unspoken question between them.

"No worries. I don't go that fast. Even if your dog took a tumble, he'd be fine. It might even teach him a lesson. Just choke up on the leash and you'll be fine. It's close by." He gestured to a golf cart bedecked with antlers and a red nose on the front parked near the office.

He made it sound so simple. As far as she knew, Max had never been on a golf cart. She moved toward the golf cart and rattled the leash as if that would convey to Max the need to sit quietly during the ride as opposed to anything else, he might normally do.

"Okey-dokey," Bob chirped and climbed behind the wheel. "If you want to sit together, the two of you will have to take the back seat."

They took the back seat. Max sat on the floor while Nala wrapped a hand in his collar.

The cart started with a jerk, the quiet electric engine allowing

Bob the ability to talk over it. "Lots of folks use golf carts in the main part of town. It's not too practical for those who live a piece away. When it gets cold, I put the sides on it. Most of the time, we don't have too many places to go in the winter."

The golf cart bounced along the path and up to the exit where Bob took a right. Slender pine trees marched up to the road. In between, she could see larger, older pines with a few deciduous trees tucked in between with orange and red leaves. A smell of wood smoke drifted on the wind, not too surprising since they were leaving the campground. Nala had her doubts about taking a golf cart on the road, but there wasn't a single other vehicle out. They went about a hundred yards when a narrow driveway fronted by a red and white striped mailbox appeared. Bob tapped the brakes before turning into the drive.

He turned back to address Nala. "I use the brakes to signal my intentions to turn since I don't have turn signals."

His desire to relay this information caused him to veer off the drive into the grass. Nala pointed ahead, not wanting to offend her driver, but not willing to get stuck in the ditch that bracketed the drive.

"Oops." He steered the vehicle back onto the road with a nervous laugh. "Good thing Selma didn't see that."

A tidy, little, brick cottage came into view with nine concrete reindeer in the front yard. Two small pines stood guard beside the cheery red door. The decorative shutters had holly leaves cutouts in them, which would have suited a gingerbread house. The man played up the Santa angle.

The golf cart came to a stop. Bob boosted himself out and stood, holding onto the frame of the cart. "I suggest we check the garage first for Chris's truck."

They hadn't done that already? Nala sucked in her lips to prevent her from saying anything. Sometimes silence was the best answer. She and Max stepped out of the cart and followed Bob to a detached garage that—not too surprisingly—was painted forest green. Instead of using his key, Bob squatted, grabbed ahold of the door, and lifted it, revealing a small red truck. The front of the truck has stenciled on it, *Here comes the fat man.* Bob pointed at the words and laughed.

He motioned to Nala. "You got to see the tailgate."

She bent to release Max so he could check for scent trails. Of course, he didn't know what Chris smelled liked yet, but she was sure he could pick out another dog. Nala rounded the truck to see the tailgate read, *There goes the fat man.* Inspired. It also showed the man didn't mind a little attention.

Best to check out the inside of the truck. With the garage door wide open, allowing daylight to flood inside, she opened the driver's side door and leaned in. Her first reaction was to inhale, pulling the peppermint scent into her lungs. On the bench seat was a schedule book and an open bag of peppermint sticks, which explained the smell.

Bob popped his head in on the other side. He pointed to the book. "That's his planner. He didn't go anywhere without it. You'd be surprised how many personal appearances he makes, and he even does private parties. Sometimes, he'd even go up to French Lick where those two fancy hotels are for special seasonal events. Chris is a popular guy."

"May I?" Nala asked and nodded in the direction of the book. Normally, she would have picked it up, knowing it would provide a timeline, but with Bob there it felt like she was intruding.

"Go ahead. That's why you're here."

On that they could both agree. Nala removed a pair of latex gloves and a large baggie from her purse. When she first started, she paid good money for evidence bags but soon discovered the bags she could purchase at the grocery store were cheaper and more durable. She blew into the gloves to loosen them up before donning them. Once gloved, she opened the planner. Pages were covered in neat printing. Unfortunately, it looked like Chris was in the habit of abbreviating words to fit into the small lines.

She flipped to today's date. There were quite a few things written in for the day. "I think this might be the winery." She pointed to the entry that read *Monk Hollow Wine Debut*, showing it to Bob but not handing him the book.

"Oh, yeah." Bob placed a hand on his chest. "That's today. I went and forgot. I better give them a call to tell them he won't be there."

"What's going on there today?" Did Chris have regular scheduled visits planned? The sketchy information she was getting gave her the feeling she came in halfway through the movie.

Bob coughed, then shook his head. "The release of the Christmas Red wine. It's sure to sell out. Chris was supposed to be on hand for photo ops. Once you locate him, he can reschedule the photo shoot."

At least Bob had confidence that she'd find Chris and he'd be well enough to go hawk wine. That was a plus. She flipped through the book, looking for any reference to a trip. She pointed out some entries to Bob. "What's that one?"

"Oh that!" Bob shook his head. "He was driving out to the Gaither Christmas Tree Farm to check on his blue spruce tree. He's very particular about the tree he puts in his house. It has to be perfect."

"Would the Christmas tree farm people notice him checking his tree?"

Bob's shoulders went up in a shrug. "It would depend on someone being in that area at the time. All he would do is drive his truck up there, get out, and check the tree to make sure no fungus had taken root. After that, he'd leave."

"Okay." The man really did schedule everything. "That's the day he didn't show for coffee. The tree place might be a good place to start." She flipped back a page. "I could start the night before. Hmm." She read the entry aloud, drawing a loud reaction from Bob.

"Woo-hoo," Bob gave a whistle. "Chris did say something about meeting a woman. He thought he'd give dating another stab. Apparently, he was meeting her at the expensive restaurant."

It made her speculate if his dating profile would include a fondness for milk and cookies. "Did you know who it was?" It would be hard tracking down someone only identified briefly as *M*.

Bob gave a little snort. "Wish I did. Chris didn't want to jinx it. I do know she wasn't local. He said that much. I think he met her on one of those pen-pal sites."

Max's barking sounded, and there was an answering bark.

"Max found something!"

She and Bob rushed out of the garage to discover Max greeting a smaller, scruffy dog of dubious parentage.

"It's Dasher!" Bob confirmed what she had suspected. His brow furrowed as he turned to address Nala. "Chris never goes anywhere without Dasher."

Chapter Eight

DASHER HAD BURRS in his coat, mud on his paws, and a pleading look in his eyes. While she didn't possess any of Max's ability to communicate with other dogs, it was obvious this canine felt sad, confused, scared, and most likely hungry. He swung his liquid-eye gaze to Bob and barked frantically.

Even though it took some effort on his part, Bob knelt and patted Dasher. "I know, fellow. I miss him, too. That's why we're here. We're going to find Chris. Right now, we're going into the house. I bet I can find some food for you."

A good scratch behind the ears had Dasher leaning quietly into Bob's hand. When the man tried to stand, it was obvious he had issues. He grunted and rocked but never got past crouching. "Ah, could you help me?"

"Of course," Nala assured him as she held out her hand. She hadn't offered earlier because some people get upset when assistance is offered due to the implication it might be needed. She gave a firm tug that had Bob upright again.

"All righty!" He brushed off his hands on his khaki pants. "Let's see what we can find inside. Personally, I'm hoping for a note of explanation, such as I decided to visit relatives or took off on a cruise." Bob glanced down at Dasher and shook his head. "Chris would never leave Dasher outside. He spoiled the dog even more than he did Rudolph, and that was a diva dog for sure."

He fished out a key from his pocket as he spoke. "I guess that should be expected. Spoiling the dogs and all. He never spoke of any children. I know for a fact he didn't have a girlfriend. What else did he have to lavish his love on?"

Since Nala didn't have an answer, she settled for a shrug. Chris may have a busy planner, but in some ways, he had a very lonely life outside of work hours. However, it appeared as if he was always working, unlike the mythological Santa who is usually credited with working a few days a year.

The key fit into the lock with no problem, allowing Bob to push the door open wide. "With most bachelors, you might be afraid to enter because of empty beer cans, dirty dishes, and mountains of laundry. Not Chris. He was as neat as they come. When we had coffee, he'd do up the dishes while I was still there. Cleaned out the pot, too."

Dasher rushed into the opening, with Max following close behind. The outside light streamed into the windows of the small kitchen, illuminating the room holding a Formica-topped table with four red vinyl chairs in the center. Encircling the room were metal cabinets and appliances that could have easily been from the fifties.

"Wow! Is everything original?"

"Most likely. Chris was not a fan of replacing something if it wasn't broken." He gestured to the snug, neat room. "Nothing out of place. I guess I'd be more alarmed if there were a dirty dish on the counter."

The sound of dog nails on the floor sounded as the two canines made a thorough search of the house. Her eyes drifted over the room as she cataloged it. Despite it being fall, the room was still toasty. For a man who wouldn't update an appliance in the last thirty years, he'd have certainly turned down the furnace before a planned departure. Could be he didn't plan to be gone that long. There was a rotary avocado wall phone, but as far as she could tell, no modern conveniences.

"I noticed there isn't a microwave or a dishwasher in sight."

Bob slapped his thigh. "That's Chris. He likes the old ways. He still owns a stovetop percolator and uses it every day. He saves the grounds for his plants. Great fertilizer, you know."

Nala didn't know. She didn't garden, and she assumed the percolator was used to make coffee. This guy really wasn't into technology. So far, she sketched out a profile of a lonely man who hated new gadgetry. It was no wonder he embraced his Santa role. At least that way he stayed well-loved and socialized. It could also be the reason his house was so neat. It's hard to mess up a home when you're not there.

"Try not to touch anything," she prompted when Bob leaned a little closer to a wall calendar. He stepped back and placed his hands in his pockets.

"I wasn't going to touch anything," he responded with a sheepish grin. "Thought there might be pertinent information on this calendar. I watch crime dramas. I know the drill."

Another person who thought everything could be solved in a sixty-minute episode. It was easy to see from this distance the large numbered blocks were devoid of any penciled-in information. "Makes sense. Let's look at the rest of the house."

What she really needed to do was go over the house inch by

inch, which was difficult with her helpful chaperone hovering nearby.

Barking and the sound of something being knocked over came from the other room. *Goodness.* Nala broke into a jog. A large dog at play could wreck a house in no time. Add in another energetic dog, and it could turn into the perfect storm of canine destruction.

"Max! Stop!"

Even in a rush, she took note of the pocket living room with clusters of framed photos on the wall and a dated plaid living room ensemble. The area rug, bunched and rumpled, was half pushed under the couch. Her hand still clad in a latex glove, Nala used it to grip the sofa and give it a little push. Nothing. Talk about solid. She wrinkled her nose as she considered how much effort it might take to move it.

"Bob?" she called. "Was the couch always like this?"

"No." His face blanched, and his chin trembled a little. "Chris always had everything squared away. I used to tease him about being OCD. I think something has happened to him."

"Ah, Bob. I thought that was the reason you hired me."

He gave a brief nod, then blinked several times. "In theory, I know we wanted you to find Chris." He chafed his arms and exhaled heavily. "Selma was sure he was missing. I went along because it's easier to go *along* with Selma. She's a force of nature. I figured any time Chris would pop up and tell me a believable story behind his disappearance. I never thought anything bad could have happened to him. Now…" He paused and audibly inhaled. "I'm worried."

Bob being worried rattled her, too. Sure, the whole purpose of the trip was to track down the Santa impersonator, but in the back of her mind, she thought it would be a bust. It still could be. Nevertheless, the furniture being shoved around told a different story. Max couldn't have moved the couch on his own. Where was Max?

A short hallway ended in a basic bathroom between two rooms. The doors to all three rooms stood ajar. The first was a bedroom with an oversized bed with both dogs crouched on top of it.

"Max!" Nala hissed his name as she entered the room.

"I didn't do it," Max whispered.

"What?" Nala hissed the word but took a few steps back to see what Bob was doing. It wouldn't serve if he caught her talking to a dog. While most people did fuss over their pets, most didn't ask them questions with the expectation of them being answered. A backward glance confirmed Bob was still in the living room, a few meters away. Currently, he was busy straightening photos that were askew, which reminded her of the rant her father would go into about civilians involved in a crime scene. The fact he was touching things meant he could be compromising evidence.

Max joined her in the hallway. "The office." Max angled his head, indicating the other room. "Dasher knocked over the candy dish."

The smaller dog, trailing after Max, acted offended and surprised. Could be he was upset that Max would finger him for any breakage without a second thought or again, it could be the talking.

Before inspecting the office, which she suspected was a mess if Max was trying to escape all blame, she visually surveyed the bedroom, making a point to note the personal touches in a modest room with two windows. One large window faced the front of the house. The second smaller window awkwardly sat near to the corner of the interior wall. What builder would do such a thing? No symmetry whatsoever, on the plus side, Chris would be able to see anyone coming down the drive or in the side yard.

The sliding door to the closet had been pushed opened, exposing several Santa suits in dry cleaner bags along with some less festive clothing options. Boots laid on their side on the floor underneath, which didn't fit the orderly Chris. The furniture was a heavy colonial-style, possibly circa 1960. The bedside table drawer stood open. Inside were cough drops, non-prescription sleeping pills, reading glasses, and a spy novel by a popular author.

Nala knelt and flipped up the white chenille bedspread. Part of her wondered if she'd find Chris staring out at her. Nothing. Not even a single dust bunny, which had to mean he hadn't been gone too long.

Bob whistled from the doorway. "This place is a wreck. Chris isn't going to like this one bit."

He strolled to the closet and started up righting the boots, causing possibly more smearing of evidence. "Bob." No response. Nala spoke a little louder. "Bob, I need you to stop."

"Just a minute. Almost finished." He straightened the final boot and stood. "That's better."

Nala blew out a breath. Her father used to joke it wasn't the criminals that made his job challenging, it was often the civilians. When he originally said it, she hadn't understood. Now she did.

"Bob, we don't know what happened to Chris, but everything that is out of order could be a clue or even evidence. Every time you touch something you are compromising the evidence. I could have picked up fingerprints from the boots.

His eyebrows shot up. "Why didn't you stop me?"

"I tried." She cleared her throat. "Remember me saying your name?" she asked and avoided the curt reminder she told him in the living room not to touch anything.

"Ah, yeah, I did." He scratched his jaw. "I'm used to a more forceful tone of voice."

Screaming at the man wasn't her style. Besides, most people couldn't decipher shouted words, they reacted emotionally, which often wasn't helpful at all. A person who stepped in front of a moving car would hear someone yell *Look out!* and stop crossing, ensuring being hit. Nala needed Bob's goodwill. He was certainly easier to work with than Selma.

"I appreciate your being here and showing me the house. Right now, I need you not to touch anything. I'll also need to come back later and fingerprint everything. You don't need to come with me because it will take hours."

"Understood." His one-word statement and flushed face testified to his chagrin at muddying up the crime scene.

She'd treat it as a crime scene. Her father would tell her to call in the professionals, meaning the police. Not every county had a CSI unit, and even better, none of them had Elvin, who could work wonders on processing. They didn't have Max, either, who could track reasonably well. As far as she could tell, Chris was better off with her gathering the evidence. If she got to a place where she couldn't go anymore, there would be no shame in calling the police. Even now, she wasn't certain that Chris wasn't wandering somewhere, confused, and disoriented.

"We'll check the office and the bathroom. You can drop us off at the campsite, and I'll return with my equipment."

Bob glanced at his watch. "Um, I need to get back. Selma and I were going to the Spencer County Library for a travelogue show. A gentleman will be presenting on Hawaii. It's like a vacation without the cost." He shook his index finger. "You got to get there early because all the good seats will be gone. It's no fun having to look around a tall man or a woman with big hair."

It also probably was no fun listening to your spouse gripe about having bad seats. "All right, we should get going. I assume we'll take Dasher with us?"

"Of course, I'll go get his stuff."

Bob made eye contact with Nala. He was waiting for something. Oh yeah, she told him not to touch anything.

"We can pick up food at the store. Maybe he has a leash by the door or something. If not, I have one you can use."

She undid Max's leash and attached it to Dasher. "There you go. Why don't you wait outside? I'll be right behind you."

Bob took Dasher as she passed the dog to him and carried him outside. He was a man used to taking orders. All she was going to do was take a quick peep into the remaining rooms. The real work would happen when she came back. So far, all she knew for sure was Chris was gone. It was a rapid exit. Possible foul play.

Max stepped off the bed and padded after her. The small bathroom had tiny green and white ceramic tile marching halfway up the walls where it gave way to white paint. A window in the wall let in daylight and allowed Chris to see anyone who might be approaching. Every room so far had plenty of windows. It could just be practical planning for light in those times you didn't have electricity. Then again, they provided a complete view of what was happening around his abode if a person needed one.

The office she expected to be a mess, and it was. Papers and books were on the floor. A desk lamp lay on its side. File cabinet drawers were pulled open.

Nala stepped into the room to examine the opened file cabinet more closely. Obviously, a burglary of sorts, but what could Chris have that anyone would want, besides multiple Santa suits?

Her dog stood inside the office, lifted his nose, and sniffed. "Smell that?"

She drew in a deep breath. *Sulfur.* It reminded her of a spent match, fireworks, or even the firing range. Not good and not something she'd mention to Bob.

"Let's go. We've got work to do."

Chapter Nine

NALA'S RETURN TO the house to investigate wasn't as soon as she'd hoped. News of her compiling a book of candid photos had a line of folks in their Sunday best dress by her cabin, waiting for her to return. Of course, everyone knew where she was staying. There were no secrets in small towns, especially when it came to the location of non-locals. Selma and Bob, already ensconced in their car, tooted their horn in greeting as they headed for the travelogue.

Little girls in princess costumes, boys dressed in their baseball uniforms, and even dogs in tutus all waited in line. Some enterprising folks had donned shirts with their business logo on it. Another couple had baskets of merchandise to be casually featured in their photograph as if they normally strolled through town toting sixty pounds or so of Mason jar candles and fruit preserves. Fortunately, a nearby picnic table provided support for the baskets while they waited for their turn.

Sunlight streamed through the trees making it easy to gauge passing time. There was no way around it, she had to take their photos. Even though she would have preferred the assembly line fashion that school photographers utilize, she knew that would be suspicious behavior on her part. It didn't help that those waiting called out advice.

"Get on a chair!"

"Shoot down."

"That will help hide Mildred's double chin."

Mildred was a fan of the suggestion, which resulted in Nala balancing on a meter-high tree stump for that perfect photo. If people went to this much trouble for the possibility of appearing in a book, they'd expect a book. Her top teeth sunk into her bottom lip as she considered she'd be long gone before they figured out no book was forthcoming. Selma would have to spin a handy excuse.

All Nala knew was she'd have to avoid Spencer county in the nearby future. What a shame, she thought, as she peered through the viewfinder at a gap-toothed baseball player. Some of the photos were just too cute. If nothing else, she could send them back to Selma to give to the right mama. This depended on if she was taking photos with actual film.

By the time they got to the end of the line, campers were peeking out of their tents and RVs to see what the commotion was. A few even strolled over for a look. One of those in line took it upon himself to inform the curious that the line was for bona fide residents only. Thank goodness for that, she thought as she slipped off her tree stump platform. No more photos since the camera button wouldn't click anymore. Saying click would be a little far-fetched. Max kept bumping her leg, an indication of boredom, and the bathroom was calling.

"That's it, folks." She needed an excuse for why she couldn't do what she was clearly there to do anymore. Not knowing a great deal about photography, she stretched to remember anything pertinent. The sun chose that moment to break through a cloud, shining an extra bright beam on them as if an epiphany or a revelation. The sun, of course. Nala gestured to the sky. "Noonday sun isn't flattering. It causes all sorts of shadows. Makes people look like they're in a horror movie. I wouldn't want that for any of you. Maybe I'll see you around town later."

The half-dozen that were left sighed and nodded. A couple dressed in coordinating square dance outfits approached with the *sushing* of a crinoline petticoat. The woman held out her hand and said, "I'm Alice. This is my husband, Mel. I totally understand about the sun. I think it would be better if you came tonight to take photos of our square dance club." She wrinkled her nose a bit. "It would just be odd if our picture was under the trees and all."

Nala shook the outstretched hand and agreed, hoping it would allow her to escape to the bathroom faster. "Sounds great. I'm sure Selma would give me your address."

They both chuckled as if Nala had just told a huge joke. Mel winked at her. "Selma and Bob are in our club. They'll bring you along tonight. All I have to do is give them a ring. Make sure you put on your dancing shoes."

What have I gotten myself into? Nala managed a weak smile as the couple walked away, chuckling. Luckily, the rest of the group had dispersed, which sent her striding to her cabin with Max bumping her leg every third step. Yes, he wanted something, and it wasn't too hard to guess what.

Inside the cabin, she unwrapped the camera from her neck, deposited it on the couch, and dashed for the facilities. Max leaped after her, but she got the door closed before he squeezed into the minuscule bathroom. Dogs weren't the best about boundaries.

He barked twice, and then said, "I'm hungry."

No big surprise there. Nala blew out a breath. Nothing was working as it should. You'd think her former career as a preschool teacher would have taught her that things seldom work out the way they should.

"Okay." She called through the door. "I'll get your lunch in a minute. We must be quick. I need to get back to Chris's house and want to come up with some great finds before Elvin arrives."

Max muttered on the other side of the door, something low and inaudible. When she opened the door, he shot her a reproachful look. "Not sure why you're in such a hurry. What does it matter if you find something great?"

"It's my job, and that's what they pay me for." No reason to add each discovery reaffirmed her commitment to stay in the private eye business. Her parents were split between being supportive of her career change and fighting the desire to say *I told you so*. As for a significant other to bolster her sagging morale, that was another thing that needed work. "I should call Tyler."

"You should," Max agreed, with a wide doggy grin. "He feeds me under the table."

"It doesn't take much to win you over," Nala teased as she strolled to the kitchen.

Overall, Tyler was a great guy. He put up with her dog and her parents. Most guys never made it to that stage. Still, she didn't want to settle for a guy because he passed both her dog and father's approval. Honestly, she wasn't so sure he was set on her. Still, the very least she could do was call and tell him she was on a case. Then again, it might be interesting to see if he was jealous of her possibly sunning on a Caribbean beach somewhere with someone else.

After a quick meal of leftover lasagna and icebox cake, Nala was ready to go. Not so with Max. He pawed at his dish filled with expensive kibble. "You expect me to eat that?"

"It's a balanced diet made from lean meat and vegetables."

He continued to stare at her. It was almost as if she could hear him saying where were *her* vegetables. "Okay. I'll put some dog treats in it."

She suited her actions to her words and stirred in some tiny treats, making certain to stir them in deep, which would result in Max accidentally eating kibble in the process of finding them.

Her pooch strolled over to the food and delicately ate from the bowl, eating as little kibble as possible and still netting the dog treats. He sat down by the bowl and looked up at Nala. "I expect something a little heartier when we return. Maybe a steak."

"Dream on." As far as she knew there were no steaks in the freezer. She hadn't been paid either. She hoped it wasn't going to be one of those things where if she didn't find Chris or the man turned up on his own, she didn't get paid. Maybe they considered the cabin and food as part of her payment, which was fine as long as they didn't think it would cover all of it.

The drive took less than five minutes and was considerably smoother in a car. Thankfully, Bob had allowed Nala to keep the key. It probably had something to do with going to the travelogue. Good chance he would have offered to bring her by again if he were home. Before she got out of the car, she texted her address to Elvin, along with a few details on how to get there. As an afterthought, she advised him to slow down before he got there. It would be like Elvin to get a ticket. While Nala tried to be low key in her choice of vehicle, Elvin went for fast and flashy. He equated them with babe mobiles. His current girlfriend, Abby, wasn't a fan of the babe mobile or all it represented.

After the text, she exited the car with Max following. "I want to walk the perimeter first."

Max matched steps with her but kept talking. "What do you think Dasher is doing?"

"Eating, sleeping, whatever dogs do." Leaves crunched under her feet as she worked her way around the various concrete elves and reindeers. She assumed they were elves, but they looked a bit more like the gargoyles usually crouched at the roof corners of buildings. The yard alone could serve as the Christmas section of a concrete figurine showcase. It had to make grass cutting an ordeal. At the edge of the door, using her feet as foot measures, she counted off the steps. "One, two, three, four…"

"What are you doing?" Max queried.

Her eyes rolled up in disgust. The interruption made her lose count. It was best to explain rather than complain, or he'd interrupt again. "The house appears bigger from the outside than it does from the inside. "I'm counting the footage on the outside, then I will measure on the inside."

"What are you looking for?"

"I don't know. Let that be your last question."

She went back to counting at the door where the living room pretty much ended. Sure, closets would take up space. She got to the end of the house and said, "Twenty. That house didn't contain a twenty-foot wide bedroom even with its modest closet. Let's go find out what's what."

"Yes!" Max gave an enthusiastic bark.

If Bob and Chris were such longtime friends, it made her curious as to why he hadn't checked out the house before. Obviously, Chris liked his house tidy, but there was also a chance he'd asked Bob not to enter when he wasn't home. If so, why had he even given Bob a key? Simply a safety measure in case he lost his key? She'd have to go to the source and ask Bob.

BEFORE SHE BROUGHT her sleuthing tools in, she wanted to check out the bedroom. Nala slipped on the latex gloves and mentally prompted herself to touch nothing. The key she tucked into her front pocket and her phone into her back pocket.

Max immediately started sniffing, forcing her to step around him. Due to the open blinds, sunlight flooded the rooms. Chris must have left during the day. Even so, if he were planning on being gone, he would have closed the blinds if only to prevent the vintage furniture from fading.

The bedroom door was still open, which allowed entry without touching anything—a win. Nala backed up against one wall and counted off her foot measurements. Twelve, the room was only twelve feet wide. Add on another two feet for the closet at the most, but that meant six feet were missing. The walls weren't six feet thick. Nala peered out the window. The frame was less than six inches. The outside wall was real. The living room backed up to the bedroom so there was no space there. A quick knock assured her the hall wall was as it should be, which left only the closet wall.

"Chris is going to kill me," Nala muttered to herself as she placed the numerous Santa suits on the bed and moved the boots aside.

She started tapping high, then waist high and was met with a hollow sound. There was space behind that wall. The question was, how did a person get to it? No doors or obvious seam marks on the wall. It was a closet wall as far as she could tell, although appearances could be deceiving.

The scratch of dog nails on the floor meant her dog had arrived to help, even though his assistance wasn't always needed.

"Whatcha doing?"

She learned a long time ago it was best to answer Max. He never grew tired of asking the same question over and over. "Looking for a hidden door."

"Whose door?"

That should be a no brainer. "Chris's hidden door. It's his house."

Max lifted a doggy eyebrow and yawned. "Figured as much. Did you sniff it out?"

"Well, no." Sometimes her canine couldn't understand why humans didn't make full use of their olfactory sense.

"Let the professional work then. Give me something you think Chris touched."

Nala snagged the book in the bedside drawer and held it out to her dog, who took a long inhale. "Peppermint, venison jerky. I have to say I'm shocked about the jerky, and there's an underlying scent." He gave another long sniff. "I think I have it."

He placed his nose to the floor, went a couple of steps forward, then a couple back. It almost appeared as if he were dancing. Then he went to a large wardrobe beside the closet door. Why would a man have a wardrobe *and* a closet? Those Santa suits didn't take up that much room. Nala opened the wardrobe to find it filled with stacked cardboard boxes.

Max barked, then sat. It was the signal her father had taught him once he found something. Personally, she didn't think Chris was in the wardrobe. Still, she had to do something to satisfy her dog. "I wonder if Santa is in here."

A low electronic hum greeted her when she leaned into the wardrobe. *Weird.* She patted the boxes, which sounded hollow. She tried to knock the top one down but discovered they were all attached. *Weirder.* She tugged on the bottom one and all the boxes swung away, revealing a small opening, and the electronic sounds grew louder. The sound reminded her of being in Elvin's home with his various computers all turned on.

A flashlight would be useful. There was one in her car trunk, which seemed about a hundred miles away. She'd peek first. That's all. The important thing was not to let the door close since she had no clue how it might work from the inside. Her body was halfway in, and her eyes adjusted to the dim light put out by the various video screens showing different views of the outside of the house. There was a police scanner, several computers, a printer, and a landline. *Peculiar.* Max scampered in behind her, trying to see.

"Whoa! This is how Santa knows if you're naughty or not."

Nala turned to try to escape being crushed by her large dog and fell in. Max tumbled after her, and the door slammed. Not a good sign. She pushed up into a sitting position and considered the room.

"I think there's a lot more to Chris than the usual mall Santa."

Chapter Ten

CHILLED AIR PUFFED into the dim, closet-like room, adding more sound to the white noise. Even though there were no windows, all the various monitors showing scenes from outside gave a feeling of being outside. There had to be twenty monitors at least. Overkill, considering the size of the house, and purposeless as far as Nala could tell. There was nothing fence-worthy in the entire house. As far as merchandise went, the most expensive thing Chris owned was the Santa suits. No cheap red polyester suits that you could usually pick up for Halloween. All his suits were a rich burgundy plush with faux rabbit fur trim. Even though each suit had to cost around five hundred dollars or more, it was hard to imagine someone fencing a Santa suit.

Max bumped up against her leg. "Smells like peppermint in here, too."

"No surprise. I imagine Chris spent a lot of time in here."

A small gooseneck lamp squatted on the table, along with a closed folder. A snap of the toggle illuminated the room but made it hard to see the streaming black and white images on the monitors. She clicked off the light and stared at the monitors. On one she saw the image of her car, but only from the door handle down. She expected any camera mounted in the eaves of the house would take a high view, therefore, the camera must not be in the eaves. None were visible on her walk around the house.

A whine filled the room as a car with a wonky transmission passed on the access road. "Too loud!" Max complained.

It *was* too loud. Nala could hear the birds outside singing. The soft coo of a mourning dove, the evocative chatter of several chickadees, and the cowbird's call, reminiscent of water dripping, were amazingly clear. "He even has microphones outside."

"Paranoid much?" Max stated and nudged her elbow with his nose. "I'll tell you what he doesn't have. Snacks. No snacks anywhere. I looked."

It wouldn't have taken long to search the small room. "Guess he didn't spend too much time here after all."

"Why would he come here in the first place?"

Max hit it on the head. Why would the man have cameras and microphones scattered about his property? Most people could observe what was going on if they bothered to step outside. It took some work to scramble into the hidden room, which would be no easy feat for an aging, rotund man. Still, he thought it was important enough to have such a setup. Could be he could remotely use his phone or a hand unit to check out what was happening when he wasn't home. Maybe he was staring at her car handle even now, wondering who was sneaking around his house. That brought her back to the weird camera angle.

"The statues."

"Have they come to life?" Max placed his front paws on the table to stare at the monitors. "Don't see anything. Wait! It's moving. The deer!"

Nala turned off the light to better search for moving statues, although she had her doubts. Still, she hadn't considered her target would have a monitoring station in his home either. A doe glanced up at the camera before leaping away. "That's a real deer."

"I knew that," Max was fast to affirm. "Just testing you."

Sure, he was. Her rescue dog was easy to understand. What was harder was a single man who insisted on playing old St. Nick for decades, which should have made him a jolly fellow. Instead, he had his house wired up like Fort Knox, except for no military police, guards, or gold. At least she didn't think there was any gold.

"It just makes no sense."

If she could understand his reasons, she might be able to figure out what happened to him. At this point, Chris was heavy on security without any obvious reason.

"Why the cameras?"

Talking to herself sometimes helped her to work things out. Before Max, it was more effective because currently, her dog assumed all comments were directed at him.

Her pooch nodded his head as if he had the answer. "Could be he was sick of kids. Cameras allowed him to see them coming. He'd crawl in his room and pretend not to be home."

"Nah." Nala wrinkled her nose. Anyone who played Santa for decades must love kids. "Besides, crawling into the hidden room is too much work."

There were plenty of times when she spotted someone making their way down the block selling magazine subscriptions or wanting to give her a free estimate on windows, and she pretended not to be home. Besides family and friends, the only person she'd open the door for was a Girl Scout clutching her cookie order sheet.

After a canine throat-clearing, Max announced, "Maybe he's a spy."

Not a spy again. This dog must have watched a James Bond marathon or something. "Why would a spy be living in Santa Claus, Indiana?"

"Retired spy," he offered with a wag of his shaggy head. "Think about it. After dodging bullets and bombs, he probably wanted a quiet life."

In a way, it could work, but there were so many issues with her dog's theory. The fact she was even considering it showed how desperate she'd become. "How many spies resemble Santa?"

One canine ear twitched forward, then the other as he contemplated the question. "None that I know. That would make it perfect. Hiding in plain sight."

She seriously doubted that. The park used Chris's smiling face in their promotional material. A man who was trying to hide wouldn't allow that. Still, it made her wonder. She clicked the light back on and opened the notebook.

Starting from January first was a series of dates. She flipped through the book that had Chris's cryptic code underneath each date. There would normally be an *NT*, which she assumed meant not a thing or nothing. Sometimes, there would be an *S* or a *D* or even an *RC*. The last may have stood for raccoon. If he were an animal watcher, he took it very seriously, spending thousands of dollars on equipment. Even Elvin would be impressed.

The sound of scampering and grunting had her turning her head in time to witness Max trying to crawl up on a cot that had been pushed under a table supporting various monitors. There wasn't enough clearance for him to get up. With a final grunt, he dropped to the floor.

"Never met the guy, but he's just cruel putting a dog bed where a dog can't get on it."

"Not a dog bed," she corrected. Why would he have a cot in here unless it was a safe room? "Besides, you should be working. Have you sniffed the place from top to bottom?"

Max sighed and rested his head on his paws. At times, he wasn't the most diligent of workers. Most police dogs were raring to go when it came to working. Those were the same dogs who were deliriously happy when rewarded with a tennis ball.

A vibration in her back pocket had her pulling the phone out and checking it. "Elvin's on his way, and he's bringing Karly. Oh…" She kept reading. "…it's Karly texting *for* Elvin. She thought she'd tag along and say hi to everyone since it was a quick down and back trip."

"Elvin!" Max wagged his tail. "Jerky treats. Karly carries goodies in her pocket, too."

She hoped they brought something along since Max expected it. Once the two arrived, Max would do nothing but shamelessly beg. "Officer Max!"

She waited until her dog sat at attention, quivering, awaiting his orders. "Inspect the room."

Without any complaints or whining, Max sniffed the room inch by inch—something you could probably get no human to do no matter how great their sense of smell was. She paged through the notebook as she waited and discovered it'd stopped four days before. This meant Chris could have been gone for four days, or he failed to fill it out before he left.

Max sat down in front of her and barked. Usually, this was a sign the dog had found something, but Max liked to use it for reporting, too. "Report!" she intoned in a firm voice.

"Smell associated with Chris found."

"Not surprising."

"Several other smells, too."

"Let me guess," Nala started, aware that when it came to reporting, Max liked to be thorough. "Peppermint, dust, mice."

He bobbed his head. "Dust, yes. Peppermint, yes."

"Okay." She reached for a box and popped it open and found VHS tapes with dates. Apparently, Chris had his information transferred to tape. At best, it could only hold about eight hours. Most of the time, closed circuit systems recorded over previous recordings. What she needed was the tape from when Chris vanished. How cool would that be to find the mystery of her missing Santa recorded on VHS tape? Each container she popped open was a progressively older tape. Maybe it was still in the machine.

"Max. Do you see a VCR anywhere?"

"A what?"

"Never mind." She kept forgetting how young he was. This was a job for someone whose memory went back past 2000. A glowing red light above the REC button helped her to find the VCR. Leaning close, she could hear it running, which possibly meant it had been left inside the VCR endlessly recording images. Luck might be on her side today. Pushing a few buttons stopped the recording and had it rewinding. Another button started it playing. She heard Bob's voice first, then hers. She squeezed her eyes shut and made a derisive snort. All she had was a recording of their visit to the house.

Max crowded her and placed his paws on the table to have a better view. "Ooh, look at me. I could be a movie canine." He continued to watch, then glanced at Nala. "I think my right side is my best. What do you think?"

Anyone overhearing Max's conservation might think the dog was vain, but she felt he was always searching for approval after he'd been kicked out of so many homes.

"All your sides are great. Right now, I'm going to get my flashlight to search this room better." Nala took five large steps and reached the door that opened into the wardrobe. With her hand on the handle, she gave it a wiggle, but the knob didn't move.

"No, it can't be. There's no way we can be locked inside here."

Max stopped sniffing long enough to bump up against Nala. "Did you say *locked*?"

"Yes."

She shook her head and gave the knob another twist. The knob slipped a little. Her heart gave a little leap at the movement mistaking it for the door opening. She wiped her sweaty palms on her jeans before trying again. That time, nothing. The slip was probably just sweat. Inhaling deeply, she tried to wrack her brain on what to do. Plenty of times she'd been locked out of somewhere, but she'd never been locked in. If it was a safe room, the lock would have to be inside. Their impromptu entrance must have tripped it. All she had to do was remain calm and find it. She couldn't breathe a word of their situation because Max would erupt into full-fledged panic mode.

When the knob wouldn't turn, she settled for beating on the door. "Come on, you can do it! Open up, you stupid door!"

Max, who had been content to watch her struggles, surged to all fours and began to bark. In between his canine solicitation for assistance, he yelped, "Too young to die! I haven't even started my film career!"

Even though it was hard to hear much with Max barking and yelling, she was certain she heard car wheels on the gravel driveway. "Max! Be quiet! Someone is here."

To her surprise, Max stopped barking, sat, and slid to lie down. Once on the floor, he glanced up at Nala with a grimace. "They're back to finish what they started."

Chapter Eleven

CARS DOORS SLAMMED, which meant there were at least two people, maybe more. Nala crouched beside Max, resting her hand on him while holding her breath. What did they come back for? Didn't they already have Chris? Maybe not. With his surveillance equipment, he could have spotted the threat and took off through the woods since his vehicle was still in the garage. Her breath whooshed out in a gasp when she could no longer hold it. She shook her head. Why in the world do people hold their breath when oxygen to the brain is the most needed?

No way could the uninvited visitors hear her through the wall. She hadn't heard the electronic white noise until she entered the wardrobe. Talking voices penetrated the walls. She couldn't make out the words, but she did notice the tone was casual, not hurried, frantic, or threatening. Whoever it was didn't fear being caught. It could be confidence in their abilities. If someone noticed their vehicle, they could claim they were lost, which would be accepted easily enough.

Remembering the monitors, she glanced at the one that featured her car. The front end of another car was snugged up against hers, but not enough to identify the model. At this angle, she couldn't see the brand or if the car sported a front license plate.

Max's ears twitched, and his muscles bunched as he surged up into a sitting posture and barked three times in succession.

"No, no, no," she shushed the dog in a whisper.

Max ignored her and wagged his tail. So far, Max had demonstrated an instinct for danger. He knew to keep his snout shut around bad guys, and he had a sixth sense about picking out culprits, often before she did. Not always, though. Sometimes if food was involved, it was harder for him to make the determination. Still, he *acted* happy.

Whoever it was must be walking the perimeter as she had because the voices were coming closer. She heard, "Christmas town creepy movie set."

Her hand went up to her mouth as she blinked. A shaky laugh escaped her lips, causing Max to regard her curiously. Elvin. It was Elvin and Karly. Of course. After all, she did give them directions to Chris's home. All she had to do was get the two of them into the house to let Max and her out. Nala grabbed her phone and texted a message. The notification chime she heard through the wall meant Elvin had it on high.

"Look," Elvin called out. "It's Nala, and she's inside."

"Why didn't she answer when we knocked?" Karly inquired.

This caused Max to erupt into a barking frenzy, drowning out what they said. No need. She'd texted they were locked in the safe room inside the wardrobe in the bedroom, which should be self-explanatory enough. All they had to do was come in and release the door mechanism. No problem unless she locked the back door. "Sugar cookies!"

Well, it might be up to her to serve as her own rescuer. That's what private investigators who have their own weekly television show managed to do. Think. Chris wouldn't want anyone accidentally discovering it while he was inside. Wouldn't be much of a safe room if that was the case. That meant she might not be locked in. All she had to do was figure out how to open the door. Jiggling the handle hadn't helped. The only way she could open the door of her ancient backyard shed was by lifting the handle before trying to swing it open. Feeling hopeful, she tried that method. No luck. She slumped against the door.

She could hear footsteps and Karly. "Nala! Max! Where are you?"

"In here!" she yelled, then realized that was probably no help. "In the bedroom. Through the wardrobe!"

Max added in his commentary by barking.

Footsteps came closer and knocking penetrated the wall as her potential rescuers tried to discover the door. Nala pounded on her side. "Pull the bottom boxes!"

"Got it!" Elvin called out. There was some shuffling noises and scratching at the door, but no opening. After what felt like forever, the door swung open, revealing her friends. Before she could say anything, Elvin did. "That's another fine mess you got yourself into."

No doubt it was from a movie she'd never seen. "Thanks." She blew out an audible breath and wiped her brow. "I think I might have a touch of claustrophobia."

Elvin tried to peer around Nala, but she gave him a shove. "Move. You can crawl in yourself after I am out."

He scooted out of the wardrobe to allow her to exit. Nala checked to make sure she had her phone and squatted in the door, ready to crawl through when Max shouldered her aside and squeezed through the opening. Typical.

Nala followed more slowly into the bedroom where she stood, stretched, and shot a hand through her hair. *Freedom!* It smelled like peppermint, although technically, the air inside the hidden room and outside were pretty much the same. The bedroom felt so much better especially with the sunlight shining into the room. No way would she be stuck in the peculiar safe room/security closet for the rest of her life.

She gave an all-over shake like what Max would do when caught in the rain. Rather than raindrops, she wanted to shake off the apprehension that had settled on her shoulders. For the briefest moment, she could see Chris's house being sold since he was never found and an unsuspecting family buying it, unaware there was a human and dog skeleton hidden behind the walls.

"What took you so long to open that door?"

"Locked back door." He arched an eyebrow as if she had forgotten this detail. "Even if Santa is missing, I don't want to get on his bad side by breaking a window of his home to gain entrance. Lucky for you I brought my burglary tools. I doubt anyone who's looking to knock over a casino will call me, but I was quick enough for your purposes."

"You're right. Sorry I didn't act more grateful." Feeling much more at ease, she decided to tease Elvin. "Tell you what. To show you how appreciative I am, I'll say nothing to my father about your burglary tools or your breaking into this house and who knows how many other marginally legal things you might have done."

"Hey!" He angled his head in Karly's direction. She had a wide grin on her face, clearly amused at Elvin's discomfort. "You'll give her the wrong idea."

"Ha!" Nala nodded in her best friend's direction. "She knows you. Any thoughts she might have about you will be close to the truth."

The wardrobe door swung wide as Elvin peered in and wrestled with the now closed hidden door. "What's up with this? It was just open."

Nala pivoted at Elvin's grumbling in time to witness his lower half protruding from the wardrobe. "Here." She tapped on his back to get his attention.

Elvin backed out, squatted beside the door, and gestured to the interior of the wardrobe. "By all means my lady."

She wrinkled her nose and glanced at his hands. "You'll need gloves. Can't have you messing up evidence."

"Puh-lease." He made a derisive snort and pulled a pair of blue latex gloves from his pocket. "I'm a professional. The entire reason I drove down here was to pick up the fingerprints. Karly told me about all the different flavors of hot chocolate, so I might check that out, too." He told Nala, "Demonstrate how you managed to open the door and then lock yourself in."

"That's an issue." She glanced around the room, and her gaze landed on the discarded black boots." Picking one up, she motioned for Elvin to move. "Let me show you. It's a trick door, and I stumbled upon it by accident. As you found, the boxes are all connected. When you pull on the bottom one it opens." The door swung open on cue. "It's a bit dim inside with no windows. A flashlight would be helpful." She wedged the boot into the opening should the door shut the way it had before.

Elvin reached into his pocket and pulled out a small flashlight and twisted it on. Surprisingly, the man was prepared even if the purple sparkly flashlight didn't fit Elvin's persona. Despite his short stature, lack of muscles, and T-shirts with comments only other nerds would understand, he saw himself as an action hero.

"Isn't that my flashlight?" she asked.

He shrugged his shoulders. "Could be. You need to keep better track of your stuff."

It wasn't worth fussing over. She might as well use Elvin's expertise while he was here. "Take a look. There are all sorts of closed-circuit camera monitors inside. Obviously, Chris kept an eye on anyone or anything approaching the house."

Elvin pushed up his slipping glasses with one finger. "Yeah, right," Elvin concluded. "I'll take a look around and get back to you." He turned and crawled into the wardrobe but made sure to use the boot to prop the door open.

With Elvin out of the room, but aware of how voices travel, Nala stepped closer to Karly to whisper, "What's up with your hitching a ride with Elvin?"

At times, Karly could be a little critical of Elvin, not willing to give him much slack on his movie quotes or his wannabe tough guy façade. Most people didn't take Elvin seriously, and those who did were usually on the Internet or were utilizing his tech services or both. Nala sucked in her lips realizing she had been almost as judgy, unaware of Elvin's skills or his gentle nature.

"You know." Karly shrugged her shoulders. "I ran into him at the coffee shop, and he mentioned driving down here. I figured, why not? I could say hi to my relatives. Maybe visit the old haunts if time allowed." She sidestepped a little closer. "What I really wanted to know was about your tropical trip with some exotic hottie. By the way, if you aren't interested in the hunky Officer Goodnight, would you mind if I decided to take a run at him?"

Not the tropical trip again. Nala grimaced, then sighed. "Look around," she gestured to the modest bedroom. "This *is* my getaway vacation. When I find Chris, he'll be my exotic male. Geesh, they say small towns have a gossip hotline. As for Tyler Goodnight." She swatted her friend on the arm. "Hands off. Thanks for reminding me to call him though."

"I expected as much." A snort emphasized her feelings. "Can't blame a girl for trying. What are your plans for the rest of the day?"

That was a good question. "My first order of business is to comb through the house in search of clues, then Chris's truck. I'd love for Max to talk to Dasher, Chris's dog, but he's locked up in Selma and Bob's home where I can't get to him. Anytime I show up in public, I'm mobbed by folks wanting me to take their photos. Tonight, I'm invited to a square dance thing. Not sure if it is an actual event or just practice."

"Okay." Karly held up a finger. "Back up a little. What's with everyone wanting their photos taken?"

Obviously, Selma hadn't shared her plans with Karly, probably afraid the information might get out, which was a legitimate concern. "Your aunt thought I needed a cover since this isn't the busy season and my appearance might pique curiosity."

"True." She raised her index finger again and gave it a tiny wave. "Are you just someone who likes to take random photos of people you've never met or does your cover have a purpose?"

The unease Nala had initially felt at deceiving folks who were so anxious to have their visage on a glossy page returned. "They think I'm making some cutesy book about Santa Claus. Quite frankly, I wish I were. Some of the photos are darling. Everyone will be so disappointed when nothing happens with them."

"Don't worry. They'll forget as soon as something else happens. There could be a UFO spotted, a local girl runs off with a carnie, a cow could have triplet calves. That's a rare occurrence. Could be a resident got onto one those reality shows, too."

Maybe she was giving her appearance much more weight than it deserved. Before she could answer, Elvin popped out of the wardrobe. He dusted off his clothes with his hands and then announced, "Equipment is old. The notebook he uses for a logbook makes no sense. The tape that's in there now had been taped over several times. I can't really say much more." He shuddered. "It gave me a glimpse of what my life might be like if I don't socialize more."

"I would have thought Chris socialized a great deal. Besides his job, which consisted of non-stop children sitting on his lap, there was also his daily rounds of the town."

Her intention had been to joke, but his expression wasn't amused. Nothing was going as expected. She shouldn't tease Elvin about desperate situations when she was relying on Max to extract vital information from another dog. Max would have to talk to Dasher or at least try to get some impressions from the terrier. At least she had that option.

"You got the fingerprints of your harasser?" Elvin changed the subject for his real reason behind the drive.

"They're in the car. I'll get them for you. No reason for you to take off right away." The prospect of being left alone in a town full of strangers didn't appeal. Never mind there was someone who wanted her out of the place pronto.

"I gotta go right now," Elvin insisted.

He turned and headed to the hall. Nala trailed after him, aware that if he didn't get going, she had no results anytime soon. It could be useful, or it could turn out to be teens playing a joke. It made her wonder how they got her number.

"Okay," she agreed as they reached the living room. Max padded beside her. Karly brought up the rear. The four of them exited the house. Nala retrieved her box with the fingerprint tape from the car and handed it to Elvin. "It was nice of you two coming down even it was for a few minutes." Nala appreciated the rescue from the hidden room plus the mood lift her friends' familiar presences brought with them. She held up a hand in parting and managed a weak smile. "Safe travels, y'all. I appreciate your making the long trip."

Elvin smirked, strolled to his car, opened the door, reached in, and withdrew a duffle decorated with dog footprints. Placing it on the ground, he told her, "Karly's staying. I thought you knew."

Nope. She cut her eyes to her best friend, who gave a little finger wave and a sheepish smile. Most people might think extra help would be a good thing, but that was only true when the person knew exactly what to do. Not knowing the details was one of the reasons teachers refused to call in subs when they should go home sick. It was too much work putting a lesson plan together with the possibility it wouldn't be followed. Lucky her, she had a novice to train while actively searching for Chris and maintaining her cover as a photo journalist. Since her trainee and best friend were the same, tact would be essential. Her day just kept getting better and better.

Chapter Twelve

THE SPORTS CAR reversed down the gravel driveway with a grinning Elvin at the wheel. He knew how Nala would feel with an unexpected helper dropped on her. Probably the same way he'd feel. Annoyed. Worse, she couldn't say anything because it would be taken wrong and would hurt her best friend's feelings. Speaking of Karly, she was practically bouncing with excitement or a sugar high if they stopped at the Candy Castle before coming here.

"Ah," Nala started, not sure what to say as Karly launched herself toward her for a big hug.

"This is going to be so much fun." Karly released her hold on Nala, rocked back on her heels, and clapped her hands together. "Ever since you became a private eye, I've wanted to help."

Nala forced a smile. She'd certainly heard enough hints and outright suggestions about how her friend might help. "You helped. Remember Comicon?"

"Yeah, right." She gave a derisive snort. "I helped Harry hawk T-shirts and other merchandise while you dashed after the culprit."

"It's what I do. Besides, we needed to be at Comicon to catch the guy. Often being a PI is a waiting game. I'm not sure what you can do right now. Obviously, I am going to go through the house, have

Max talk to Dasher, then apparently go to a square dance meeting. Not sure what there is for you to do." Even though there wasn't anything obvious her friend could handle, Karly's only mode of transportation was tearing up Highway 69 even as she spoke.

Karly delivered a playful arm slap with a grin. "That's where you're wrong, partner. This is a small town, and you're an outsider. No reason for folks to open up to you. In fact, they might hide any information they think might reflect badly on themselves, the town, or Chris."

Even though Nala had never lived in a small town, she understood the dynamics. Outsiders received the blame for everything from license plate switching to picking morel mushrooms from a guarded secret location. Poor economy along with new-fangled ideas was laid at the feet of outsiders, too. Someone already was trying to run her out of town. Perhaps Karly's influence as a former local could be helpful. "Are folks going to come up to you and tell you all their secrets?"

"No need. I know most of them." She held up her index finger. "Remember Aunt Selma. There's not much she doesn't know. What I'm hoping for is some small talk. Anything new or different is always up for discussion. Someone could have noticed something that might be helpful in your investigation. It might not be a thing by itself, but several different oddities that together could become a lead. Even Aunt Selma can't be everywhere. As hard as it may be to believe, some folks avoid Selma. They find her a bit overpowering."

"Oh, really?" Nala feigned surprise by arching her eyebrows and covering her mouth with her hand. "That's preposterous!" They both giggled at the idea.

Maybe it would be helpful to have Karly as her assistant. More than one time she could have used a hand, especially when she was being shot at or pursued. "Throw your duffle in the car. We need to go over the house and see if there's anything someone might want."

"Wouldn't Chris have taken any valuables with him if he'd left on his own?" Karly straightened to her full height and pushed back her shoulders. An air of confidence settled around her. This wasn't her area of expertise, but she was asking some good questions.

Nala waited for her friend to stow the duffle before answering. "I thought that. I also wondered if Chris was what they wanted, for whatever reason. Maybe he's a billionaire. It could be he has a secret treasure map tattooed on his back, or maybe he was part of a bank heist and his partners just got out of jail. I'm hoping to find some type of a clue that might help us locate him. Apparently, a Christmas themed park doesn't work well without the jolly old elf."

"Wow," Karly shook her head. "I thought *I* had an imagination. You got me beat. Let's go see what we can find." A pivot had her heading back to the house. Max, who had peeled off when Karly made the decision to enter the house, loped around the side of the house. His ears were tented forward as he sniffed the ground, which meant he was onto something.

"You find anything?" Nala queried.

He paused in his sniffing and glanced up. "Dunno. People have been around here. I picked up the scent of popcorn, taffy apple, cheese on a stick, and pistachio ice cream."

Nala didn't doubt his summary since food smells were his specialty. "They all sound like theme park foods. I imagine anyone who came to visit him would have been by the park where all those foods are available." The impression she received from the cameras and Bob's reluctance to enter the house was Chris was not a fan of visitors. "No Chris scent trails?"

"Lemme see." He put his nose to the ground and moved a few feet toward the house, then came back in the direction of the garage. "Ah, several trails going from the house to the garage. Dasher is all over the place. That dog felt the need to mark everything."

Nala fought back a smirk. For a canine, Max could be remarkably sensitive about things. No need to mention his habit of peeing on anything over six inches tall. "What's your most recent trail for St. Nick?"

"Who?" Max stared up in confusion.

"Chris," she clarified. There were times she thought Max could read her mind. More often, she had to explain what she meant. Even though her dog could speak due to the gift of enchantment, his vocabulary was somewhat limited as was his ability to reason.

"Okay." He shook his shaggy head, then moved his snout about an inch from the ground, slowly surveying the area, sweeping his head back and forth as if it were a metal detector. He stopped, sniffed audibly, and then picked up his pace moving past the garage and into the woods. This could be it.

Nala darted after her dog, crunching through the fallen leaves, and giving wide berth to anything that resembled poison ivy in the slightest. The trees were far enough apart to allow passage, but only if she turned sideways and sucked in her stomach. After a hard scramble of tripping over tree roots and surprising squirrels who scolded her with their high-pitched chatter, the trees thinned out some. In any action adventure movie, she'd have stumbled into a secret staging area for ominous activities.

Instead, there was the happy gurgle of a creek splashing its way through the trees, causing Max to toss a backward glance at Nala, who motioned him forward. "Go on. We have to cross the water."

Many dogs loved splashing in water. A few even had their own child pools to play in during the hot summer months. Not Max. He could be a bit fastidious about the oddest things. Creeks must be one of his issues.

"Go! Go!" Nala encouraged without any luck.

She bent to give the canine a little nudge toward the water, which caused Max to shoot her a dark look. "No pushing!"

Nala raised her hands to demonstrate she would not engage in forcing her crime-solving partner into the water. Satisfied, Max gave a slight nod before daintily stepping into the water that reached halfway up his leg. He crossed slowly, glancing back and forth for something that could possibly knock him down or pull him underwater. Once he reached the other side, he called back to Nala, "Your turn."

Despite the diminutive size of the creek, Nala had no desire to muddy her feet. Surely there had to be another way. Maybe a log had fallen across the stream. A quick visual survey up and down the stream revealed a basic bridge that consisted of a few planks but no handrails. The weathered wood matched the landscape, which explained why she hadn't noticed it before. Nala jogged up to the bridge and strolled across it. Once across, she joined Max, who was sulking.

"There was a bridge, and you tried to push me in the water?"

Yeah, it did look bad. As much as she loved Max, he was always pointing out examples of how people victimized dogs by treating them like, well, animals. "I didn't see it until just now. You can use it going back."

"I will. I just need to pick up the path on this side of the trail."

He sniffed and walked a few feet, retraced his steps, and headed in another direction. By the time Max had tried out three of the cardinal directions, a childish shriek brought his head up. A pair of children dashed by where Nala and Max stood hidden in the tree shadows. They were back at the campground. This wasn't exactly helpful. Maybe Chris *did* dart through the woods to escape someone.

"Max?"

He blew out an audible breath. "Dunno. I was following the candy scent. Lots of candy scents here. Some are much newer." He cleared his throat. "This isn't my specialty. You need a bloodhound to untangle these scents."

Even though they were half-hidden by the trees, someone spotted them. "Look, it's the photographer!"

Exactly what she didn't need. Without giving it too much thought, Nala whirled and plunged back into the woods, hopefully going back the direction she came. In a rush, she stepped into the creek, which was as cold and muddy as she expected. The sound of leaves crunching and branches breaking accompanied Max surging past her. At least he'd know the way back. Some shouts behind her and even the sound of a possible chase, spurred Nala on even more. This must have been how Chris felt, except his pursuers could have been much more deadly as opposed to wanting their faces immortalized in a coffee table book.

A stitch in her side made it hard to run and breathe at the same time. Fingers pushed into the problem area eased it somewhat, but she had to slow to a fast walk while keeping her eyes on Max, who had cut his pace, too. You'd think they'd be back at Chris's house by now. They certainly returned at a much faster pace than they left. A tree stump to her left served as a platform for an indignant squirrel who fussed at her as she passed. Wasn't that the same squirrel she had passed earlier?

The sun filtered through the trees picking out a path. This *must* be the way back. Chris must have taken a short cut through the woods to visit his friend Bob. Could be Bob used the path to visit Chris as opposed to the golf cart. Confidence returned with the appearance of the path. Nala whistled for Max, and the two set out on the revealed passage for about eight feet until the path split into three separate paths.

"Really?" she questioned. Unlike anyone familiar with the area who would know which one to pick, she didn't.

Her gaze moved to Max who sat and said, "I got nothing."

"What about your famous tracking ability?"

"Hey, I was escaping, like you." He lowered his head to the ground and gave a couple of loud sniffs before answering. "Nope. We haven't been this way before."

"That's no help." She placed one hand on her hip and peered at the trees. It wasn't as if they were lost in 200,000 acres of Hoosier National Forest. They were in a strip of woods. If they kept walking, they were bound to hit a road eventually. Not exactly the plan she had for today, but few things went as planned.

"Yoo-hoo!" a woman's voice called in the distance. "Max! Nala! Where are you?"

"Karly! We're here!" Nala shouted. "Keep calling and we'll find you!"

In less than five minutes, they scampered out of the wood, discovering they were only about eight feet from where they first entered. *Geesh.* All those trees tended to look the same. Her city roots were showing, and an outdoor survival course might be in order.

The first thing she did was hug her friend. "I'm so glad you're here. We could have been lost in the woods forever."

"Hardly," her friend replied while returning the hug. "When I realized the two of you didn't come back into the house, I came outside. For the most part, I could hear you crashing through the woods, or at least I hoped it was you. Not sure what I would say if some stranger popped out of the trees. I considered yelling *this is private property, and you're trespassing.*" Her shoulders went up in a shrug. "I had no plans after that. I thought it was you since anyone else would try to be quieter."

"Ha, ha." Sure, Karly was right, but it didn't need repeating. "Max was on the trail of Chris. He apparently went through the woods, but Max lost him at the creek."

Max coughed and managed to raise his doggy brows. "*I* lost him?"

"Yeah." She knew Max was offended, but it was a fact. "We got to the creek, and you couldn't pick up the scent again."

"Thanks for reminding me. I'll make sure to remind you of all *your* failures." He snorted a few times letting Nala know he was hurt.

Quick to react, Karly withdrew a dog treat from her pocket and flipped it in Max's direction. He snapped the delicacy out of the air with the precision a baseball player would envy.

Karly gestured to the woods. "Chris headed to the woods because he probably felt safe there. After living here forever, he's walked the woods often. I wouldn't be surprised if he walked in the creek to hide his scent and didn't get out where it might be expected. It wouldn't matter since he knew the woods."

Nala clapped her hands together. "That's it. We need to go back through the woods, over the creek, and up and down the other side to pick up the scent."

A doggy groan sounded. "Couldn't we have lunch first? My nose needs a break, especially after all that sniffing in the dusty room."

Maybe he had a point, or more likely, he was stalling. "Okay. Lunch break."

Karly waved her hand as if in class awaiting permission to speak. At least she waited, as opposed to Max, who tended to blurt out everything. Then again, Max had never been to school.

"Go ahead."

"I know a Mexican restaurant in Dale. Not so close where every-one wants their photos taken, but close enough to pick up on local gossip." She pointed to herself. "See, it helps having someone who knows the area."

Chapter Thirteen

T HE INDIAN SUMMER weather allowed the Mexican restaurant to keep their outdoor seating section, complete with open red, white, and green striped table umbrellas. Another plus was having someone familiar with the area guiding her. Nala pulled into the parking spot and gave her friend a thumbs up.

"Good call. I always prefer an outdoor table when I can get it because of Max. I also don't like to talk about a case inside a restaurant. I've been in plenty of restaurants and heard conversations most wouldn't care to have overheard."

"Like what?" Karly asked as she swung open the car door. Max, possibly imagining being left in the car, had his feet on the back of her seat ready to surge into the front if needed.

Nala jumped out of the car and opened the back door to derail her dog's unsavory behavior. The car might be used, but it was new to her. She intended to keep it in good condition. She whistled, getting Max's attention, and pointed to the open door. He emerged with head and tail up as if that had been his intention all along.

Returning to the conversation, Nala said, "Mom and I went out to eat, and there was only us and a couple of women in the entire restaurant. They put us in back to back booths. At some point, my mother motioned to me to be quiet, and we just listened to the women behind us talk. They were planning to spy on one of their husbands. They had it all laid out from using a cellphone taped underneath his car to track his movements to checking his voice mail while he slept."

"You should have offered your services," Karly quipped as she led the way to a table a bit farther away from the rest. The isolation was probably designed to be used for romance as opposed to business.

The restaurant door opened as several women exited, allowing Mariachi music to slip out along with spicy mouth-watering aromas.

"Maybe I would have if I had been in the business at that time." She pointed to the ground, and Max took his place under the table without a fuss, which was unusual. "The conversation impressed upon me how easily other people in the restaurant could hear private conversations. After that, I always wanted to sit where I wasn't practically sitting in someone's lap. It's not always possible."

"Hear ya." Karly nodded and selected a laminated menu standing between two bottles of hot sauce. "I see they still have lunch specials. When I suggested this place, I was half afraid they might not be in business. Glad to see I was wrong. How about we order, then you can tell me everything you have found out so far."

A dark-haired man attired in black pants and shirt backed out of the restaurant carrying a round tray loaded with ice waters, salsa, and chips. That was fast. He must have seen them getting out of the car.

"Bienvendios," he said with a wide smile. "Welcome. Are you ready to order?"

Karly, who had been perusing the menu, answered first. "The

Speedy Gonzales Special."

The appearance of the server had Nala grabbing a menu and scanning it. "Dora the Explorer for me. I'll need some more water, too."

Their server wrote down their orders and glanced at Nala's untouched water glass. "Más de aqua. More water, right away. Maybe you are part camel," he teased.

"Maybe," Nala agreed, not pointing out the large dog under the table. Since the table was open wrought iron, it would be hard to miss Max. Still, some servers could be a bit wonky about a dog, even in the outside area. A few were uneasy when it was a large canine. Never mind that most dog bites come from small, fearful dogs. This meant she'd need to be on the server's good side. She acted amused and grinned at the server. "Just call me dromedary."

Karly muffled a giggle as the man walked away. "I don't think he knew you were talking about a type of camel. He may have thought that was your name."

If so, it wasn't the casual flirty attitude she was hoping to convey. Oh well, flirty was never her forte.

Nala retrieved a stainless-steel dog dish from her purse and poured her water into it before setting it on the ground. Max slurped up the water and gazed at his now empty dish, which resulted in Karly upending her water into the dish.

"He'll call us both camels," Karly wiggled her eyebrows. "What's the name of the other type of camel? I can be that one."

I don't know." Nala shrugged. "It's best we say nothing. You see how well my attempt at humor went."

"True." Karly picked up a tortilla chip and crunched down on it. "Look at us. Mexican restaurant again. Is it my turn to pick up the tab?"

Money was such a necessary evil which became very apparent when working for herself. One of the positives about working as a teacher for the school system was a regular paycheck. "Depends on if you can get your aunt to part with the money she offered as my retainer but never paid."

"Sounds like Aunt Selma. She's a bit of a tightwad." Karly pointed with her chip. "You need to ask Bob. He's the reasonable one of the pair. On the surface, he may not say a great deal, but he knows much more than most realize. I wouldn't be too surprised if he doesn't know what happened to Chris."

Nala slapped both hands down on the table rattling it. "Why am I here if your uncle knows what happened to Chris? Better yet, will I still get paid?"

"Chill," Karly held a finger to her lips, then dropped it. "Some folks took a table behind us and are staring. Don't get so hyper. I didn't mean Bob *knows* he knows. I meant he might have noticed details which, put together, could be legitimate clues. He's not a gossip and wouldn't dare say anything aloud because Aunt Selma would spread it around." She pointed to Nala, "Your job is to put together the clues. You need to talk to Uncle Bob."

The memory of her first visit to Chris's house complete with Bob's escort hadn't been exactly illuminating. She doubted Bob knew about all the cameras and the secret room. All the man did was hover and fuss about how Chris liked things just so. Then again, it could be construed as if he were afraid of her finding something. Maybe he *did* help install the cameras. Elvin commented that the technology was well dated.

"When will I be able to talk to Bob?"

"We're going to the square dance meeting later." Karly moved her shoulders as if dancing. "You can try some of that ambush interview technique as you do-si-do."

Max tried to stand, bumping the table, getting both their attention. "I never heard you order for me unless you plan on sharing."

He had a point. With the waiter ready to take their order, Nala had rushed to pick out her own meal, but had forgotten his. "I brought your kibble. It's nutritionally complete and makes your coat shine."

"Cardboard. You are torturing me with bland food with no smell. At least cats get food that smells good."

Karly coughed and scratched her neck. She whispered, "Couple staring. I think they can hear Max but can't figure out which one of us eats cat food or wants to eat it. My money is on you. Oh, look, here comes our food."

"Food," Max blurted the word, then lunged out from under the table, tripped the server, and sent the dishes flying. Tacos, enchiladas, and rice separated from the plates that landed with a rattle. Thank goodness it was all plastic. The former playful waiter glared at Max, who ignored the man and gobbled up the pavement buffet.

"I'm so sorry," Nala started and cut her eyes to Max, who made haste to lick up every bit of food before he was stopped. "He's usually better behaved than this." He wasn't. "Ah, could we order again?"

The server bent to pick up the plates and shook his head. "I have a dog at home. I should have expected him to dash out like that, especially when food is involved. His tummy will hurt tonight. The food is too spicy for dogs."

"You're so right." That was the reason she never gave Max anything other than chips or a cheeseburger from the children's menu. They'd have to stop by the drugstore for some medicine and getting Max to take it should be listed under the labors of Hercules. He was not a fan of pill taking, but he *was* a fan of cheese if she had any to hide the pill in.

Even though Nala suspected it would serve no purpose, she snapped her fingers and pointed to the area under the table. Max gave her a *who me?* look, glanced around for any missed food, then finding none, lay down beneath the table. Once the server picked up all the dishes, he stacked them on his tray and left. Only the curious couple still eyed them.

Karly coughed into her hand. "Didn't you tell me a private investigator has to keep a low profile?"

"Please." Nala covered her face with her hand. "Think hard. Who thought I needed a dog, especially one who talks and demands cheeseburgers?"

"Ah," Karly started, putting her hand to her neck. "The talking part I'll own, but you're the one who spoiled him by feeding him fast food."

No need to point out that Karly often gave Max fast food tidbits, as did Elvin and Tyler, plus her parents—although they would all deny it. She leaned a little closer to make it harder for the couple to eavesdrop. "You try to ignore a talking dog who follows you around chanting cheeseburger, cheeseburger. With an ordinary dog, you could give him dog food, and he gives you sad eyes, and you make up a story he's sad because the cat next door bullies him. With Max, there's no question of what he's thinking."

Max nudged her leg. "You say that like it's a bad thing."

Then there was his excellent hearing. She cleared her throat and added, "Max has been an excellent help in all my cases."

"I solved most of them," Max added.

"Helped," Nala clarified.

The sound of chairs scraped the pavement as the couple got up to leave while the woman whined. "I don't think they're dangerous. I still want my chimichanga."

Oh my! The last thing she wanted to do was ruin the lunch crowd business. "We ran off that couple."

Karly waved aside the matter. "I thought the woman looked familiar. The whine brought it back. No worries. Aunt Selma told me about her. She likes her margaritas, so they'll be back. Let's talk about your info gathering at the square dance."

Why was it everyone who wasn't a private eye had ideas about how it should be done? Besides having her father turn every childhood activity into a learning lesson on observational skills and understanding motivations, she did take courses in investigations but probably learned more from Sawyer by helping him with his insurance fraud cases.

"I don't know how to square dance."

"No problem. Square dancing was made for people who can't dance. That's why they call out the moves. None are that tricky." She gave a thumbs up and a broad wink.

"Thanks for the vote of confidence in my dancing skills, I think." She grimaced. "Anyhow, I don't think people talk while square dancing."

"You'd be surprised. Most of them *do* talk. Sometimes, it's just a hello and how are you kind of thing while others have punctuated conversations interrupted by partner changes."

It sounded doable. "Not sure how this wouldn't attract attention.

Excuse me, Bob! When did you and Chris put up all the surveillance equipment?"

"Surely you can come up with something not so obvious. Isn't that what you PIs do? Just make stuff up?"

"All the time." It was sad this was what her best friend thought she did. "I'll come up with something like an excuse to talk to Bob while not skipping across the floor."

"Sounds like a plan," Karly enthused as the server reappeared. Just to be safe, Nala wrapped her hand around Max's collar to make sure they received their food this time.

Their server kept a wary eye on Max as he placed the plates on the table. "Enjoy."

IT DIDN'T TAKE too long to square up their check with the server for their meals and the ones Max ate. Karly picked up Max's leash as the three of them wound their way around the outside tables and to the parking lot. The sizable sedan sat exactly *where* she left it, but not *how.*

"Um." Karly narrowed her eyes as she read the windshield. "*Leave now before it's too late. Exclamation point. Exclamation point. Exclamation point.* How did they know which car was yours?"

Good question. It might be she was followed or, as the only new person in a town of two thousand, her appearance and car were noted. Nala turned slowly, scanning the parking lot for any fleeing individuals, only spotting a slow-moving elderly man leaving the optical center. Nope, not a suspect, or if he was, she'd have to congratulate him on his disguise. Her attention shifted back to the car as she approached it and wiped the *l* with her finger, smearing it and making it look more like *ate.* Shoe polish perhaps wasn't the preferred tool of vandals. On the plus side, she did have window cleaner in her trunk.

First, she needed a photo for evidence, which would require her phone.

"Damn punks!" the elderly man growled as he walked past their car. "The world is going to hell in a handbasket."

Karly grinned and waved at the man. "Mr. Nelson. Hello!" She waved hard only to have the man shoot her a suspicious glance.

The man reached into his pocket and withdrew a pink canister and yelled, "Stay away, punk!"

Nala recognized the bright pink cylinder as pepper spray. They usually sold them in pairs in the gun shops as a mother and daughter set. "Watch out! He has pepper spray!"

"What?" Karly asked, but Max heard her and lunged to hide, dragging Karly along.

They both tried to hide behind Nala. As for the old man, he kept walking and grumbling to himself. People assumed small towns were filled with cute, cheerful folks while the dangerous people lived in cities. Ha!

Once he was tucked into his car, Nala asked, "Who was that?"

"He used to be Aunt Selma's neighbor. Maybe still is." Her shoulders went up in a shrug. "Didn't recognize me though."

"He's a bit paranoid."

"Always was."

Nala used the camera to capture the message. No way was she driving while peering through the various letters. It might spark a conversation that she didn't want. Before spritzing the windshield, she leaned closer to see if a convenient handprint was visible. There wasn't. She spritzed away.

"Isn't that evidence?" Karly asked, angling her head to the windshield.

"Not really. No obvious prints. Besides, I'm certain it's the same prints I sent with Elvin. I hate to think I have someone else trying to run me out of town." She returned to the trunk to look for paper towels, followed by both Karly and Max.

"Who's threatening you?"

Nala turned slowly and raised her eyebrows. "Did you miss the part about Elvin driving down here to pick up prints to analyze?"

"Ha, ha." Karly grimaced as if the forced laugh hurt. "I know you don't have a *name* for the individual, but who do you think it is? Someone who doesn't want you to find Chris? Could it be an unhappy customer? Maybe it's some cheating husband you unmasked. What do you think?"

Nala tried to shake off the idea of so many people having it in for her. Spotting the paper towel roll, she ripped off a few and headed for the windshield while Karly padded after her and nudged her with her elbow.

"Well?" Karly insisted.

"It has to be someone around here. Whoever it is, is asking me to leave. No one was threatening me back in Indy."

She sighed. It seemed like forever since she was home. Make a mental note. Call Tyler. It would be nice to talk to someone friendly. Yeah, that's what she'd do. Didn't have an excuse to call him, except she wanted to.

"Earth to Nala!" Karly said, cupping her hands around her mouth.

Brownies! What was wrong with Karly yelling in a strip mall parking lot? "Shush." She placed a finger up to her lips and lowered her voice. "Remember, we're undercover."

"Okay," Karly enunciated in a loud whisper. "What did you do to tick off a local?"

Never one to be left out of the conversation, Max added, "Yeah, what?"

Truthfully, she hadn't been here long enough to annoy someone—or at least she didn't think so.

Chapter Fourteen

Most of the drive back consisted of Max hanging out the car window, barking at any other dog who happened to be out for a drive. Nala, who'd had enough of his antics, yelled, "Stop that!"

Max pulled in his head and rested it on Nala's shoulders as he spoke. "I have to bark when the other dog barks first. It would be rude not to."

Yeah, that sounded totally bogus like something Max would make up, only Karly cleared her throat. "Um, he's right. Dogs have feelings, too. How would you feel if someone snubbed you when you delivered a cheery welcome bark?"

Sometimes, Nala felt her friend spent much more time communicating with animals than she did with people. "Well, ah, if I barked at anyone, I imagine they'd not only reply, but would definitely keep their distance."

"Ha, ha!" Karly forced her laughter. "You know what I meant."

They were passing through Santa Claus, causing Nala to slow. Not only did the speed limit drop significantly, but due to the small size of the town, she could overshoot the narrow drive to Chris's house if she wasn't careful. It reminded her of what she needed to do before she went to the square dance ambush interview session.

"How's the old tummy, Max?"

He yawned, releasing a cloud of doggy breath. "I could eat."

"Not exactly what I was thinking. We need to pick up on Chris's trail while the light is still good."

A groan filled her ear. "Work. Work. Work. That's all you ever want to do."

"It's the reason we're here," Nala reminded him and wiggled her shoulders, hoping to dislodge Max but didn't succeed. "I need you to talk to Dasher, too."

"Listen to you. Where would you be without me?"

"He has a point," Karly pointed out as the car slowed and made the turn into the gravel driveway.

You'd think Karly would take her side as opposed to the dog's. "There are a lot of things Max can do." No reason to point out that often he didn't do them, or they didn't work out as she planned. "Without my helpful canine, I'd have to talk to more people or peep through social media accounts."

"Yeah," Max agreed loudly. "Think about that next time I ask for a cheeseburger."

Leave it to her dog to bring everything back to food. No need to mention he wasn't getting any special treats after devouring their lunch. The best he could hope for was some liquid antacid or some grass to ease his belly. She pulled the car behind the house and parked. If anyone happened to drive by, they wouldn't notice the strange car at Chris's house.

"We're here. Let's go. I want to take another look through the house. The first time, I saw nothing that might tempt a thief since most everything is about three decades behind the time."

Nala bounced out of the car, ready to track down Chris. The

meal had energized her. She waited for Karly and Max to make their exits a bit more slowly. She pulled out the key Bob had given her and put her hand on the knob when it moved under her fingers. The door was already open. The memory of her locking and checking the door surfaced. No way was she leaving the door wide open for anyone who wanted to take a stroll through Santa's abode. Besides, Bob had impressed upon her how particular Chris was about his home. He wouldn't have been all too thrilled about their going through the house. The very least she could do was make sure she'd closed the house up tight.

She cut her eyes to Karly and whispered, "It's unlocked."

That meant someone could be inside—possibly the same person behind Chris's mysterious disappearance. If they had Chris, why come back? Her heart skipped a beat while her mind raced. Here was one of those touchy moments when the wrong decision could either solve the case or possibly endanger her life and Karly's.

Apparently, she failed to relate the gravity of the moment because her friend smirked and said, "You probably forgot to lock the door."

"Did not," she hissed the words. "Someone could be inside right now."

Karly's eyes grew large, and she edged closer to Nala. "What should we do? Call the sheriff."

The whole reason behind hiring an investigator was to keep the matter low key. A sheriff or his deputy barreling in with lights flashing wasn't that. Besides, what if there wasn't anyone here? She would have drawn attention to herself and the missing Chris for absolutely no reason.

"Ah, we'll send Max in first. He'll tell us if anyone is in there."

Max must have heard her plans because he was slowly backing away from the house, shaking his head. When Nala slapped her thigh to get him to advance, he sat down. Max wouldn't be going in low. She thought of putting him at attention, but waved Karly back and reached inside her chambray shirt for her weapon instead. It was up to her. Even though it would be a felony if anyone reported her pretending to be a cop, Nala pushed open the door and went in low, holding her pistol with both hands in a firing stance. Her head swung side to side as she surveyed the small kitchen for anything that shouldn't be there, such as a dangerous stranger dressed in black with evil intent. Nothing.

Her father was a big proponent of using her senses. Nala straightened up, lowered her Glock, and inhaled deeply to bring all her senses into play. Someone *had* been here recently. It would be hard to explain beyond saying things felt different or that there was a disturbance in the universe. She took another deep breath. Whoever snuck in while they were at lunch wasn't here any longer. The house felt empty. Being overconfident, however, might end up with her being shot, too.

"Police! Come out with your hands up!"

Karly shouted from the outside, "I'm calling 911!"

She didn't need that. She backed up to shout out the door. "I got this officer! No need for backup."

Her friend gestured to her phone and mimed calling. Maybe she didn't understand that Nala didn't want her calling unless it was an emergency. Hopefully, lip-reading was a hidden talent for Karly as Nala silently enunciated *Don't call.*

"What?' Karly asked, holding her hand to her ear.

Television sleuths never had these issues. Nala closed her eyes and audibly exhaled. "Don't call. I think the house is empty. Let me do a walk through."

She turned and did a quick walkthrough of the house without spotting any intruders. Inside the bedroom, she made a point of peeking into the wardrobe, the secret door was pushed shut. Nothing there so she might as well pull in the rest of the team. Odd, she was almost certain someone had been in the house, but there was no sign of anything. Maybe she *hadn't* locked the door. When she turned, her eyes went to the dresser drawer that had a sock stuck in the edge of it. That wasn't there before. She'd have remembered it after Bob's insistence that Chris liked everything neat and tidy. Someone *had* been in there, which meant she needed to take prints. Her lips tilted up in a grin as she jogged back to the car to grab her fingerprints supplies. Too bad Elvin had already left for the day because she'd soon have another set of prints for him.

"What's happening?" Karly asked when she passed her.

"Prints. Possible prints. It might be best if you stayed out here." Nala tried to push out her friend's hurt expression when she announced, "You should stay outside. The more bodies in the room, the more likely evidence could be compromised."

Karly was her best friend. When you got to a certain age, it wasn't all that easy making friends. But then, it hadn't been exactly easy on her when she'd been younger, either. Nala spun around, standing inside the back-door frame. "Never mind. Come in but don't touch anything."

"I won't," Karly promised with a radiant expression. "I'm so excited. It will be like an episode of one of the crime dramas, only, I'm in it."

"Not hardly. Crime drama is only about fifty minutes of content.

Sure, it would be nice to solve a case in that time frame." She held up a finger. "Elvin can be a miracle worker, but he's never been able to get me a lab result by the next commercial break."

True to her word, Karly touched nothing and watched as Nala dusted for prints. On television, fingerprints often solved the case, or the mention of having them caused the local guy to suddenly confess. It wasn't so clear cut in real life. Fingerprints usually ended up being a smear of several prints. Even when she did get a decent set, it wasn't the smoking gun, especially if the person had a legitimate reason to be there.

After the fingerprinting, Nala decided to give Max's tracking skills another run, but Max was less than thrilled. The dog brushed his nose with his paw. "I don't like tracking. Everything smells, and it tickles sometimes."

Nala knelt beside Max and rubbed his head. "I know. Out of the three of us, you have the best nose. If I could do what you do, I'd do it."

"Would you?" Max acted mildly intrigued.

"I would. Just think of all the crimes that have been solved due to the sensitivity of a dog's nose."

"You're right." Max agreed, and his ears tented forward, a clear sign of his interest despite his initial refusal.

"I couldn't do it without you. Those bloodhounds got nothing on you." Nala knew she was doing it up a little brown, but the more over the top, the more Max liked it. No need to mention bloodhounds could track a scent twelve days old, follow a suspect in a closed moving car, stay on a trail for a hundred and thirty miles, or had a nose a thousand times more sensitive than a human's. That information she'd keep to herself. Hearing about how great another sleuth was would only dishearten her, so why do that to her dog? "Okay. Let's hit the trail. You ready?"

Max barked twice, assumed a standing position, and then pranced in place.

"Officer Max!" She waited until Max sat and assumed the attention pose. "Find."

Without any smart-alecky remarks, Max surged into action with his nose to the ground. Nala and Karly had to jog to keep up as he followed a definite path. This time he trotted over the bridge, which was different and maybe a slight detour. Knowing Max, he didn't want to get his paws wet. Like before, they ended up at the campgrounds.

"Well," Nala shot a hand through her hair, dislodging some leaves she picked up in route. "Chris came to the campground, but Max keeps losing him here."

"Too many conflicting scents or maybe Chris used a golf cart or car even," Karly said. "It makes sense he'd come here. He *is* familiar with it and all the outbuildings and cabins offer lots of great places to hide."

"True," Nala concurred as she surveyed the various campers moving around the facility: an older couple had a golf cart like Bob's and were tooling along the path; a mother and school-age daughter riding a tandem bike—possibly homeschooled; the aroma of charbroiled burgers drifting from someone's campsite; a country music station competing with the squeals of children at play and the yapping of an unhappy dog.

"He could definitely get lost in the confusion, but where would he go from here?"

Chapter Fifteen

NALA AND KARLY stood in the shadow of the woods bordering the campground while Max lowered his head to the ground and sniffed. He'd shake his head as if ridding himself of the scent, turn, and try again. This he did several times before sitting and letting out a long sigh. "This is impossible. So many scent trails, so many with candy, plus, too many dogs in the area. It's hard to ignore a urine marker."

On that point Nala would have to agree. She tended to avoid any place that smelled like urine, including public bathrooms. "Nothing?"

Max sighed again. "This is the work for a trained bloodhound."

Never mind that bloodhound's trailing ability was seventy-five percent instinct and relied on its facial folds and long ears to channel the scent to its superior nose. German Shepherds, on the other hand, were natural herders. Max's few forays at herding children and smaller animals demonstrated that history. As for his other bloodlines, it had to be opportunistic eater or a dramatic performing hound.

"Okay. I guess this brings us back to Bob." Nala cut her eyes to her friend, who nodded and spoke.

"Uncle Bob is good at keeping secrets. He must be living with Aunt Selma. I'd almost say she's as good as you at ferreting out information, but she has a much bigger time window to do it with and knows everyone involved, which probably makes it easier."

Ah yes, everyone was certain they could be a private investigator simply because they happened to be unusually curious or nosy, as in Aunt Selma's case. "Much bigger time window," Nala felt compelled to point out. "Holiday weekend starts on Friday."

The clatter of steel wheels on a wooden roller coaster track carried across the small lake. Both women turned and watched the empty cars climb, then plunge down the steep incline.

Nala pointed to the roller coaster. "They're running the rides, and it's only Wednesday."

"Checking the rides for any issues, which is a whole lot easier when no one is in them. They also clean the park and stock up before the crowds hit." Karly placed her hands on her hips and gave the place an approving look. "It gives the locals a few more days pay, too. I have to say the Christmas Land family is good about looking after their employees."

Nala agreed. It also meant whoever ran Christmas Land had to have a big investment in Chris. The possibility of the park owners having a huge life insurance policy on the jolly old elf occurred to her. It wasn't that uncommon for businesses to insure high-value employees. People died all the time from various causes, and it would take time to replace a specialized employee. During that period, a business could take a nosedive.

"How's business at Christmas Land?"

"Good enough to employ the majority of the town, especially during the season." Karly's eyes rolled upward as she considered the matter. "My grandmother told me it started after World War Two when people needed something to uplift their spirits. It was much smaller, then. Ever since, it's kept growing. The secret must be there's nothing like it for miles and miles. It's great for people who don't want to fly to much more expensive parks. They keep tweaking the place with the water park, which is second to none with two water coasters and endless slides. They also provide free parking, free drinks, and free sunscreen. What's not to like?"

Her friend's enthusiasm for the local park made Nala give in to the urge to tease her. "You sound like a commercial. You're not getting paid for this endorsement?"

"No." Karly punched Nala on the arm. "You know I can't be bought. What surprises me is you've never been here."

"Well," Nala started remembering her childhood years with her family. At any time, her father would dash out of the house even when he wasn't on duty. It seemed like he was always on call. When he reached the rank of captain, he couldn't help micromanaging things, which must have been as annoying to the officers as it was to her. When he wasn't working, he insisted on training her by using observational games. Even a simple trip to the grocery for a few things had her eyeballing the folks in the store to see who might be shoplifting or switching labels. Once, she heard him bragging he would make her into a super cop.

As for her mother, she wasn't the theme park type. Her idea of a treat was a shopping trip to Chicago or getting a mani-pedi at the local salon. "You know my family. We went to Florida once to visit cousins or maybe it was a wedding. Anyhow, we stopped in at that Mouse Park, but it was so crowded and hot my mother insisted on leaving. My father didn't disagree since he spent most of his time on the phone trying to delve into police business from hundreds of miles away. He could do that much better at the quiet, cooler hotel."

"Wow! You must have been disappointed."

She had been. "The hotel had a nice pool with a waterfall. My mother bought me tons of Mouse Merchandise so I could tell people I'd been there, which was true to a degree." She shrugged her shoulders and asked, "Does the Christmas Land family know Chris is missing?"

"Good question." Karly pursed her lips, considering the possibility. "Aunt Selma never mentioned if they did. All the same, I assumed the family who owns Christmas Land would be the only ones with deep pockets and willingness to pay to locate Chris."

Tired of sitting, Max stood, glanced back at Nala, and started walking. Even though Max returned when called about eight out of ten times, it was the two times that worried her. Nala jogged to catch up with him and snapped his leash on just to be on the safe side.

This resulted in a small groan. "Treating me like a dog again."

"Think of it as being undercover. You're only pretending to be a dog so you can interview Dasher. Let's check to see if Bob is back."

The three of them changed their direction and headed to the large camp store and swimming pool complex. Bob and Selma's vintage silver Airstream trailer squatted next to the store, looking a bit like a piece of contemporary sculpture with its rounded edges and shiny finish. Its location allowed the couple to facilitate any emergency requests for firewood, marshmallows, or help with getting into a cabin. Running a campground couldn't have been anyone's first choice when it came to a career, or so Nala thought.

"Have Bob and Selma always run the campground?"

"Yep." Karly didn't even break her step to answer. "The

campground has been around forever. Well, maybe not forever. The park used to be pretty small with Santa, some little kid rides, and a train. It probably would have taken a family only an hour or two to get through it. When they started building it up with roller coasters, coaster fans would visit, and they needed someplace to stay. There really wasn't anyplace else. A few showed up with RVs, and some even slept in their cars since they had driven so far. The story I heard was Uncle Bob let them stay on his land, but Selma felt he should charge them, which turned it into a campground. It's a pretty nice campground, and they'll even shuttle the guests to the park entrance."

A tired woman exited the store, clutching a grocery bag and holding onto a squirming toddler with long blond curls who was yelling about wanting to see the unicorn again. Max yipped and wagged his tail, ending the whine-fest.

The distracted child pointed at Max. "Big dog. Can I pet him?"

The woman's expression turned hopeful as she directed her attention to Karly and Nala.

"He's friendly," Nala told her. "It's okay."

The child rushed Max and threw his arms around his neck giving him a hearty squeeze. Worried about her dog, Nala knelt beside the child. "Dogs like little hugs."

Fortunately, the child let go and asked, "Can I hug him again?"

Behind him, Max shot her a wild-eyed look and shook his head emphatically *no*. To soften the blow, Nala said, "Maybe tomorrow."

The child skipped back to the waiting woman and announced, "I get to see the dog tomorrow!"

Max groaned. Still kneeling, Nala informed her canine in a low voice, "Hush. It's not a given. We have lots of work to do. Speaking of that, let's go check on Dasher."

"Then let's go," Max whispered back, stood, and waited on Nala to do the same.

"Be nice," Nala cautioned Max.

Having the ability to speak in English to people often made the shepherd mix consider himself better than other dogs. Previous attempts at communicating with other dogs had Max complaining about the other canines having one-track minds, as if *he* didn't. Instead of addressing the comment, he pulled at the leash, probably anxious to get the task over with.

More people exited the store with bundles of firewood and chatting about the fire they'd build later. Nala and Karly nodded as they passed them. A bell affixed to the screen door jingled as they entered.

Bob had his back to them as he fiddled with something behind the counter. Still, he replied, "It's a wonderful day to camp. What can I do for you?"

He turned, holding a box of lanyards, with each one rolled into a tight bundle and kept closed with a rubber band. When he saw Nala, he coughed. With Karly, he did no more than lift his eyebrows after not seeing her for so long. "What can I do for you girls? I bet you're on the hunt for a frozen treat. We have fudgesicles, popsicles, and push-ups. For the selective palate, we have dark chocolate ice cream with chocolate chips in pint containers."

"Whoo!" Karly said, "Since when?"

His sales spiel sounded just like something he repeated over and over throughout the days. It probably worked half the time. It was odd he acted surprised to see them. As for Karly, how soon she forgot why they were here. Nala cleared her throat. "We're here to help you out. We thought we'd take Dasher for a walk. Let him have some time in nature with another dog."

Suddenly remembering her part, Karly nodded and added, "We've made a canine play date for Dasher."

Bob's forehead furrowed. "Well, that's a thoughtful thing to do, but Dasher is out right now."

There was a whiteboard behind the counter listing the activities for the day, including candy bear bingo, decorating a pumpkin, a scavenger hunt, and a miniature golf tournament. The idea of the dog being out must have struck Karly as weird, too, because she asked, "Is he at candy bar bingo or is he perfecting his shot on the windmill hole?"

"Ha, ha, ha!" Bob pretended to laugh, then slapped the counter. "I keep forgetting how funny you are."

Originally, Nala thought Bob was the nice guy, the one she could go to for a straight answer, but now she wasn't so sure. "What *is* Dasher doing then?"

"Groomer. He needs the full-day treatment after his time in the woods." Bob put down the box of lanyards and started removing the rubber bands around them one at a time, which required him to look down at the box.

Nala was willing to accept the groomer as an excuse, but his behavior up to that was a bit strange.

"Who?" Karly picked up a loose lanyard and shook it out. "I don't remember having a dog groomer in town."

"Well now, you don't know everything, missy. Lots have changed since you and your folks moved to the city. We have two dog groomers now."

Instead of appeasing her, Karly chose to repeat her earlier question, "Who? Who's your dog groomer?"

"Not that it would matter to you. Wouldn't be anyone you know." Bob fumbled with the lanyards to the point he knocked a few out of the box.

Selma came through the side door talking. "What are you doing, Bob? I just rolled up those lanyards. We don't want everyone touching them." As she came closer to her husband, she grabbed the box of lanyards away from him.

It was then Selma realized someone else was in the room and turned to acknowledge Nala and Karly. "Oh, hello." She nodded in Karly's direction. "I heard you blew in with your boyfriend in his expensive sports car." She craned her neck to look around them. "Where is he?"

Karly gave an elaborate sigh. "He had to go back to work. He has an important job."

"I remember," Selma paused as she searched her memories for the right one. "Your mother said he was a heart surgeon. I imagine many folks are relying on him."

Heart surgeon? Elvin? Before Nala could say anything, Karly grabbed her arm and pulled her toward the door while hissing, "I'll explain later."

At the door, Karly held up her hand to wave. "See ya at the square dance."

Outside on the dirt path, Nala shook free of her friend's grip. "Snickerdoodles! What was all that about? By the way, did you notice your uncle was lying?"

"Yeah, I picked up on that. It's something our family does."

This was news to her. All her life Nala had envied Karly's big rambunctious family. "Why lie? Especially about Elvin being a heart surgeon."

"That one wasn't mine," she snorted. "That was all my mother. I think it started when my parents made the move to Indianapolis. My father's goal was to get a better job, which he did, then he lost it almost as fast. Embarrassed, he lied about his job. Mother joined in lying about everything from how well the kids were doing in school to my heart surgeon boyfriend. There's occasionally some truth mixed in, such as my work in the animal shelter, only in mother's version, I run the shelter. It's unfortunate that Aunt Selma talks so much. I chose to go to Dale for lunch because I didn't want everyone in Santa Claus asking me about stuff my parents have said previously."

Wow! That certainly changed the way she saw Karly's family. Maybe the grass wasn't always greener on the other side. "All right, people make up stuff. Why would your uncle lie about Dasher? All I wanted was for Max to get some impressions from him."

"Dunno," Karly shoved her hands into her shorts' pockets and stared down at the ground as she walked. "Maybe he doesn't have Dasher. Maybe the dog is missing just like Chris."

"Yeah, I kind of thought that, too. I might as well do what I can do. Use the cell phone to call Elvin, then Tyler."

"Oh, Tyler," Karly said and raised her head. "What type of story are you going to give him for calling?"

Numerous possible reasons for calling had gone through her mind. In the end, she thought she'd go with the truth. That should surprise him, especially since men complain women were always playing mind games. "I think too many stories are already floating around. Figured I'd be straight with him. Tell him what was going on and *if* he wanted to see me, I would be interested in seeing him."

"Whoa! The truth. Guess I would never have tried that approach."

"Not surprising, with your family." She smirked just a little to let Karly know she was joking. "Before you get too excited about my honesty plan, you should wait and see how it works out for me."

Chapter Sixteen

I NSIDE THE CABIN, Max sat by the fridge. Karly delved through the contents, her voice muffled by the fridge door and the fact her head was almost inside the unit.

"Ooh, look! It's Aunt Selma's lasagna and icebox cake! That alone is worth the trouble of coming down here."

"I prefer cash," Nala commented from her location in the living room. Phone in hand, she typed out a few numbers and put it up to her ear to listen. Her lips twisted to one side, and she sighed heavily at what she heard. "It's Elvin's voice mail. The prints I took were mainly mine. There were others, but they were smeared under my own prints, which made them unidentifiable. The good news is I'm in the fingerprint database. Otherwise, I'd be looking for an unknown person who wasn't in the base when it was me all along."

Cake pan in one hand and a fork in the other, Karly strolled into the living room. "Why are your fingerprints in the base?"

"Yours aren't?" Nala asked as she scrolled through her messages. When she glanced up and spotted her friend in the act of eating out of the pan, she wagged her finger. "Plate, please. You weren't raised in a barn."

"Nag, nag, nag. I was just checking to see if you were paying attention." It only took three steps to return to the kitchen where she plated a hefty slice of cake. "You never answered me about the fingerprints."

Nala leaned to the side to see into the kitchen. "I'd appreciate some cake, too. As for the fingerprints, did you somehow miss out on the big push to fingerprint your kids just in case they were kidnapped or something?"

"Obviously." She took a bite of the cake and assumed a rapturous expression. "The icebox cake is as good as I remembered. Maybe better. With all my siblings, if someone decided to take one of them, I'm not sure my parents would have noticed immediately. They might even be grateful. Since you stumbled onto the fact my family makes up stuff, they might insist the missing child never was or the royal family had dropped by to pick up their secret prince. No prints anywhere, I think. Wait. I did have to get fingerprinted so I could go into schools to talk about the shelter and how students could help. Not sure if that put me in the system or it was just to check if I had any prior arrests."

"Probably the latter," Nala concluded, then held up her phone. "I'm going to duck into the bedroom to call Tyler."

Karly's mouth dropped open. "You're going to deprive me of eavesdropping on a one-sided, awkward conversation?"

It would be awkward. "Yep. You can pick out clothes for square dancing. Oh, and check out the camera." She gestured in the direction of where she left it. "It stopped working or something. Not totally convinced it even has film in it, but didn't you used to take photos?"

"I used to do those lonely heart photos for the shelter. Big softie looking for someone to snuggle with and watch romantic movies together. For the dogs, athletic male looking for a running partner. You know the drill. Eventually, I switched to my phone since it was easier. I can look at the camera. What are you going to do with the photos you have?"

"Apparently not what people expect, which is a book about the town. I think there are some good photos. It would be nice to do something with them. Sure, I'll be gone, but it doesn't seem fair to all those people who are expecting something."

"Hear ya," Karly managed to mumble through a half-full mouth. "Maybe we could put up a website like the book. Elvin could help us."

"True." Nala liked the idea. It'd make her feel a little less like a liar when she snapped the locals' photos. "You could leak the information to Selma. I'd put some disclaimer that the publisher didn't go through with the book, but I wanted to share the smiles and the happiness I found in Santa Claus."

"Sounds doable," Karly concluded with a smirk.

Not receiving any attention, Max padded into the living room and used his head to nudge Nala's arm. "Stop that!" she ordered. "You're not getting any cake. Besides, you can't expect to eat again so soon"

Max could be lazy and consistently focused on food, but that could be said of most dogs who weren't working dogs. "I'll see you two in a sec. Just going to make a call or two."

Nala stood with intentions of sliding into the master bedroom and shutting the door. Before she could do so, Max barreled into the room. He didn't like to be left out of anything. Most pets wouldn't be an issue listening in on a conversation, but they didn't blab what they heard, either.

There was also a good chance Karly would be on the other side of the door with a drinking glass up to it or even using the special auditory enhancer which could be used to listen in on conversations, although it wasn't as easy to use as people might think. You had to be close enough to deploy it, meaning the investigator had to be in front of the house or even in the driveway. Shifty types and cheating spouses usually noticed random strangers sitting in cars outside, tending to make it not all that effective. Still, it would work fine for Karly, who needn't bother. She'd get a recap of the conversation.

Nala kicked the door closed with her foot, then sat on the bed-spread which featured a happy cartoon bear carrying a Christmas tree. It might have been more appropriate for a child's bedroom, but this was one of the Christmas cabins. She didn't expect Tyler to be home, but she felt she needed to call. The longer she put it off, the weirder it would be when they did talk.

Her mother labeled Tyler a *catch*, but the woman also wanted to be a Glamma, a glamourous grandma, in the worse way. People are always emphasizing to teenage girls that a baby isn't an accessory. It wouldn't hurt to reiterate the messages to wannabe grandmas. The problem was her mother had already done pretty much all she wanted, including being a wife, mother, and successful business owner, as well as having a magazine-worthy decorated home—magazines aimed at the average woman as opposed to the super-wealthy. Gwen Bonne didn't let a small thing like her daughter's unwillingness to marry and pop out babies slow her down too much. If her parents didn't care so much about the relationship or lack of one, things would be a ton simpler.

She tapped out his number, and let it ring while she considered what was good about the man. He liked dogs or should she say, he liked Max, who didn't consider himself to be a pet. Personally, she found the reticent veteran easy on the eyes with his wide shoulders, trim physique, and easy smile. Somehow, he tolerated her parents, who could be very transparent in their effort to matchmake the two of them.

The phone was on its fourth ring when it picked up. "Hello?" Tyler said, sounding a bit breathless. "Nala? Is that you?"

Of course, it was her. Didn't he have her name attached to her number? "Ah yes, it is. You didn't have to run for the phone." The fact he had made such an effort to answer did please her, however.

"I did. The only time I don't have my phone with me, you call."

"Sounds like you were expecting me to call." Nala made the mistake of glancing at Max, who was making faces. He rolled his eyes and hung his tongue out of his mouth. She wasn't sure what that meant. It caused her to lose the sassy attitude she was feigning.

"*Hoped.* I hoped you would call so I could apologize so you wouldn't think I was in your business and all."

"In my business?" she echoed his words, surprised at them.

"Yeah. I shouldn't have dropped by your house just because I happened to be in the area."

She thought it was rather sweet. On the other hand, if she had been entertaining another man, it would have been problematic. Of course, she'd have to get out a calendar and count backward to remember dating anyone before Tyler, or she could just ask Karly. "Ah yeah, about that."

"Big mistake, I know. Even worse, I listened to your gossipy neighbor. To be fair, the way she ran out of her house, I thought the woman might have an actual emergency."

"I can imagine."

"Anyhow, I can understand your being upset with me."

"You can?" It was a little hard to believe since she *wasn't* upset with him. Nevertheless, she *was* picking up on the assumptions. He assumed it would be okay to drop by as if they were exclusive, which they weren't. She could also have been wearing her rattiest clothes and had a mud mask on her face. Calling would have been much more considerate.

"Even worse, I asked your father if you were on vacation. That was so unprofessional." He made a derisive snort. "I'm ashamed of myself. I understand if you never want anything to do with me. It was kind of you to take time out of your vacation to call me."

"Ah, right." Now it was her time to explain all the misconceptions. "It would be better to call than to swing by the house. I'd really appreciate it if you didn't ask my father questions unless it has to do with police work, or carpentry, or such. If you want to know something, ask me."

There was a pause at the other end that made her wonder if Tyler had accidentally muted his phone or had quietly put the phone down in her gutsy, gal speech. Maybe that was the result of honesty. If so, it was very overrated.

"Nala, I do have something to ask you."

"Go ahead."

"When you get back home, I'd love to take you out. I hate to think I screwed everything up by being too impulsive."

"Sounds like a good plan to me."

Max, who had been quiet during the call, added a firm bark.

"You took Max on vacation? Don't they have quarantine rules about animals?"

Nala squeezed her eyes shut. *That's* what she forgot to mention.

"I never went on vacation. I'm on a job. My neighbor assumed I was jaunting off to somewhere tropical, and I didn't correct her. Maybe I should have, but I was running late and, of course, you've met my neighbor."

A low laugh sounded. "I understand. I also knew you were on a job. Your father told me."

Normally, her father was the reticent parent. Go figure. "Okay. So, you were just testing me with calling from your vacation nonsense."

"Maybe."

"All I can say is talk to me. Don't talk to my neighbor, my parents, my friends—just me. It will make things a whole lot simpler."

"Got it. Will you be back this weekend?"

"I certainly hope so."

"Text me when you know. I'm glad you called."

"Me, too. Bye."

"Bye."

The bedroom door cracked open, and Karly inserted her head, proving she had been listening from the other side. "How'd the call go?"

"Surprisingly well." It had, which was a minor miracle. Instead of the awkward explanation of why she might lie about vacationing with someone else, Tyler apologized for his behavior of assuming she'd welcome an unannounced visit. Such behavior could be referred to as *checking up* on her. If she had been home, he'd have discovered there was very little to check up on. All the same, he was assuming his appearance would be greeted with open arms. She could have been working on a case, hanging with Karly, or even enjoying a bubble bath. Apologizing for showing up unannounced was the right thing to do.

"Sugar cookies!"

Karly snorted, then made a tsking sound. "What's got you upset?"

"Not upset, exactly." She pursed her lips as she cobbled together a reasonable explanation. "It's hard to explain. Tyler did the right thing by apologizing for nibbing into my business by coming by unannounced, then listening to gossipy Gloria, and worse, asking my father if I was on vacation. At least he understands what he did, which is a whole lot better than the previous guys I've dated."

"Okay," Karly enunciated the word slowly. "So, what's the problem?"

Nala rolled her eyes. "You know. I don't want to like someone my parents like. It just seems wrong somehow."

A giggle greeted the pronouncement. Karly smirked, then giggled again. "I know what you mean. You're not a teen anymore so you don't have to rebel. What you find attractive about Tyler is not the same thing your father likes about him." She stuck out her tongue and made a gagging sound. "That would be yucky!"

"You're right. Let's plan out our square dance strategy. Did you pick out my clothes?"

The question made her friend sigh heavily. "I tried. You have nothing playful or colorful. There's beige, khaki, and navy or…" She held up both hands with a wide-eyed expression. "…wait for it…more beige, khaki, and navy. Woo-hoo! Is this your dress to impress wardrobe?"

"Come on, you know better. It's my dress to *blend in* clothes. Show me what you picked out. With any luck, we might have time to cruise the main strip. I'd also like to know why Bob is lying to us."

Chapter Seventeen

MUSIC STREAMED OUT of the open doors, along with laughter and an order to promenade. Just as Nala thought, they had started without them. The call to Elvin slowed down their progress, along with Karly's desire to revisit her old home. Whoever said you can never go home again was right. On the way to the dance, all her friend did was complain about how her former home had been changed for the worse.

Nala, Karly, and Max strolled toward the open doors. Little bits of conversation floated out, demonstrating that people did manage to talk while swinging their partner or whatever they did.

"Um," Nala started, "how am I supposed to join the dance since they already started?"

"Do you know *nothing* about square dancing?" Her friend enquired, skipping ahead, twirling, and then curtseying in her direction. "Didn't you have to do that in gym class? I know we did."

"Yes, we did, too," Nala agreed, but grimaced in the process. "All I remember is wanting to be Trace's partner, which I never was, and trying to avoid the guy with the damp hands, who always seemed to be my partner. The gym teacher paired us up alphabetically. I may have mentioned how dreamy Trace was or something that could have put him on the gym teacher's radar." She blew out a breath. "Not too surprising, he didn't pair me up with my secret crush."

"You're in luck." Karly danced beside her friend. "Now you can dance with anyone. Unlike school, these dancers get tired and drop out for a drink or a smoke, which gives you time to join. Make sure you greet everyone so that talking to Uncle Bob doesn't look obvious." She elbowed Nala and added, "You can thank me for fixing your camera by fixing me up with one of Tyler's hot friends."

"Oh, the camera!" Nala slapped the palm of her hand against her forehead. "I left it in the car."

"No worries. I'll get it after we get you inside and introduced to everyone. Want to hear how I fixed it?" She managed to bump into her friend with all the subtly of a rambunctious puppy.

"I imagine you're going to tell me."

Max, who had been veering off the path to sniff at bushes, trotted back in time to say, "I want to know."

"Okay," Karly chirped. "You needed film. You used up all of yours. I unloaded yours and replaced it with another roll. You'll able to take thirty-six more shots before that runs out. It was lucky Aunt Selma included film in the camera bag,"

"Yes, lucky me," Nala murmured, although her tone suggested something other than good fortune. "Let's get this over with."

They stepped into the brightly lit room. Long foldable tables with checkered tablecloths covered one wall. Two middle-aged women in vivid square dance ensembles manned the table loaded with two-liter drinks, a bowl of ice, plastic cups, and an iced tea dispenser. The second table had plates loaded with cookies, cupcakes, and fat slabs of pound cake drizzled with strawberries. It didn't look like any of the dancers were watching their weight.

Karly waved to the two women and guided Nala over to the table for the introductions. "Hello!" she called out in a loud voice. "Bob and Selma's niece, I'm sure you remember me."

The woman with the tall hair lacquered in place appeared a bit perplexed, but her shorter friend wasn't. "Ah yes. Selma talks about you all the time. Aren't you engaged to a surgeon?"

Perhaps smelling her distress, Max helped with a large *woof*.

"Oh look, a dog," Ms. Tall Hair announced. She nodded in Max's direction. "He'll have to go before Suzanne sees him. Hurry! Quick!" Her eyes cut to the dancers, who were slowing down.

Karly snagged Max's collar and guided him down a dark hall. Nala trotted behind. "Where are you going?"

"Looking for an empty room so Suzanne doesn't spot Max. She's dreadfully allergic to all animals. Can't even step into a home where an animal once lived. I heard she refuses to date men who used to have a pet. Somehow, pet dander lingers on for years or so she believes. Good thing we got Max out of there when we did. If she erupted into one of her massive meltdowns, your opportunity to question anyone would vanish."

So far, she hadn't been impressed with her opportunity to dance and ask questions. Maybe she could handle slow dancing, but all this skipping around and changing partners would be confusing.

"I guess that *is* a plus." She knelt to pat Max. "I know this isn't the ideal situation, but I don't think we'll be here long. Think of this as a break for you. Maybe take a nap. We'll be back before you know it."

They slipped into the hallway and partially closed the door. Closing it all the way might be better, but they needed a way to identify which door Max was behind. Only the illumination from the main room and the parking lot lights coming through the windows provided enough light to see where they were going. Since she'd followed Karly's directions that consisted of turn here, no here, back up, you missed it, she was rather clueless about their destination. Since they came in the back way, she missed any signs. "Where are we?"

"School. Used to be the middle school, but I'm not sure what it is now. We just put Max into one of the supply rooms near the cafeteria or at least it used to be. I'm not so sure if they even use this building anymore."

The last thing she needed was Max running amok in an over-sized pantry. "They don't use this place anymore?"

"Pretty sure."

It wasn't as strong a confirmation as she might like. Oh well, she had a limited timetable. Friday was coming faster than she'd like. No need to mention previous things her bestie had been pretty sure of during the years, which included drinking lots of orange soda would turn you orange, pop rocks and soda in your mouth would cause your head to explode, and super glue was great for sticking fingers together. The last one was true, but there was no useful reason to have your fingers stuck together.

As they walked into the room, Tall Hair waved at them and pointed to a third middle-aged woman attired in a glittery cowgirl outfit. "Madge needs a break. Go take her place."

What place? Many folks were standing in groups talking while a few strolled to a specific place and posed as if waiting for their close-up on Square Dancers Magazine or something. Since she hadn't seen where Madge had come from, it was hard to know where to go. Tall Hair and Madge kept emphatically pointing to the far wall. Nala looked back and shook her head.

A man picked up the microphone and climbed up to a small

podium. Nearby, a woman placed a vinyl record on a turntable, which had Nala staring. She *had* heard turntables were coming back. The woman spoke before the man spoke into the microphone.

"Our next dance is about to begin as soon as we get all our squares formed." The discussions ended as everyone dashed into a spot. Four couples made up each square, except for a forlorn elderly man who was shrugging his shoulders and attempting to signal Madge, who waved away his invitation.

She yelled across the room. "My feet hurt! City girl is taking my place!"

Without being told, Nala was sure she was city girl, and she hurried over to stand by the octogenarian. "Hi. I'm Nala."

"Jim. Glad to meet you. We'll have to muddle by the best we can since my girl has deserted me to go gossip."

The lively music started, and Nala waited for the caller to give some handy directions, but he settled for just saying, "Star Pattern," then he picked up a drink. Was he clueless about his job?

Jim grabbed her hand and pulled her close to the other dancers who were all holding hands. She couldn't remember if she ever did this in school. Probably not. She'd avoided holding her partner's clammy hands. Even as she shuffled to the left with the circle, she remembered this was supposed to be an information gathering session. Surely the women would know if Chris was dating someone. If Bob knew, he was playing possum.

As the circle galloped in the other direction, moving much faster than people her parents' age should move, she managed to say, "Does Chris ever come to these dances?"

She could have sworn the music stopped. It must have been a pause because it started again with people weaving through the square, taking arms for half a turn.

When Nala drew close to one lady with tight red curls, the woman hissed at her. "City girl! Don't come chasing after our Chris."

Another turn had a different woman glaring at her and asking, "Did you run through all the men in *your* city?"

Snickerdoodles! Talk about mean girls. They had nothing on these women. Well, maybe they didn't understand her question. She'd have to try something different, but the complicated moves took all her concentration. Even with watching everyone's feet, she stumbled.

The third woman in the square snickered and smirked in her direction.

Red Curls sashayed by and said, "Takes more than youth to square dance," with an arched brow.

Who thought this was a good idea? Oh right, Karly. The caller who had been having a nice chat with Turntable Lady finally realized he had a job to do and spoke into the microphone. "Promenade."

Jim made a grab for her hands at the same time as a whistle split the air. Karly held up the camera and waved it. Thank goodness for small favors. It would be no problem taking folks pictures while her friend chatted them up. "Sorry, Jim. That's my cue. I'll send Marge back to you."

Instead of looking sad, her partner acted delighted. "Do that. You can't dance at all. Just makes me look bad."

Before she could answer, she heard a shriek, then, "What's that?"

She suspected she knew, but she turned back to watch. Max rounded the corner at full speed. Anxious to get out of the closed room, he leaped over a pair of discarded cowboy boots and slammed into the table of yummy desserts. Oh no! She started running, aware that it was already too late to reverse the damage. Why had she never mentioned to Karly not to whistle. Her father had trained Max to respond to one no matter what.

Behind her, she heard a woman shout, "It's a dog with dog hair, and dog dander, and dog germs!"

It was time to leave. She jogged past Karly, signaled Max, and waved at the crowd. "It's been fun. We'll just leave."

As they trotted toward the parking lot, she heard someone say, "The cookies were dry, but I sure hate to see the pound cake go to waste."

The music started again, signaling all wasn't ruined as she'd supposed. Max, who had been herded outside, waited until they got to the car before speaking. "My bad."

Her first instinct was to agree, but he was responding to training even if he did cut that corner a little close. "Ah, what can they expect when they leave the doors open. I'm sure a possum or raccoon would have come in uninvited. One probably has for all we know."

Nala dropped her hand to scratch behind Max's ears. If nothing else, he got her out of square dancing. For that, she should be deeply grateful. She knew Jim was. "Where to now, gang?"

"Candy Castle," her bestie answered. She had her hand on the passenger door and the camera bag slung over her arm. "I think we could use a hot chocolate fix."

The dome light came on as the car door opened, spotlighting a large teddy bear wearing a striped cap and muffler. The bear itself was rather cute. Not so the knife stuck where the bear's heart would be if it had one. A piece of paper lay on the seat. In large black letters worthy of a wide permanent marker, it read, *You're next.*

Not exactly friendly by a long shot.

Chapter Eighteen

S HE MADE MAX smell the bear before bagging it for evidence.
After the bear and knife were carefully bagged and stowed in
the car trunk, Nala and Max prowled the night-darkened parking lot
for the culprits. Karly settled for staying in the locked car with the
engine running, radio playing, and devouring a bag of leftover candy
she found in the glove compartment.

Music and light poured out of the open doors, giving the autumn night a touch of festivity that bypassed Nala. Why did all the
cases that appeared easy on the surface turn out like this? It would
have been simple for a square dance participant to sneak out and
leave the bear, then slip back inside with no one the wiser.

She slid from car shadow to car shadow with teeth gritted, knees
bent, weapon out. Max followed a similar path with his nose
hovering a few inches above the ground. Waiting next to an older
sedan that carried the stink of an oil-rich exhaust, Nala blew out a
heavy breath. The cool breeze brushed against her skin causing
goosebumps, or it could be the thought that she'd encountered her
troublemaker that made her shiver. Whoever it was knew where she
would be almost every minute of the day. While she didn't broadcast
her intentions, as a non-local with a large, black shepherd mix, she

was noticeable and easy to track. Who could it be? The most likely folks would be Bob and Selma. They hired her, but had yet to pay her.

Mentally, she reviewed all the photos she'd taken of gap-toothed youngsters sporting cowboy hats or unicorn shirts, often both. Nope, it couldn't be any of the under ten set. They still believed. Who would want to get rid of Santa as well as the person who could locate the old elf? The local business owners, brandishing wares or displaying their websites on their clothing, would want people to come to the town, which meant it wasn't them, either. It had to be someone who didn't wish the town well. Who would want the town to suffer? Once she solved the crime, the motivation would make sense, but currently, she had nothing.

Max moved ahead as if on a scent trail. Some odd murmuring came from her left. With her knees aching from the continual squatting, Nala stood to see if she could locate the sound.

A shriek sounded, and a car door slammed open. "It's your girl-friend! She has a gun!" a woman cried.

Nala only had time to catch sight of a woman's full skirt flutter-ing as its owner sprinted toward the building. The other occupant of the car, a man, exited more slowly with his hands up. Speaking to Nala, in a trembling voice, he said, "Mary Ellen, it's not what it looks like. Don't shoot." Then the man did a doubletake. "Wait, you're not Mary Ellen."

Great. She had stumbled onto a clandestine couple making out during square dance practice. This town was ruining her image of cutesy villages. She lowered her voice. "You're in luck this time. Better watch your step."

The man's gaze was riveted on the gun clutched in her hand. She holstered it and signaled he should go. No one had to tell him twice. He tore out of the place leaving a plume of exhaust. Yet another car that needed work. Max padded back to Nala and nudged her leg.

"Hey, boss."

Her dog didn't usually call her *boss* since he was aware of who called the shots. When he did, she felt it was a trifle patronizing. "What is it?"

"The trail ended."

While her rescue dog may not have bloodhound skills, he could be decent about new scents, which this one was. "How?"

"Drove away. It ended at an empty parking space."

Sounded right. She couldn't expect Max to run along the road trying to pick up a scent. Maybe there was a way they could identify the car. "Anything unusual about the car?"

"Did you miss the part about the empty parking space?"

Smart-aleck dog. "Use your much-vaunted scent skills. Where the car was, did that smell different?"

Even in the limited lighting, Max's doggy brows went down into an expression of suffering. "Okay, I'll give the parking space another scent check."

Nala trailed behind him as she walked to an empty space located next to an RV about the size of a school bus. The large vehicle could have hidden their culprit as he or she assembled the intimidation tools. It showed some intelligence on the culprit's part. Just what she didn't need—clever harassers. Even though the trail ended before the RV, what bothered her was who drove their home-on-wheels to a dance practice?

Her dog took a few steps, sniffed the ground, and then cocked his head as if considering. It reminded her of the wine tasting event she'd attended with Karly. There was one male participant who would get the same expression as Max before launching into some detailed description of earthy notes and citrusy undertones with references to other wines he had known. Max traveled to the four corners of the space and repeated this behavior.

Growing impatient, Nala asked, "Anything?"

"Lots. Old and new smells. There's a spicy tomato that reminds me of pizza."

There were a couple of pizza places in town. It might make her look like a friendless loser to eat pizza in the parking lot, but plenty of people did eat their lunches in parking lots, especially if they were delivery people. Pizza might not mean much, but she'd keep it in the back of her mind. "Anything else?"

Her dog made a choking noise, then shook his head violently. "Cologne. Too much."

She wanted to ask how he knew it was cologne as opposed to perfume but she didn't. Those types of questions tended to baffle her pooch. "Male or female?"

"Male."

So far, she expected as much. The threats felt like something a man would use to scare away a woman. Being such a fragile creature, it would only need a message spelled out in dog treats to get her running. *Not.* A female culprit would know it would take more. She would have come in harder and faster, possibly with threats to make small children run from her due to an acid in the face incident or by simply implying Max was in danger if Nala didn't vamoose.

A male with too much cologne would be a sizable portion of the male dancers. Most must have thought since they'd be close to someone other than their spouse, a hearty splash of cologne would forgo the need for showering.

"Well, that's something." Just not quite enough for their situation. "Try a little harder."

"Nag, nag, nag. You're never appreciative. Let me remind you this is not my natural calling. I think I should get paid extra for this service. Hey, wait a minute. I don't get paid at all."

Not this again. It was hard to tell if Max thought he was being funny or had a legitimate grievance. Before she could address his attitude, he went back to wandering across the rectangular space, sometimes with his head slightly tilted, other times with his nose close to the ground. Finally, he stopped. "Motor oil."

That could mean a possible oil leak, which might not be as helpful normally, since oil-rich fumes tended to be more of a standard than an exception in this locale. A black cloud of smoke could signal his arrival if driving.

"Good job!" She meant it but was a little downcast that there hadn't been a smoking gun among the scents. What she did know was it was a male wearing too much cologne and drove a vehicle with an oil leak.

A weird expression passed over his canine features. Max shook his head and walked back to a spot and examined it again.

"What is it?'

"Dasher. I smell Dasher."

Bob had mentioned he sent the dog to be groomed, which seemed possible considering how muddied and matted he was. However, there'd be no reason for Dasher to be there. "Are you sure?"

Dogs are quite adept at expressing disgust with minimal facial movement. Max was an expert at it. He snorted. "Excuse me?

Excellent canine nose here. I know who I smell. It's the same smell. There's a reason I'm always sniffing things. I have a brain like an elephant. Come to think of it, maybe better than an elephant."

There was no need to mention it was *memory* like an elephant since an elephant never forgot. Instead, she focused on the possibility that her harasser had the small dog. It made no sense. Last time she saw Dasher, he was in Bob's arms. Well, one thing was for sure, he did know her phone number and that she'd be at the dance tonight. How would he know about the Mexican restaurant, though? Better yet, why?

Her failure to respond to Max's comments must have confused him as she pondered the most recent info. He nudged her leg. "Better than an elephant, right?"

"Oh yeah, right."

She turned and walked slowly toward her car, which was lit up like a proverbial Christmas tree with soft rock issuing forth from within. Karly should know if Bob was the type of guy who would be out to ruin the town. On the surface, he seemed so sweet and unassuming. Not exactly the type of person who would hatch a devious plan such as this. It could be he held a grudge that he nursed, waiting for the right opportunity for payback.

Was he who he appeared to be, or was he someone entirely different? Should she be afraid of whoever left the threats or was it merely a smokescreen? Her father was a big fan of being cautious, since you never had any way of knowing sometimes when it was too late.

"Hey!" The sound of running dog feet sounded behind her. A breathless Max appeared at her side. "What was that about? You left me. Didn't say you were leaving or anything."

She had just ambled off while contemplating what was next. "Surely you'd be able to follow with that better than an elephant's nose."

"I could," Max agreed. "I'd probably just catch a ride with Bob and Selma, though."

Dogs had a way of disappearing around Bob. "Don't do that!"

"Whoa. Way to get overdramatic. Just joking."

Maybe she had been a bit over the top. She forced a laugh. "Me, too. You can ride with whomever you want, but how would you tell them where to take you?"

"Duh. There's no place else I would be. Everyone knows everyone here and would know if someone had a gorgeous dog like myself, which means I must belong with a stranger. The only place for a stranger would be the campground."

"Yes, you're right." If a dog could figure that out, her harasser knew it, too. Back to where she started, except helpful Bob had now become a person of interest.

Chapter Nineteen

AFTER DEBATING WHO she could trust, plus the accumulated caffeine of sampling various hot chocolate flavors, Nala had a restless night of tossing and turning. She finally dozed off in the wee morning hours, only to be awakened a few hours later by a wet nose and bad breath.

"Hey. Hey! You awake?"

She considered feigning sleep, but that would result in Max scampering onto the bed like he usually did when she tried to ignore him. One eyelid popped open as she rested the rest of her face into the pillow. "What?"

"I need to go out."

"Karly?" Why not have her friend pick up some of the dog care duties. It would give her a feel of what it was like being an actual investigator.

"Gone."

"Huh?" This unexpected development caused both eyes to snap open as her sleepy brain processed the information. Nala pushed up into a sitting position, peering at the sunlight streaming into the room. "Where'd she go?"

"Geesh. What do you think? I'm a gatekeeper? Maybe she's

doing some healthy stuff like running or meditating."

"Karly?" It didn't sound like the woman she knew, who insisted on sampling six of the thirty hot chocolate flavors before they returned to the cabin. Maybe she had a secret athletic side Nala knew nothing about. The thought made her shake her head. Couldn't be. The woman would announce anything healthy she did since it would be so out of character.

Max shrugged his shoulders, directed a significant look at Nala, and then strolled to the open doorway leading into the hall.

"Okay, I'm coming." Even when her pooch didn't use English, he still made himself clear. Nala swung her bare legs out of bed as she considered her dog decorated nightshirt. Since it didn't exactly strike a professional note, it wasn't something she wanted to be seen in. She should change. The sounds of dog nails striking the floor drew her eyes to Max, who was doing his version of the potty dance. No time. She darted to the outside door and swung it open as she instructed Max, "Do your business and come right back."

He lunged down the steps and inspected the ground for the correct spot. As she stood on the stoop, she surveyed the area. A few of the nearby campers were gone, along with their oversized vehicles. Their absence made the cabin a little more secluded. Despite the early morning stillness, something was wrong.

Robins chirped in a nearby tree, and voices carried as a pair of campers power walked the trail. Before she could step back inside, they waved at her. Nala put her hand up even though her first instinct was to dive back into the cabin. It would be better if there was coffee brewing in the cabin, which would jumpstart her deductive reasoning.

Her eyes widened as she realized what wasn't right with this charming, pine-scented scene. "My car's missing!"

Max trotted back to the porch with an inquisitive expression. "I hope you're not going to pin this on me."

He made it sound like every bad thing was placed at his doorstep. Only the ones with his pawprints on it were.

"No," Nala answered as she stared at the spot. This small burg was not rife with crime. Just the opposite. Before she could eliminate any suspects, her car came around the curve with the windows down, music playing. Karly sang about getting retribution on a cheating ex. Relief flooded Nala. Although, a knot of annoyance still bunched her shoulders.

The car slid into the empty spot, the music stopped, and Karly's head appeared above the auto roof. She called out, "I got donuts!"

Max barked with delight, causing Nala to shoot him a look. "Running? Meditating?"

"It may happen someday."

Not likely, but she kept her opinion to herself as she rounded the car. As much as she hated to, she really needed to say something about taking off like that and not telling her, especially since the sedan contained all the sleuthing tools and evidence.

Karly balanced the rectangular white box against her belly, and the other hand gripped one of those cardboard drink containers filled with two steaming cups of varying sizes. One probably held a cup or so of a coffee-size drink while the other could almost accommodate the whole pot. No wonder Karly was having trouble balancing it.

Nala stepped barefooted onto the path and headed toward her friend with the same mindless obsession zombies demonstrated in the movies. When she was within a foot, she asked, "Is that coffee?"

Karly grinned. "I thought about getting you some milk to go with your donuts, but I know you better than that. What else would it be besides coffee? I decided to check out if Ethel was still making the best donuts ever. She is. Be prepared to be amazed."

"Bless you." Nala asked, "Which one is mine?"

Her inquiry caused her friend to chuckle. "Please, which one do you hope is yours?"

"The ginormous one." More than a few people told her she drank too much coffee, but the beverage had helped her stay alert on several late-night assignments and cleared away the cobwebs from those late nights the next day.

"As I thought." Her friend nodded in the direction of the tall cup. "Besides, the other is a chai tea latte. Ethel makes a decent latte, too."

"Thank goodness I didn't pick up that one."

They both giggled at the possibility, and Nala decided not to say anything about the impulsive borrowing of the car, this time.

Breakfast was consumed at the picnic table after Nala donned a jacket, pants, and shoes. Max hovered nearby, hoping for a bit of the delicious yeast donuts. Hands wrapped around the still-warm cup, Nala inhaled deeply. As a child, her mother was no fan of camping, but Nala began to understand the appeal of being outside among the tall trees.

Karly rubbed her hands together, always an indicator she was going to say something she considered important. "Okay. What's our schedule today?"

Even though she did have a tentative plan, Nala put her cup down and caught her friend's gaze. Her friend's arrival was a bit unexpected, despite Karly's many mentions of wanting to help. Most people confused PI work with a movie of the week. "Normally, this time of the week you're working, usually prepping for the big weekend rush at the shelter. Why are you really here?"

Karly chose that moment to stuff half a donut in her mouth and chewed. An obvious stalling procedure since the yeast donuts were mainly air and sugar glaze. Still, her friend chewed and chewed. The sugary bread had to have long since dissolved.

"Come on, come clean."

Instead of answering, Karly reached for her cup. Nala grabbed her wrist before she could touch the cup up to her lips. The lack of liquid sloshing indicated the cup was already empty.

"My stars!" Karly exclaimed and tried to pull her arm back, but Nala held on.

"What's the big secret?" Nala angled her head to make better eye contact with Karly, who was examining the weathered picnic table. Nala assumed she and Karly shared almost everything. Her hand loosed on Karly's wrist, and she held it up. "Go ahead and nuzzle that empty cup all you want."

"Sometimes I wish you weren't so observant." She set the cup down on the table, placed both hands on the bench, leaned back, and sighed. "This is supposed to be my vacation."

"Here?" Nala gestured to the park. "With me?" She pointed a thumb to herself. "It's well past summer."

"Yeah, I know. Most of the shelter staff has a family. It's only fair they get off for summer vacation. As for here, I do know the place, you're here, and so far, it has cost me almost nothing. You're letting me help with the case. Basically, it's been better than the last five staycations I've had. I didn't want to tell you because it made me sound pitiful."

Did the woman not know her? Nala pointed her index finger at Karly. "Tell me about my exciting, fun-filled vacation last year."

Her friend's brow wrinkled, and her lips pursed. "I can't remember anything."

"Exactly. Last year, I worked all year at the pre-school with investigating on the side. When summer came, I was down to only one job. What did I do the year before that?"

"Can't think of anything. Did we go to the state fair?"

"That was one day." Nala arched an eyebrow. "Today, we're going to do something slightly edgy. I got the idea from a television show. You and I are posing as Theme Park Inspectors. I even have an instant photo camera, mobile printer, and a laminator to make us IDs."

"Woo, sounds fun. Any special outfit I should wear?" Karly's hands went to her hair, which she skimmed back. "Should I pull it back to look serious? An FBI type of look?"

Even though the ID kit rode around in her car trunk, she'd never used it. While the characters on television got away with it, Nala felt like it might be a little like tempting fate. Sawyer, her partner in disability fraud, often told her all he needed was an official sounding title, and it was easy to get information out of people. Once, he called the target and said he was coming by with a sweepstakes check for a woman who was supposedly bedridden. When he climbed out of his shiny sedan with balloons and an oversized check, he made sure to go to the neighbor's house, only to have the woman run out of the house calling him. Nala stayed in the car and filmed the whole thing, which ended up with the woman not getting the sweepstakes check or any more disability checks. It just seemed mean to Nala. She wasn't out to deprive anyone of their checks, but perhaps it was a way to get the necessary information. Someone might have a clue they didn't even know they had, just as Karly suggested Uncle Bob might. She certainly hadn't thought about attire, though.

"Probably not the bun. A ponytail should work. As theme park inspectors, we might have to test some of the rides."

Max placed his large head on the table and cut his eyes to the box of donuts. "Do I get to test the rides?"

"No." Nala felt sometimes a *no* served much better than a long-winded explanation. "No pets at the park."

"That's a very unenlightened viewpoint." He sniffed as if trying to inhale the donut box. "What am I supposed to do while you're gone?"

The downside of the talking dog was he never hesitated to say you how he felt. Those with dogs who settled for yapping and barking had their owners making up pleasant translations devoid of any whining or complaining. "We won't be gone long. You stay in the cabin and watch television. Who knows? There might be a show you haven't seen."

One ear went up as he considered the prospect, then he gave a slight nod of assent. "I *could* use a break. All that sniffing has worn me out. I'll expect a treat when you get back."

"I know." Nala stood, picked up the cups and holders, leaving the donut box for Karly. To her, she said, "I think a pair of khakis and a polo shirt would work. It's the type of outfit someone would wear if they expected to be active. It's okay if we don't have matching polos. We can use the name tags to hide our lack of matching company logos. Even athletic shoes would be the shoe of choice."

"I think I have everything." Karly untangled herself from the picnic table and scooped up the donuts. She followed Nala while

Max came last, following the donuts. "Did you notice theme park inspectors spells out TPI. We could also double as toilet tissue inspectors. Ha!"

Why did she have to go and say that? "I'll spell it out under the initials. We'll only be there for a short time."

"Got it," Karly said as they mounted the steps to the cabin. "What if some other inspectors have already been there?"

Was she like this when she worked with Sawyer? Probably. It might even explain why the man traveled so much. "We'll say it's an impromptu inspection or we're following up on a complaint."

As much as she might dislike Karly's questions, it was a great way to brainstorm before she was asked similar questions in real life. Max squeezed by her to be first into the cabin and launched himself onto the couch. "I hope they have my favorite channel."

The idea that Max had a favorite channel made Karly laugh. "Lemme guess. Animal Planet?"

Even though her friend was the first one to encounter Max and his ability to speak, she was still thinking of him like a dog, which was something Max never did. He answered. "Go ahead and tell her."

"Classic movie channel. There might be a movie on about Christmas being canceled due to a missing Santa."

Chapter Twenty

ADOZEN VEHICLES consisting mainly of pickups and older compacts were parked near the entrance of the theme park. Turrets complete with colorful flags waving in the wind gave the place a festive appearance. Each parking section had a placard of an animal to help them remember their parking section. Since it was Nala's first time there, everything was unfamiliar.

"Big parking lot."

"Oh, this is only the main one. There's an overflow parking lot and even staff parking lots. What's your plan to get in?"

A parking place close by might be best in case they needed to leave fast. Her father was always a fan of backing in to the space to prepare for a swift exit, but pulling through two slots worked just as well and was a whole lot easier.

Since she picked up the idea from a combination of Sawyer and television, her money was on bluffing. "I was hoping flashing our badges would work, as well as mentioning we have an appointment."

"We *don't* have an appointment," Karly quickly pointed out. In some ways, she was a bit like Max, stating the obvious.

"I know that." She pointed to a twenty-something pair attired in theme park shirts. "Them. We can go in with them." Nala grabbed her notebook, the better to take notes on, but her hand hovered over her purse. A park inspector probably wouldn't be lugging around a handbag, especially if they had to check out a ride. At least she'd need her keys, which she pocketed. She jogged in the direction of the employees, leaving Karly to follow.

The two were almost at the gate which had another staff member behind it. The two called out a greeting and pushed through the unlocked gate. One of the employees turned and spotted Nala. "Hey, you came to take photos! Cool. Probably better without the park being swamped."

She never considered the photo angle. Nala placed her hand over her badge. "You're right. Photos. Silly me. I forgot my camera. Let me tell my assistant."

Breathless, Karly jogged up to the gate, placed her hand on it, and bent over slightly. When she stood upright, Nala stepped in front of her, blocking everyone's view of the TPI badge. "Assistant, I need you to bring the camera equipment I forgot."

Still winded, Karly grimaced and gasped, "Camera equipment!"

Her friend would have a great deal to say to her after their visit was finished. With her back to the employees, Nala removed her own badge and gestured for Karly to do likewise, which she did. "Yes, I'm so embarrassed. Here I am to take photos of the park for the book, and I forgot the camera."

"Oh! That camera!"

"Yes, you know the one I've been using around town. Bring the panoramic film, too." It seemed like something a professional photographer might say.

Karly, aware that others might be listening, lowered her voice to a whisper. "You don't have panoramic film. I loaded the camera with 200, but you might want 800 for action shots."

Improvising must not be her friend's strong suit, but then there wasn't much call for it in the animal rescue business. "Ah yes, that will be fine. I'll wait here."

After a heavy sigh and a look that promised some serious retribution, Karly turned and walked about five yards before returning to Nala with her hand outstretched. "Keys?"

Oh yeah, she forgot. She passed the keys over with a forced smile, then turned to address the remaining employee, who sported a name tag identifying her as a VIP crew member named *Mia*. The slender brunette grinned at Nala.

"What photo would you like to do first?"

The whole purpose of the trip is to get information. One thing she'd found to be true was people enjoyed talking about themselves and sometimes in the process, they revealed vital information. It wasn't always a given, but worth trying. "What's *your* job here?"

"I'm the head of security." She angled her head to the gate. "That's why I'm letting in all the employees. I'll lock up after your assistant comes back with the camera."

"Oh." Nala found herself momentarily wordless as she contemplated the idea of this diminutive female overseeing security for the entire park. "That's interesting."

Mia chuckled and smirked. "You know, most people who don't know me get the same expression on their faces. They assume a security head would be male and some musclebound goon." She gestured to the surrounding park that featured a large statue of Santa plus bubbling fountains. "This is a family fun park. It was originally created for small children, which is still its base audience. There's no alcohol, no weapons, no fireworks, no skateboards, and no shenanigans. About the worst problems I have is line hopping and disgruntled patrons when it rains."

All she needed to do was direct Mia to focus more on Chris, but she couldn't jump in and say *What about your Santa? Anyone threatening him?* "I imagine the other folks in line handle the line jumpers."

"Pretty much, especially if it's teen boys." She audibly exhaled. "Teen boys are always looking for a fight, especially if there are girls nearby to impress. In that case, I usually make both parties cool down, rather like taking a time out. It tends to work. As for my grumbly folks, we usually hand out half-off coupons for a future visit and others I give a courtesy pass. The latter I save for those who are polite and not screaming at me."

Karly's red polo made her easy to track as she walked very slowly back, which gave Nala even more time to pump the chatty security head. "Wow. Some people really do over-react. Ever have anyone threatening an employee?"

Her brow crinkled as she considered the possibility. "The life-guards at our waterpark can get a little terse with each other. Apparently, there are more cushy positions, such as the lazy river, as opposed to being seven stories up on one of the water slides. When it comes to break time, it takes most of the guard's time going up and down the stairs. We fixed that by rotating the guards. Every guard is trained for *all* the positions. Those who had the easiest positions didn't like it, but everyone else did."

Not at all what she wanted, and Karly was almost back, which meant they'd have to walk around the park and take photos, leaving possibly her best-informed person behind. "Ever have maybe someone's ex come in and cause trouble?"

Karly must have heard the last question. While Mia's eyes rolled up as she searched her memory, her friend brandished the camera bag and blurted out, "Does anyone ever go after Santa?"

The abrupt comment had Mia wrinkling her nose. "Haven't you heard Santa sees everything you do and say? Every now and then, we have a few kids who have bones to pick with our Santa, Mr. Natale, because they didn't get the gift they asked for the previous year."

Kids were a lot bolder than when Nala was a kid. You got what you got, and you liked it. "How does that work out?"

"Surprisingly well." Mia patted the area over her heart. "Chris has the touch. I heard from Kelly, one of the elves, that he convinces the children whatever they got was the better fit. Sometimes he settles for telling them the elf in charge of making that toy was sick. The elf sends apologies."

"So, basically what you're saying," Nala often resorted to paraphrasing, a talent she learned from working with demanding parents in the academic setting, "is that your Santa has no issues. No one harasses him or anything of the sort?"

"Pretty much. Chris is a cool guy. You should meet him. Unfortunately, he's not here. No need for him to practice since he's been doing this for decades." A goofy grin spread across her face. "You could tell him your Christmas wishes. Lots of adult women want their photo with Santa. Not so with the guys. Anyway, you all have fun. If you have any more questions, you can get one of the employees to call me."

Karly pushed the camera bag at Nala. "You should get a photo of Mia."

"I should," Nala agreed, thinking it might endear the security chief to them. She pulled out the camera, powered it up, then looked around for a suitable backdrop. "Why don't you pose with the Santa statue?"

They followed as Mia scampered over to the statue and wrapped her arm around Santa. Luckily, the jolly old elf rendition wasn't too tall. Nala fussed with the camera and changed her position until she got a clear photo, free of shadows. "It looks great, but I should take another one."

Once the camera was returned to the bag, they were ready to walk around the park. Mia held up one finger, signaling them to wait, and then ran back to the gate and locked it. She jogged back with a happy expression. "I have an idea. You want to see the park? I usually walk the park to see what's going on. There's basically nothing happening now, but I could show you around which would make my day a lot more fun. Even point out some of the better photo spots."

Would this cramp Nala's style when she asked other employees questions? You couldn't brush off the head of security without looking suspicious. So far, Selma's plan to pretend to take photos was working out great. "Sure, that would be wonderful."

Along the way, they went through kiddie land and took a ride on the carousel. Nala pulled out her phone and shot a pic of Karly riding the carousel pony. A dog shot by as they headed to another ride. "You allow dogs?"

"Owner's dog. He isn't here when the park is open or Santa is here."

It smelled like a story to her. Since Chris wasn't seen without his dog, he must like dogs. "What's with Chris and dogs?"

"Well," she held up a finger. "Don't get me wrong. He likes dogs or at least those who don't attack him. We do allow *guide* dogs at our park. Dogs that have been specifically trained for that purpose. Some people take advantage of that."

Was she going to stop there? Drop a juicy piece of gossip, then say nothing more? That was more Nala's mother's style. She'd wait until Nala begged for the rest of the information. Her father never begged. Either he didn't want to know or had better methods of finding out. Probably the latter.

While she was trying to think of a subtle way to get more information, Karly exclaimed, "You have to tell us!"

"Not sure if I should." Mia gave a small sniff. "I'm sure you'd get the tale if you asked anyone in town, but you'd probably end up with a story of Chris being mauled by a teddy bear come to life or some other nonsense. As I said before, we allow legitimate guide dogs in. The dogs can't ride on the rides and generally, those with guide dogs are with an accompanying family. I'm sure you've seen the guide dog vests you can buy online."

Nala schooled her face to show no emotion as she gave a short nod of acknowledgment. With any luck, Karly wouldn't mention they had one in the trunk along with a white cane.

"Well, we've had more than a few people try to slap one on their dog to get them into the park, which isn't a treat for the dog at all. Too many smells, too much noise, being bumped by strangers, and don't forget how the hot pavement would hurt their poor paws. It's obvious those dogs are not trained, especially when the owner ends up carrying them everywhere. It's more like they are guide *people* for the dog."

Mia laughed at her joke, which forced Nala to laugh. In turn, Karly laughed about a minute after the fact.

Rides meant for teens as opposed to toddlers crowded the next section. Mia pointed to one known for its ability to twirl around and make the rider slightly nauseous. "Hey, how about a go on that one."

"Love it," Karly enthused and rushed up to the ride as if there were a herd of other folks she had to beat.

"Child at heart," Nala explained with a smile while wondering if it were possible for her dog and friend to switch bodies. Even now, Karly, encased in a canine body, could be watching movies, and lapping up the last bit of the icebox cake.

"We all are if we're willing to admit it," Mia picked up her pace as she headed for the ride. She called out to a young man standing by the ride's controls, not witnessing Nala slowing her pace to almost a shuffle. Theme parks had never been in her family's vacation plans. Even the carousel with its slow twirl and circus-style music made her a little nauseous.

Ensconced in a red shell-like structure sat Mia and Karly, grinning like goons. Nala had half a mind to wave them on, but she had no clue what might be said on the ride. So far, everything was fine. All she needed was a little more information on the attacking dog or dogs. Could it have been deliberate? Mia acted like there were tons of folks slipping guide dog vests on their ill-trained dogs. What if someone stuck a vest on a dog who was trained to attack? Fudge! She smacked her fist in her hand. She'd have to get into that contraption that resembled something from a nightmare, her nightmare.

The vinyl seat was warm, but not hot. The ride operator made a point of checking to make sure the handle locked properly, possibly illustrating what a model employee he was for Mia. He strolled down to the controls and called out, "Ready?"

Mia must have signaled they were since Nala never would. Their car made slow circles as it went over the uneven surfaces. This wasn't too bad and to think she was worried. "About that attacking dog. What was the story there?"

"Weird. The man was an adult traveling alone. Not typical for someone who is blind. We've had a few blind roller coaster fans, but they came in a group along with sighted friends. This guy had no girlfriend, no kids, and he strolled straight to Santa's castle as if he knew where he was headed. There's a decorative wooden gate…"

The ride picked up speed, whirling even faster. Karly leaned forward to grab a metal disk. She kept pulling her hand over hand, moving it a little bit, possibly to stop the gyrations.

"It's not working!" Nala shouted as the ride accelerated into another sickening spin.

"Sure, it is!" Karly yelled as they whipped into several fast turns.

One took out Nala's stomach, or it felt just like it. Might be best to leave the stomach wherever it was flung since this was not a ride for dicey digestive systems. The ride operator decided it would be a good time to blast them with some 90s rock. No doubt chosen for the teen riders' parents if they were in the vicinity. After what felt like a lifetime, the ride slowed, and the music stopped. The operator hopped on the ride and walked to their car with no visible balance issue.

"Okay, ladies, the ride is over." He reached down, unlatched the handle, and pulled it up, releasing the three of them.

Karly vaulted out, giggling. Mia followed a little slower while Nala stayed seated. "Are you sure the ride has stopped? My head is still spinning."

"Yes." Mia held out her hand to Nala. "It's obvious you're not a theme park fan."

"My parents weren't, as far as I know. As an only child, you don't have a lot of bargaining power. My mother's version of a stomach-churning event was to find something on sale she just bought at another store and paid more for."

"You're quite the comedian," Mia said as she tugged Nala to a standing position. "Any other rides you want to go on?"

As far as she could remember, she didn't ask to go on this one. "How about the one where you just sit and enjoy the ride? There's no spinning in circles or being flung about."

Mia grinned. "I know just the ride."

Why was no one getting the message that she didn't want to go on another ride? Still, Mia was her current informant. She pressed her lips together, trying for a smile, which probably wasn't happening. "Lead on." If she were truly a photographer, she should take a photo of the ride. "Wait. How about a photo of the ride?" She gestured to Karly and Mia. "Why don't the two of you get in a car as if you're just sitting down." She pointed to the ride operator. "You can be closing the handle."

The three posed for the photo before they continued the tour of the park. As they strolled, some of the rides and decorations took on more of a dated look. It reminded Nala of something she might have seen as a youngster.

Mia pointed to her right. "This is the oldest part of the park. In the beginning, the park wasn't big. You could probably spend an hour and be done. This was Christmas Land's first ride."

With her luck, it would be a catapult. However, there were no towering roller coasters in evidence as in the previous part of the park.

"Here it is," Mia sing-songed.

A large wooden structure decorated with bunting, which looked more like an oversized porch, squatted in the near distance. Not sure how that could be a ride, but things were different long ago. Maybe she wasn't a big fan of the more traditional carnival rides, but she wasn't even sure what this was supposed to be until a train whistle tooted in the distance and a small engine pulled under the porch area, trailing several cars behind it. Nala relaxed. This she could do.

"Just in time. I bet we can convince Janey to take us through Storybook Land."

Karly twirled around and clapped her hands. "Storybook Land! I went on this when I was a kid, then I became too cool to ride it. Now I can't wait!"

At least Karly was having a good time. It would be a win if she could just get a little more information on the dog attack.

The crew member must have seen them coming. She dinged the bell and yelled, "All aboard!"

"Maybe you'd like to get a photo of the train," Mia suggested.

Mentally she thought *why* but thank goodness didn't say it aloud. When would she ever get used to being a photographer and taking photos? Probably by the time the assignment ended.

"I'd love to." She pulled out the camera, took a few shots, and stared down at the film number Karly had pointed out to her. There were plenty left before the film had to be changed.

Karly raced for the caboose and shouted from her position. "I always wanted to be back here, but it was always full!"

The train engineer rang the bell, and then sounded the whistle before chugging into a forest populated by nursery rhyme characters. Even though the train made a clackety sound, it wasn't too loud to prevent conversation. "You were saying something about a gate before you were interrupted? Guy with a guide dog or something."

"That was no guide dog, and the guy wasn't blind. Not sure why an adult male would want to see Santa, anyway. Once he got into the castle, the dog went straight for Chris. There's a little fence around where he sits with a gate, which is usually open. When Kelly, our elf, saw that loose dog charge for Chris, she slammed the gate shut. Chris took cover behind the chair. Since the display is part of Mrs. Claus's kitchen, there were people nearby. Someone grabbed a fire extinguisher and sprayed in front of the dog, which confused him. Nikki, who works in the kitchen, caught the dog. She's a regular dog whisperer. We ejected the man and his dog but did give him his money back. Weird situation. Not quite up there with the Santa stalkers, but strange all the same."

"Any reason for the attack?" Whoever was behind Chris's disappearance may have had something to do with the dog incident.

Mia shrugged her shoulders and pointed to concrete statues portraying Peter, Peter, Pumpkin Eater. "That was one of the first ones. As for the dog attack, I figured the dog must have responded like a bull seeing all that red. The man didn't have enough sense to hold onto his pet."

"Dogs can't see the color red." She had picked up this tidbit from Karly, who'd explained dogs see in the ranges of yellow and blue.

"Really?" Mia's lips twisted to one side as she considered the possibility. "Maybe Carl was right. We usually call him Conspiracy Carl because he knows them all and embraces most of them."

The train bumped a little as it went over a bridge section. A whoop sounded from the caboose, proving Karly was still with them. "So, ah, what did Conspiracy, I mean Carl, say?"

Mia leaned a little closer and spoke. "He thought it was a deliberate attempt to get rid of Chris. He figured the guy came from that new park they set up across the river. They're having a bit of a tough time getting started. No name recognition, no free drinks, no water coasters, and no Santa Claus. It seemed far-fetched to me at the time, but lately, it seems whatever we won't do, the other park will do to attract paying guests. They recently posted you could bring your dog into *their* park. Not a smart idea, but I am sure it will appeal to many."

Alarm bells went off in Nala's head as she knew where to head next. At the very least, Max would be thrilled he could get into the other park, but he'd better wear his vest, just in case the info about bringing your dog to the park was false.

Chapter Twenty-One

THE SUN BEAMED directly overhead as Nala headed for the park exit. The security head gave her a lot to think about, although she wasn't buying into the dog attack being the result of an untrained dog. No adult male in her experience who was able to drive himself to a theme park ever wanted to visit a random stranger dressed up as Santa. Most dudes would avoid showing up alone at the park as to not look pathetic. When asked, Mia assured her the man was alone. From the park security's viewpoint, all they wanted was for the man and his unpredictable dog gone before it bit someone.

They still had plenty of time to grab lunch, get Max, and head to the competing park. This time they'd have to rely on their badges as opposed to her bogus photographer rep. Nala picked up her pace, aware she was racing against the clock.

Karly broke into a jog to keep up. "Slow down. You're just being cruel."

"How so? We got all we were going to get here." It made no sense to hang out at the park, especially when she hadn't found the fellow who made the park so popular.

"Nala." A pleading tone entered her friend's voice. "We haven't even seen the water park."

This might be a job for Nala, but she kept forgetting that it was a vacation for Karly. Unfortunately, the two activities weren't compatible. Still, she hated it when her friend directed that sad puppy dog look her way. She probably mastered it by working with all the sad, puppy dogs.

"It's a water park, and it's past Labor Day, which means it's bound to be closed."

"Oh." Her expectant expression melted into a frown. "I keep forgetting since it's so warm."

"We're farther south than Indy, and it's been a long, hot summer that never seems to want to end. I imagine the water park is a bear to deal with kids running wild and with all the screaming."

Nala shook her head, wondering how the lifeguards decided what was simply playing around and what was a visitor in actual distress. Most likely the water wasn't that deep, and people could just stand up.

It was a shame her friend couldn't get the vacation she wanted. "Tell you what. My parents haven't closed their pool yet. When we head back, we could take a detour. You know my mother would love to see you. First things first, though. Find Santa. Do you know anything about this other park that just popped up?"

"Foreigners." Karly said the word with a bit of a dismissive tone in her voice.

"Oh." Nala nodded as if she knew what Karly meant. "I guess that's why they didn't know there was a park a few short miles from theirs."

Karly snorted. "They knew Christmas Land had plenty of business they hoped to snag."

As they approached the park exit, a few employees mugged and posed, which made Nala stop and take a photo. She sure hoped there was something she could do with all these great photos. "Wait! I need your names."

"Ronnie."

"Betts."

Since she'd left her purse behind, she picked up a park map and scribbled in the names, along with a short description consisting of Christmas Land employees by an oversized Christmas tree. *Male. Ronnie. Female. Betts.* Hopefully, she could make sense of her notes later for the website she might create with the photos. She penned in Mia's name, too. "Thanks."

Both she and Karly waved as they exited and headed for the car. Her friend glanced back over her shoulder. "We had a lot of good times there."

"I'm sure you did. I'm surprised you didn't run into more of your acquaintances."

"Me, too. I guess most of my old classmates moved away. On the bright side, we didn't run into Keith."

"Keith?" When it came to past crushes and actual boyfriends, Karly was seldom silent. A dim bell rang in Nala's memory. "Ah, was he that guy from your summer romance when you helped with the campground?"

"Stop there." Karly held up her hand. "This is one topic that should remain in the past." She grimaced a little. "So not my type. I may have even thought that at the time. Too much eager puppy about him. Let's go with I learned my lesson."

This *I learned my lesson* refrain popped up every time Karly experienced a relationship disappointment. Although truthfully, calling first dates a relationship was an overstatement. Comparing past dates to types of dogs was another way Karly grouped men. It was hard to know what would be wrong with puppies besides chewing up everything.

"Let's pick up Max and head for that other park. What's it called?"

"I'll look it up." Karly pulled out her cellphone and ordered it to find nearby theme parks. "Hmm," she murmured as she scrolled. "It has to be Vacation Land. It's the only one nearby besides Christmas Land.

They'd reached the car, which Nala unlocked with her fob. Karly spoke as she swung open the car door. "What kind of name is Vacation Land anyhow? It sounds more like an RV and camper sales center. Theme parks should have happy names that evoke pleasant feelings."

"Christmas Land was taken. Besides, most people like vacations."

"Point taken."

They both slid into the warm interior for the short trip back. By the time they pulled in front of the cabin, the air conditioning hadn't even dissipated the heat. "Let's leave the windows down."

After parking and powering down the windows, Nala opened her door at the same time as her phone rang. "I should get this." She pushed her purse toward Karly. "Key is in there."

The phone chimed again as she picked it up from the console, expecting it to be Elvin or possibly a friend. Ever since she started the agency, her parents, especially her father, believed they were consultants and often offered advice when none was wanted. Tyler's name showed. Odd, but a good kind of odd, too. "Hello there."

"Hi, Nala. Sorry to bother, but I was a little concerned about you."

Ah, he worried. How sweet. "Not much to worry about. The hunt for Santa progresses slowly."

It would probably be best not to mention the latest threat. Tyler might give her unwanted advice, which would irk her. "You called just to tell me you're worried about me?"

"Well, yes and no. I was talking to a friend of mine. He works not too far from where you are now, and he's trying to nail a drug distribution ring. Crystal meth in large quantities passes close by. You might stir up some suspicion even though you aren't looking for drug lords. I know you'll tell me to mind my own business, but I just wanted to give you a heads up."

As far as minding his own business, she might not have put it that way. "I appreciate the information. So far, I haven't stumbled across any drug rings. If I do, I will let you know. Promise."

"You do that. Stay safe. Remember we have a date when you get back."

Nala managed a flirtatious laugh that even surprised her a little. "I know. I have to be safe because Karly is here with me."

A slight groan sounded. "I think I would have been better off not knowing that. Promise if Karly suggests anything you think is a bad idea, you won't do it."

"Of course. I would never..." She hesitated as she remembered some of the questionable activities she and her friend had participated in before, but they were much younger back then. "...blindly follow a stupid suggestion. See you soon. We're headed to Vacation Land."

"Talk to you later."

The call disconnected, leaving Nala staring at her phone. *Talk to you later* wasn't wildly romantic, but at least he wanted her to be safe, which meant he cared. She'd take that. The mention of a drug ring had her analyzing all her interactions. While not everyone had been overwhelmingly friendly, she figured people acted the way they would normally. Besides, her father had done some drug training with Max, convinced it would be useful. Personally, she thought her father might try to subcontract her dog for the narcotics unit. If there were drugs around, surely Max would have reacted unless her father hadn't trained him for that drug.

Nope. She didn't want a run-in with any drug lords, be they homegrown or international. With that thought foremost in her mind, she walked into the cabin. Max greeted her from his place on the couch. "What took you so long?"

Really? That's what she got? Other pet owners were greeted with excited dancing and delighted yips. Even though the shelter couldn't peg Max's exact age, Nala would have to say he'd reached the sullen teen stage. "Work. That thing we came down to do. By the way, did Captain Bonne train you on recognizing any drugs?"

One of Max's ears tented forward even though his eyes remained on the movie. Images of people milling about the seashore meant it could be Jaws or Baywatch or a knock-off of either. Personally, Nala thought evoking her father's title would have gotten more of a response, but then, the crowd on the beach parted to reveal a wet Samoyed pulling a human to shore.

Max let out a lusty sigh. "Oh, the Frost Empress could rescue me *any* time."

Yep, he was at the teen stage. Nala cleared her throat. "Captain Bonne?"

Max lifted a paw, which meant wait for a second. The hero dog on television did an all-over shake that the producers thoughtfully slowed down for all the dogs in the audience. "What a dog!"

Fudge! It might be hard to get any work out of her dog unless she was devious. "Frost Queen is quite the hero."

"It's Frost *Empress*. I'm sure it's Frosty to those she knows well." He winked one eye, indicating he would be one of the privileged few.

It was nice that her dog had a healthy self-esteem which also worked to her advantage. "I'm sure a dog like Frost Empress would be impressed with an equally courageous dog who closed cases."

"That's me," Max replied with a wide grin.

Time to reel her hopeful dog in, so she cocked her head to one side. "You do realize Santa is still missing."

"Not my fault. I sniffed everything you asked me to sniff. I ran as far as I could. It's now all about you and your computer skills."

If it were that easy, she'd be back home by now, possibly prepping for a date with Tyler. "Not exactly. No one left information online about where Chris is. I got a tidbit there's some drug distribution going on in the area and was curious if you smelled anything."

Max rolled over on his back and waved his four paws in the air. "Peppermint. Candy. Cinnamon. Bug Spray. Sunscreen. Venison jerky. Cologne. Smoke. Oil. No cocaine, no weed, no meth." He rolled to his side and yawned.

"I'm making lunch," Karly called from the kitchen in a cheery voice. Her despair about the water park being closed must have been forgotten.

"Sounds good," Nala called out, heading for the kitchen.

After a quick lunch, Nala and Karly dumped the dirty dishes

into the sink. Max, on the other hand, gave his untouched bowl of kibble a disgusted look. Used to his dramatics and aware her dog wasn't starving, Nala nudged him as she passed him. "Eat up or not. You got an important role to play. You're going to be an undercover dog."

"Really?" He sat and lifted his head. "Will I be a life guard and rescue one of you from drowning? Will the Frost Empress be there?"

He was really fixated on that movie. "I can't guarantee she'll be at Vacation Land, but it could happen. Your job will be to sniff out anything suspicious. That includes Chris and drugs. Only you don't get to go all crazy the way Captain Bonne showed you. Oh, no." She shook her head and held up one index finger. "You're a spy dog."

He cleared his throat. "Dog, James Dog, at your service. I'll do it for a cheeseburger, shaken, not stirred."

Chapter Twenty-Two

T HE SOFTLY MODULATED tones of the GPS directed them to Vacation Land. As Nala drove up to the entrance, she stared hard at the name. Yep, in twelve-foot letters it read, *Vacation Land.* Despite the fact she crossed the river and was in another state, she would have sworn she was back at Christmas Land. Everything was almost the same. Turrets with flags waved over the entrance. The same animal cut-outs reminded folks to remember they'd parked at Red Rooster Nine or whatever animal they parked beside.

"Weird," Karly commented, echoing Nala's thoughts. "I heard some foreigner started up the park, but they must have visited Christmas Land because it's almost a mirror image."

"I noticed that." Nala parked the car and switched off the ignition. "I'm no expert on theme parks, but if you're going to put two parks so close together in a non-resort area, wouldn't you want one to be different?"

"I'd think so." Karly adjusted her badge and checked out her image in a compact. "It might be different inside, though." She gestured to the vehicles in the lot. "Looks like they're in business. I'm surprised. Christmas Land never ran on a school day. Most of their help is high school employees and a few of the teachers, too.

Besides, too many kids would skip school to go to the park."

"I can see that," Nala remarked as she pushed up her pants leg and attached an ankle holster.

A touch of alarm entered Karly's voice as she gave her friend a concerned look. "What are you doing? Are you worried that whoever left the teddy bear might be here?"

This is what came from bringing civilians on the job. Time her friend knew to take cover if anything happened. "Teddy bear killer never entered my mind. Personally, I think my culprit is not too serious. Come on, no one has taken a pot shot at us, and the car tires haven't been slashed."

"You say that like you expected it to happen."

"Pretty much if someone was serious about encouraging us to leave. So far, all the attempts have been more like something from a children's movie." Nala pulled her gun out of her purse, checked the safety before inserting it into the holster, and smoothed down her pants leg. It stuck out a little, making one leg appear wider than the other. No one would notice unless they were looking for such a thing. "There's something I need to mention."

Karly gave her a long look while Max stuck his head between the two front seats. "Are you going to tell her about my being a spy. It's not much of a secret if you tell everyone."

No need to point out to her dog that he just had. "Actually, I was going to tell her that Tyler warned me about a drug distribution ring in the general area and to keep clear of it. Those guys are not just leaving stabbed teddy bears as calling cards."

"Whoa…" Karly pushed out the word on a long exhale. "Is that why you're armed?"

"Hey, I have a permit for a concealed weapon. Anyhow, every

time I made the mistake of not having a weapon on me, it turned out I needed one. By bringing one, it's an insurance policy ensuring I won't need it. Please, if anything goes south, take cover. Don't worry about me or Max."

A series of barks greeted the pronouncement. Max tended to revert to his first language when upset. Nala held up her hand to stop complaints and questions from Karly and Max. "It's a routine visit. We go in, walk around, ask some questions, then leave. I don't expect to find Chris. I've got a feeling he's tucked away back at the campground, and Bob knows about it."

"Possibly." Karly nodded as if in agreement, but forgot to tell her face, which still featured narrowed eyes and twisted lips. She inhaled, relaxed her face a little, and said. "If we hurry, we can visit the Apple Fest in Mt. Zion. I hear they are making the world's largest apple pie. It will take all night to cook. Probably won't cut it until Saturday. Still, it would be nice to see all the booths selling apple butter, apple jelly, apple dumplings, apple wine, and—"

"I get the idea. Let's go. We need to decide how to present Max. Obviously, they let dogs into the park so it shouldn't be an issue, but why would an *inspector* bring a dog in the park?"

Both women considered the issue while Max threw out suggestions. "I could be a lifeguard."

"I don't think they have a water park," Karly replied.

"I'm a performer. I could do diving or a high wire act."

Nala wasn't sure where that idea came from, possibly another show he had watched. She cut her eyes to her dog. "You will do neither. Besides, they'd know if they hired a performing dog."

Before Max could make another outrageous comment, Karly shouted, "I got it!"

"What?" Max and Nala said in unison.

"Medical alert dog."

Nala had heard the term before but wasn't sure what it consisted of. "What does a medical alert dog do?"

Grinning, Karly alternated eye contact with both as she explained, speaking quickly, and gesturing extensively while doing so. "Folks that have diseases such as epilepsy that can result in seizures may have a medical alert dog. The dog barks when it detects an approaching seizure. It warns the person so they can take medicine or assume a position where he or she won't fall. It also put its body between the person's head and the floor. It can go get help when needed."

"Sounds workable." Nala gave her friend a thumbs up. "There's no way anyone can prove you don't need a medical alert dog." She turned her head to Max. "Be alert. Pay attention. I'm not expecting to fake a seizure, so there shouldn't be too much acting on your part."

His bottom jaw dropped as he groaned. "Boring."

"Maybe." Nala swung open her car door. "Boring beats running for your life any old day. When we get back to the campground, you can be super tracker dog and see if we can't pick up Dasher or Chris's scents. There *will* be a delicious bonus."

His eyes gleamed, and his lips tilted up in a momentary grin, then faded as he asked, "It's not going to be one of those healthy treats made from sweet potatoes, spinach, and blueberries? Yuck. I still can't get the taste out of my mouth." He stuck out his tongue and grimaced to make his point.

It would do no good to point out those treats were organic and expensive. "No. I'll never get you those again. We're talking cheeseburger here."

"All right then, I'm ready to work." Max hopped over the seat, crowding everyone, and forcing a mass exodus.

Because the park was running and the lot was about a third full, they had a much farther walk to the entrance. Many of the cars sported out-of-state license plates, and one even had Canadian plates—a long way to come when your country had its own theme parks. That introduced another quandary, but currently, she needed to concentrate on getting into the park.

Even though most television private eyes were constantly posing as people they weren't to get inside somewhere, Nala expected someone to point at her and shout *fraud*. When she pretended to be pregnant based on a comment that no one ever noticed pregnant women—which was wrong—she expected those she'd met while wearing her fake baby bump to ignore her. Instead, many hit up her mother for details on the possible father.

Her anxiety grew the closer they got to the park entrance. The private eye business taught her two things, the first one being that the lowest lackey was the least invested in a company, which meant they often didn't care what happened. They most likely wouldn't block her entrance and would happily bad mouth the company, leaking valuable info in the process. The second thing she picked up from her father was to imagine the worst-case scenario and how to handle it. Once she did this mentally, nothing else seemed that bad. The worst-case usually never happened, either.

Various families and a few with school-age children crowded the diagonal path to the entrance. They probably had different school schedules or were possibly homeschooled. A gaggle of college-age girls attired in skimpy shorts with sweatshirts jogged past them.

Looked like a girls' day in progress. What did surprise her were the numerous people who appeared to be alone. She monitored them, taking care not to look directly at them. The majority were under thirty. Many had the fast gait and determined headset of a person on a mission as opposed to the relaxed attitude of a vacationer. One couple had vacant expressions on their gaunt faces which sparked her investigator sonar.

A thirty-something man in a *I Love Vacation Land* shirt waved at them and called out. "Karly? Is that you?"

Instead of responding, her friend groaned. "Not him."

"Is that who I think it is?" Nala asked. The man's happy expression was somewhat reminiscent of an excited puppy.

"Yes." She sighed. "It's Keith. He thought I was the most wonderful thing to happen to Santa Claus. Everything I did was either cute or perfect."

Most women didn't complain about being adored. As far as she could recall, Karly complained about men who didn't have time for her because of their workaholic habits or need to constantly hang with the boys. "This was a problem?"

"Uh-huh. At the time, I liked it, but I was younger. It got to be too much. All that gushing made me feel unworthy. I wasn't this wonderful angel that he thought I was. Even saying it now makes me feel guilty. He was always complimenting me, and bringing me gifts like stuffed animals and my favorite chocolates."

"Ah yeah. I hate it when men do that," Nala teased.

"Exactly." Karly slowed her step as if to avoid the inevitable confrontation. "It was too much, too soon."

Needy was the word her friend didn't use, but it came through all the same. Women tended to avoid nice guys who showered them with attention while yearning for bad boys who gave them none. No wonder many men thought women played mind games. Speaking of men, there was another intense guy to her right who wasn't walking toward the entrance. She'd swear he was walking straight at them.

A short glance allowed a quick survey of average height, fit, determined gait, and a super short haircut, which meant military, police, skinhead, or Mormon. She'd discount Mormon. He wasn't wearing a tie. The long summer weather kept most people in shirt sleeves, especially when walking around on the theme park pavement which created an urban heat island effect with the blacktop reflecting the heat. This man had on a jacket, which was weird, but it could easily hide a weapon.

Nala sped up her pace, hoping to lose herself in the wave of visitors before Mr. Intense reached them. That was not to be. The person Karly most wanted to forget didn't want to forget her. He scampered out in front of an on-coming shuttle only to have the shuttle honk and shudder to a stop. The excited employee waved at the driver as he continued to gallop toward them. Karly jumped behind Nala and grabbed her arm. "Hide me."

"Not sure how I can. He's already seen you. Here's your chance to be an investigator. Obviously, the guy is crazy about you. Maybe he can get us through the gates without us paying some ridiculous park fee. Then you can pump him for information. A regular Mata Hari."

"Didn't she die by firing squad?" Karly asked, still crouching behind Nala.

"He's almost here. Act normal. No one is going to get shot to-day."

The clutching hand released as Karly stepped out and managed a pleasant expression. "I had to beg Elvin to bring me here, then I had to listen to all his lame impressions on the way down. Now this. If Max gets a cheeseburger, what do I get?"

No one told her that part of being a PI was bribing everyone. It was no wonder most television investigators were usually broke, something she should have remembered when making a job change. "I already promised you the use of my parents' pool. Along with that, think of it as something to put on your resume, and I'll do the apple fest with you."

Their discussion slowed their procession to the entrance, and it should have allowed the former military dude or possibly clean-cut serial killer to draw closer, but not too close. He must have slowed so as not to meet them, which set off all sorts of alarms. What did he want? She'd rather deal with him head on as opposed to having him lurking behind her. Nala pivoted, trying to keep him in sight, but he had vanished. The lanky man with the goofy grin galloping toward Karly was only a few feet away before he stopped short of running into them.

"How's my princess?" he asked.

Nala glanced over her shoulder, expecting some pint-sized girl in full princess regalia. While her mother never allowed her to go out in costume, many modern moms did. No precious little girls in fancy long dresses and capes were around. Was he talking to Karly?

Her friend coughed, and then managed to say with a bit of squeak to her tone. "Hi, Keith. I'm fine. You work here?"

"I do," Keith replied and fell in step with them as they continued toward the entrance. "You must be coming to the park."

Nala blinked. It was all she could do to prevent rolling her eyes. Not exactly an inspired opening, but what did she expect? He wasn't the one who got away, but rather the one her friend didn't want mentioned.

"We are," Karly said the words in a robotic fashion no one would call flirtatious.

This might not work out as Nala had planned. She coughed hard into a raised fist and tried to insert the words *Be Charming* into the hacking.

There was a heavy sigh from her friend, but then she turned to her male companion and said, "I was hoping to see you."

"Really?" There was so much open-faced delight in the man's expression that it made Nala cringe. It would be like shooting fish in a barrel.

"Oh yes," Karly replied in a stilted manner. It was apparent she had never harbored a secret desire to go into acting. "We have to get in since it's our job to inspect the park. It sure would be nice if there was a secret entrance we could go in and not wait in line with the crowd."

"I should have known you'd have an important job. Heard you were in town and hoped I'd run into you, and this isn't a big crowd." He pointed to the people hustling toward the entrance, anxious to beat others who might delay their entry by mere seconds. There was even an older lady with a walker, but no one was around her. "Weekends are worse. Most of these people don't even bother with the rides."

It was peculiar if people didn't use the rides. Could be they had excellent shows. They'd find out soon enough. Karly, who was supposed to be charming the man, was doing a poor job, and not asking the right questions. Nala's father always used to say some things you must do yourself. She would and demonstrate how it was done.

"As an important man around Vacation Land, maybe *you* can get us past the crowds."

His pale face colored up at the remark. "I was one of the first hires due to my uncle owning the place."

Wait. Hadn't Karly mentioned a foreign company started the park? She assumed Keith's uncle was probably a local man. "I thought a foreign company owned the park."

Keith winked broadly and chuckled. "That's what Uncle Eb *wants* folks to think. In truth, it's only partly true. He got some financial help from Scandinavian investors. Since they didn't know much about this area and what would work here, Uncle Eb helped them out with that. At first, the park wasn't doing that well, which had us all worried, especially, Uncle Eb. It was important for the park to succeed because of, um, previous family issues."

He glanced away after this comment, making Nala wonder if he was speaking out of turn. There had to be more to that story, and it might be pertinent. Max chose that moment to tug on the lease, pulling her in the direction of a male who was stumbling toward the entrance reminiscent of a zombie, possibly stoned, which explained Max's reaction.

Even though she was about a foot away from Keith and Karly, she still heard her question rendered in a slightly less wooden voice. "I've been gone for a while. I must have forgotten about the family issues." Karly held up a hand, "Please don't tell me if it's too painful for you."

Did Karly just say *don't* tell her? Nala's eyes rolled upward but stopped when Keith answered. Maybe it was a brilliant move on her friend's part. In college, Karly majored in psychology and joked she often used it to match up pets and adopters.

Nala gave the leash a jerk, which earned her a censorious look from Max. She angled her head in Keith's direction as an explanation. Max reluctantly gave up his pursuit of zombie guy, and they stood in place, allowing the couple to catch up just in time to hear Keith's response.

"I'm surprised you don't remember, but it isn't your family, either. Great Grandpa Donnie built Christmas Land after the war to cheer folks up. In the beginning, all the employees were family. People assumed when Donnie died, the park would go to his kids. It did, the first time around. His kids didn't live all that long, and there was third passing down. Uncle Eb fully expected to inherit a major share. That didn't happen. Apparently, favoritism was shown."

Karly gestured to the surrounding area. "That's why Vacation Land is so important to him."

"Yep." Keith nodded his head vigorously. "I'd be the first to admit Uncle Eb isn't the hardest worker, but he chose to hire hard workers like myself. He's determined to show everyone he can make a success of the park."

The story did make some sense, but the Scandinavian investors part felt a bit off. Why would they want to invest in an amusement park so far from home? If they'd done their research, which she assumed most investors did, they had to have been aware of Christmas Land close by and doing great business, although that may have been a selling point, too. Still, parts of the story didn't make sense.

Keith herded them away from the general group toward a narrow door he opened with his fob. They strolled in single file, and it must have been the first time Keith managed to look at something other than Karly because he smiled at Max.

"Fine looking service dog. Is he part of the park inspection?"

Before Nala could answer, Karly did. "Mental health dog. My partner has suffered a great deal of trauma."

This wasn't the story they'd discussed going with. Keith gave a slight nod before giving Nala a curious once-over. Most people thought they could see a mental health issue as if it were a wart or an extra arm. Keith was no exception. "Ah, what does the dog do for you?"

Once again, Karly answered. "It keeps her calm and keeps people at a distance." She gave her head a slow, ominous shake. "She doesn't do well if people get too close to her."

Snickerdoodles! The description made her sound like a ticking time bomb. Keith thought so, too. He took a backward step, then another.

The walkie-talkie on his belt beeped, and a staticky voice said, "Keith? You're needed in Jungle World."

Holding the device near his ear, he answered with a strained smile. "On it." Hooking it back on his belt, he told them, "Got to go. Do you need any help getting around the park?"

Karly gave a little finger wave. "We'll be fine, thanks. I appreciate your help, handsome."

Reluctant to leave, Keith held up his hand in response. "I'll try to get back to you before you leave."

"Sounds good," Nala responded while Karly kept a forced smile in place.

They watched Keith walk away before speaking. Karly's smile dropped as she asked, "What now?"

"Don't be surprised if Keith decides to relocate to Indy with that *handsome* you tacked on."

"I was afraid of that." Karly exhaled and leaned against a nearby building. They were still in a narrow alley of plain windowless sheds that bore *Staff Members Only* signs along with hefty padlocks. "It's hard to know what's the right amount of moxie when playing an undercover role."

"Ahem," Max cleared his throat. "Pay attention to the master." He pointed his nose upward, pushed his chest forward, and posed.

"Ah..." Karly started, then in a whisper direct to Nala, asked, "What's he supposed to be?"

"This is Hero Dog," Nala explained. She'd watch her canine posturing in front of the full-length mirror on numerous occasions. Anyone who thought dogs couldn't see their image in a mirror had never met Max.

"Oh! I see it." She clapped her hands together. "Great job. I'll keep that in mind if I ever have to play the part of the hero."

Because he expected her to say something, Nala did. "Max is great at being Hero Dog. Unfortunately, right now, we need him to be Service Dog and Secret Scent Hound."

As if remembering her badge, Nala patted it with one hand. "I'm unsure if we should wear our inspector badges. While Keith might be cool with it, someone else might report us to management. Don't get your hopes up as far as free rides. So far, we do know a Christmas Land family member is behind this park, which would mean they'd know tons about the park and possibly a great deal about Chris, too. All we need to do is get something incriminating to attach to Uncle Eb and whoever he hired to scare both Chris and me."

"That's all?" Karly said in a forlorn tone.

Nala arched an eyebrow. "You say that like it's an impossibility."

A derisive snort answered her, but Karly wouldn't leave it at that. "Are you going to march into his office and ask him why he's trying to ruin his family legacy, then announce you recorded the whole thing?"

Truthfully, the resolution of the case was still up in the air. Usually, it came together when she had dug up enough facts. Something told her she was close. Call it instinct, intuition, her investigator-sense, or whatever. "Of course not. A recording made without the acknowledgment of the person is inadmissible in court. My best bet will be to catch our harasser in the act. Then put pressure on him until he confesses. After all, spelling out *Leave* in dog treats isn't exactly hardcore. Even the teddy bear thing wasn't too bad. It makes me think whoever is supposed to be harassing us doesn't want to actually hurt us."

"Point taken. I wonder who it could be. Someone local or else they had to take a campsite while they pursued their reign of pseudo terror." They conversed as they strolled down the walkway, which emptied into a noisy main area where people congregated before splitting off into whatever world they chose to visit, which included Jungle World, Alpine World, Beach World, and Disco World. The last one didn't fit, but it didn't stop people from heading in that direction.

The buildings tended to funnel the sound, making it even louder and more chaotic. Pushcart vendors selling snow cones and cotton candy were doing brisk business. Near the oversized globe emblazoned with *Vacation Land* stood Mr. Intense. Not good.

"Come on. We need to go," she warned Karly before joining a large group heading into Alpine World.

Chapter Twenty-Three

POLKA MUSIC BLASTED from the speakers as people passed under the Alpine World arch. To the left were painted plywood mountains with a few grinning cows wearing daisy crowns. A man in lederhosen carried a wooden frame loaded with hot pretzels. Most people swerved around him in their effort to reach their destination. Nala knew it wouldn't be so simple with her companions. A quick backward glance confirmed they'd lost Mr. Intense, which was good.

Max bumped against Nala and said in a low whisper. "Is this where the Frost Empress is? I heard she came from the land of ice and snow."

She almost made the mistake of asking *who that was* but caught herself. Instead, she steered clear of the crowded walkway to address her dog. "It could be. I'm not saying she's here, but if she were, this could be the place. The important thing is to be on task. Did you smell anything on the way in?"

A couple pushing a baby stroller gave her a peculiar look. They probably talked to their baby, and yet were all judgy about her talking to her dog. At least Max answered, most of the time in full sentences.

Max grimaced. "People smell. They have to be the smelliest of all the creatures."

Not this again. Nala wouldn't deny humans could work up a bit of an odor. Some more than others, but it was a topic Max consistently came back to when asked to check for a scent. "Yes, I know, which makes them easier to track. Anything else besides body odor?"

"Sweet floral smell."

Karly, standing nearby and giving the pretzel man's wares a lingering look, replied. "Body spray. Probably someone trying to cover up B.O."

"Could be," Nala agreed. "It could also be cocaine. The scent of some strains can smell like that. Anything else?"

"Cat pee. I didn't see any cats, though." He gave his head a hard shake to rid himself of the possibility.

"Owner of an incontinent cat," Karly suggested. A passerby gave her a doubletake, and then scurried on his way.

"More likely meth binge or a meth producer. It's sounding more and more like we've stumbled into distribution central. Any other smells of note?"

Max lifted his nose with all the hauteur that would do a debutante proud. "You rush me around, then demand results." He made an audible sniff before proceeding. "Fortunately for you, I am used to working on the run. Some of the visitors had a skunky smell."

Karly and Nala said in unison, "Weed."

Marijuana, while legal in some states, was still illegal in both Indiana and Kentucky. If a person wanted to smoke, they *could* take a road trip to Illinois unless there was a closer, local option.

As it probably wasn't for the best discussing drug dealing out in public, Nala motioned Karly closer.

Karly asked, "Do you think they're selling in the park?"

Nala's eyes rolled, and she sucked in her lips as she considered it. "Well, there *are* some sketchy visitors. Loners. People who don't exactly look like roller coaster fans as well as very few families."

Karly gave a dramatic shudder.

Part of Nala wanted to head back to the cabin to keep her friend out of danger, but the investigator side had other plans. "Let's walk around some more."

It certainly wasn't on Nala's checklist to break open a drug ring, but it would be nice if she could pass on major information while Tyler handed it over to a local LEO. If her father knew anything about this, the man was so overprotective there would be undercover cops casually lurking about watching her. Most of her life she considered her dad a person who always went with what was the absolute worst things that could happen, but he'd witnessed too many worst-case scenarios on the job. Discretion was the better part of valor.

Coming up on their right side was a series of gift shops painted to look like Swiss chalets, filled with stuffed animals, oversized sunglasses, and T-shirts with *Vacation Land* across the chest. Nothing that different from Christmas Land, except the quality was much poorer: it felt like the animals were filled with sawdust, and they weren't cuddly. They soon reached the first ride, a series of cars that raced forward, then backwards while loud music played and lights blinked. Only a half-dozen people stood in line, proving Keith's point.

Karly nudged Nala. "Remember the ice cream man?"

She assumed her friend was referring to the scruffy character who'd shown up in neighborhoods during the spring playing Pop

Goes the Weasel or simply dinged a bell to get children and adults out of their house for overpriced frozen treats. "In theory. My parents were against getting ice cream from a stranger."

"Mine, too. In my case, it was because it was too expensive." She wrinkled her nose and arched her eyebrows. "Not exactly what I was talking about. There was some guy selling drugs from his ice cream truck. There was a write up about it in the paper. Pretty bold since it was right under everyone's noses. He still sold ice cream, but apparently, there were code words for drugs. He passed them out wrapped up like an ice cream sandwich. In the end, the proverbial little old lady kept noticing more and more adults and teens were visiting the ice cream wagon, and no one was ripping into their ice cream and eating it. She reported it, of course. They planted people along the route to buy ice cream, and he often didn't have any of the things listed on the side of his van. Anyhow, I wonder if something like that could be going on here?"

Yellow supports held up a water flume ride entitled *Fondue Falls*. As flume rides went, it wasn't very tall. An empty log bounced by, followed by another one filled with a doubtful little girl clutching the sides, along with her mother. As they drew closer, it was easy to see the water had been dyed yellow.

Karly nodded at the water. "I guess it's supposed to represent cheese?"

"Not a good look." Nala wasn't even tempted to put her hand in the water to test the temperature. "So far, the local county fair has this place beat. Not sure what the draw is."

"Everyone has to check out what's new for themselves. It doesn't mean they'll ever come back."

Max tugged on his lead and turned to look behind him. More

people were filtering into the park. The fact they were standing by the flume ride and not moving was probably an irritant. Things were starting to come together.

To accommodate her dog, she went back to a leisurely saunter and pitched her voice low. "Obviously, Keith believes in his uncle. This isn't much of a park. I'd say it was no competition, which might lead Eb to try to push Chris out."

"I can follow that, but what did he do that would send Chris fleeing?"

It kept coming back to that. What would send a grown man hotfooting it through the woods, deserting his beloved pup? She let out a long breath. "It had to be something other than spelling *Leave* in dog treats. Then again, what if Chris being gone has nothing to do with Eb or Vacation World?"

A few high-pitched squeals came from children shooting down an oversized slide called *The Abominable Plunge*. It would have made more sense if it were white as opposed to a faded red.

Around them, the buttery scent of popcorn floated in the air. "Popcorn!" Max gave the words a certain reverence.

"I know. Work first, eat later. I promise."

There was a low canine grumble but no distinguishable words.

So far, the park did not wow her. The families she noticed hadn't seemed particularly thrilled with the experience. A suspicion coalesced in her head as she made her way to the exit of the flume ride. Maybe she'd catch the apprehensive girl and mother. The two in question came through the ride exit turnstiles ahead of them, and they were about to get away.

Nala handed off Max's lead to Karly and broke into a jog before the mother and daughter vanished. "Excuse me. Excuse me!"

The woman kept hold of her daughter's hand and darted an anxious look in Nala's direction. "Are you talking to me?"

"Yes, I am." Since the woman stopped, Nala smiled and held out her hand. "I'm Nala Bonne." Most people wouldn't use their real name, but she was winging it here. "I'm with Theme Park Inspections, an independent organization not affiliated with Vacation Land. Could I ask you a few questions?"

The mother appeared a bit unsure, but she hesitated long enough for Karly to catch up with Max, who struck the Hero Dog pose, capturing the daughter's attention. "Mommy, look. It's that dog from television."

"That's Max," Nala squatted to be eye level with the girl. "He's a special helping dog. Normally, you shouldn't pet a working dog, but he's on a break now, so you can."

The little girl's eyes grew big with the possibility and gazed up at her mother. "Can I, Momma?"

"Be gentle. Remember the evil cat."

Nala didn't want to ask, but it sounded as if things didn't go well with the cat. She hoped the girl had learned her lesson for Max's sake. The little girl skipped over to Max and gave him careful pats with Karly's instruction.

Thankfully, Nala had abandoned the clipboard and resorted to a small tablet and pen in her back pocket. She pulled out the tablet and clicked the pen. "Just a quick note that we rate parks for value, safety, and atmosphere," Nala stalled, as she tried to think of what might be important regarding a theme park.

"Also, fun," Karly added from her kneeling position beside the dog.

"Of course, fun." Nala forced a chuckle. "I should have led with that. May I have your name?"

"Julia Owens. My daughter's Taylor."

The pen raced across the paper recording the names, place, and date. "Is this your first visit to the park?"

"Yes." The word was pushed out through pinched lips that announced it would probably be the last visit to the park, too.

"What brought you to Vacation World today?"

"I got free tickets. My father used to tell me stuff was worth whatever you paid for it. I have to say on this occasion he was right."

Nala thought as much. The young families didn't seem a good fit with the various slackers she'd seen. Walking toward them, she spotted Keith and behind him a little bit farther away, Mr. Intense. It was amazing how they all kept ending up together like this.

"Did you win the tickets?"

The woman shook her head slowly as if bemused by the suggestion, and then she spotted Keith heading toward Karly. Julia stabbed a finger in his direction. "Him. He's the one that showed up at my daughter's pre-school with a stack of tickets."

Keith turned slightly and nodded in their direction. "Every visit at Vacation World is a vacation!"

The remark caused Julia to scrunch up her face as if she'd bitten into something sour, which wasn't hard to interrupt as this *vacation* wouldn't merit being included in the family scrapbook. Unfortunately, the arrival of Keith distracted Mom, who kept shooting daggers at Keith. He had stopped to talk to Karly but was too near Taylor for comfort.

"I see you're ready to go. I don't want to keep you. What would be your major complaints against this park?"

"There's not much here. Also, it feels wrong. I wouldn't recommend it to people with young children. Taylor, we're leaving."

The little girl's bottom lip trembled at the thought of leaving Max, who had rolled to his side for a tummy rub. All the same, she stood up and went with her mother. Nala waved as they left, then turned to try to regard Keith as a mother would see him. Big, goofy guy handing out free passes to a sketchy park at a pre-school. Very suspicious.

Most basic parks charged around forty dollars admission, although discounts were given on children and multiple days. Giving out tons of free passes meant Vacation Land needed the visual of families roaming the grounds to legitimize the park setting. Keith showed up where there were bound to be young families. It made her wonder where else had Keith passed out tickets. Too bad she didn't have a stack of Christmas Land tickets to hand out to unhappy families, although after today, she doubted some of the unhappy visitors would take her offer. They'd be more like, fool me once, shame on you. None of them were going for fool me twice, shame on me. What she needed to do was talk to more visitors, which might be hard to do if Keith decided to stick with them.

If nothing else, she'd go with the ambush questioning under the guise of civility. Max had rolled to all four feet and barked at something in the distance. Keith glanced back at Max. "I thought he was your medical dog. You were talking to people, too."

"I do that," Nala explained with a wide smile. "It's part of my job. It's when people are touching that tends to bother me."

"Better stay away from Disco World then." The words were uttered in a no-nonsense voice that just might border on threatening for Keith. A quick look at her friend whose mouth was partially open demonstrated her surprise, too.

"Oh, I will. I've been talking to some folks visiting the park today. They tell me you were kind enough to give them free tickets. Who else did you give tickets to?"

"Locals." He shrugged his shoulders. "Uncle Eb figured if we got the locals to see the park, they'd spread the news. He called it an investment. I went to churches, schools, scout meetings, afterschool care, even stopped by a nursing home. Mainly the employees took the tickets there." He inhaled deeply, and then asked, "No one actually said my name, did they? Keith Beals gave me a free pass? Anything like that?"

"Nope," Nala assured him. "Besides, I think giving out free tickets would make you a hero. You'd want people to know your name."

"You'd think." An expression of distaste crossed his face. "Some people don't always understand. I'm helping my uncle who needs someone to help him. Most of the family just dismiss him. They complain about his get rich quick plans. At least he *has* plans. Not like the rest of the family, who expect to work at Christmas Land the rest of their lives."

It wasn't hard to see which side Keith decided to support.

"That's sweet of you. I'm sure your uncle appreciates it." Karly strolled forward and handed Nala the lead. Max went from well-behaved canine to dog on a scent. His ears tented forward, and he tugged against his lead, not exactly the image of a medical alert or therapy dog. He'd picked up a scent or something, and they needed to get rid of Keith.

With any luck, his walkie-talkie would crackle to life. It remained quiet. Just her luck, but here came Mr. Intense, walking their way. Good, she was tired of his ducking out of the way when he was tailing them. Time to have it out and let him know she was no pushover.

"Hey! Hey you!"

The man ignored her and approached Keith. "Mr. Beals, just the man I need."

Keith acted alarmed but nodded at the man, telling Nala, "Be with you in a minute. Remember, avoid Disco Land. You wouldn't like it there."

Nala watched the two men walk off to the Swiss Chalet gift shops. Weird. It opened all kinds of questions like did they know each other and why was the one dude following her?

Karly slid up next to her. "Are you thinking what I'm thinking?"

"Disco World."

"You bet. It makes me wonder why Keith was so insistent we'd not go."

"We'll soon find out."

The burble of wheels on concrete sounded as two employees pushed a vendor cart meant for frozen treats up the slight incline. Max sniffed the air, barked twice, and stared in the direction of the cart. "What do you want to bet they're going to Disco World. Remember the rules. Take cover if things go south."

Chapter Twenty-Four

MOST THEME PARKS are populated with signs pointing to different areas with arrows to shows, ride entrances, and exits. Vacation Land didn't splurge on signs. After tromping through Jungle Land which contained plastic trees, vines, and ominous drumming music but with very few actual attractions, they wandered into Beach Land. The fake palm trees were taller, and the music was happier. Blue and white pool loungers were scattered around an empty pool, which was probably meant to be a wave pool. There were a couple of slides, but only a handful of guests taking advantage of the loungers.

Max glanced around and was the first of the three to speak. "Boring. Isn't there supposed to be water?"

"You'd think so." Nala knew her dog could be counted on for stating the obvious. Underneath the shade of an oversized umbrella, a young woman attired in Vacation Land clothing opened her brown bag lunch. Unlike most of the employees, who were far from friendly and helpful, she looked nice, normal, and possibly a resident from across the state line in Santa Claus.

The trio veered in her direction. When they drew near, Max sniffed, then shook his head, which meant she was clean. Nala turned sideways to diminish the appearance of her makeshift badge, not certain if it would make the employee less talkative. She should have removed it, but to do so now would only draw attention to it.

Part of her wanted to return to the campground that needed to be explored more. Unfortunately, another part of her wanted to unearth the mystery of this park, which was far from the happy place it promoted itself to be. Still, a third warned her bad things were ahead and to leave now. Talk about being conflicted. Her doubts could be placed directly on Tyler who told her there was a drug distribution ring. Even in the Midwest, drugs were an issue. Small towns were ideal. Their law enforcement members were slim or non-existent. Paired with folks who thought it couldn't happen in their town and who refused to recognize the signs, it made small towns a perfect setting. After all, their neighbor couldn't be making and selling meth—that is, until their garage blew up. Even then, they still had their doubts. All she'd do is get some vital information and pass it on.

Nala smiled at the employee who looked up when they stopped a foot from her table. "Sorry to disturb you, but we're lost."

The girl sighed. "Boy, are you ever! You probably want to be at Christmas Land, which is across the river." She glanced at Max and added. "They don't allow pets there and aren't open until tomorrow."

Karly inserted, "He's a medical assist dog."

"Well, it might be okay then," the girl concluded, unwrapped her sandwich, and bit into it.

"It's pretty hot today," Nala said with her desire to ask about the missing water in the park. "It sure would be nice to take a cool, refreshing dip." She gazed in the direction of the pool.

"Good luck with that because it's not going to happen here. The park opened in July, the perfect time for a water park. We had water initially to check out the water slides." She made a derisive snort. "Not anymore. The park has water fountains, but even they aren't running. If you want water, you have to buy it at the stands." She shook her head, then pointed to Nala's badge. "I see you're inspectors."

"Ah yes." It was hard to deny it with the words stenciled on her chest. She made sure to use the girl's name printed on her name tag. Her mother insisted the use of a person's name made them more likely to buy. Her father on the other hand felt it humanized the officer and made the suspect more likely to confess. "No worries, Staci. We wouldn't include your name in the report. We might say the water park was not running due to…" She waited for Staci to feel in the blank.

Staci shrugged. "I didn't start when the park first opened. A friend did though. He told me the wave pool was full and the water fountains worked. So, it passed inspection back then. Rumor is there's a water main break. That's why they shut the pool down." She shook her head. "I don't know. Heard they couldn't get lifeguards, but with Christmas Land closed for the season, we should have plenty. It doesn't matter, though. It'll soon be too cold to swim."

Even though Max chose to sit during the conversation, Nala still handed the lead to Karly, and reached for her notebook. There was a trail of clues or possibly steps on how to not run a business. She wanted to get them down and to the right person. "I can see that. Anything else unusual going on?'

Instead of answering, Staci reached into her bag and pulled out a baggie of carrot sticks. After chomping down on one, she grew reflective. "It depends on what you consider *unusual*."

"Anything. Sometimes, you never know what's important."

The girls she had seen earlier wandered through, grumbling loudly about the lack of cute guys and the various rides that were shut down or even missing. Staci waited until the girls were far enough away. "That's one of the issues."

Nala didn't know if girls traveling in a pack or the general discontent was the problem. "I'm not sure what you mean." A heavy *sigh* greeted her remark, making Nala feel a bit like a parent who inquired about the meaning of the latest slang.

Using a carrot as a pointer, Staci made an arc with it, encompassing the entire area. "This is a theme park. People are supposed to be happy to be here. It's a day off from their regular life. When I started, there *were* happy people. It was summer and families were coming in along with teens who could drive. We had shows for the old people who needed regular breaks from the sun. We had more food vendors, too. Now, everything has changed. It depresses me to come to work."

This must have been how her parents felt, trying to talk to her when she was young. There were plenty of words, but none that told her anything. "Customers are no longer happy?"

She pursed her lips. "It depends. We get plenty of icky characters who show up and act delighted to be here. They're never here long and leave smiling. Personally, I'm glad to see the last of them. All the same, they buy admission tickets. Some have passes. The guys with passes are a little less icky, but they don't even act like they're here to have fun. And, most have backpacks, which I thought was weird."

Nala turned to make eye contact with Karly. She bobbed her

head, demonstrating she caught the backpack remark, too. "Did you notice if their backpacks were fuller when they left?"

"Um," Staci stalled and unscrewed a water bottle. "I don't really know. I see them walk by, the guys with the backpacks, since I used to work the front gate, but I rarely saw them leave."

"Another exit?" Nala suggested, hoping to jog the girl's memory.

"Nope." She held up one finger. "Nothing public, but there's another way to get in that's just for upper management. Peons like me use the front gate. Rumor is the park isn't doing well no matter what changes are made. I've got my application in half a dozen different places around here. I'm not waiting to get laid off like some of my co-workers."

"A lot of people have been laid off?"

"Some." She gave another shrug. Pulled out her phone and checked the time. "I need to go."

Staci packed up her uneaten lunch, stood, and walked away without saying goodbye. Outside of three visitors sleeping on loungers, Nala didn't see anyone else, but something had spooked Staci. There could be security cameras recording the meeting. That had to be it. Pocketing her tablet and pen, she motioned to Karly and Max, and they were back on the trail.

They moved forward past the sleepers with slack mouths and over the bridge that led to the kiddie pool. Karly gestured to the brightly painted mushrooms when working dribbled water onto pint-sized guests. "This could be nice with a few tweaks."

"I agree. Seems to me that Keith's uncle wanted everything that Christmas Land has and all at once. Never mind it took decades of hard work. What do you think about the missing workers?"

"They quit."

"Could have. Why not say they quit? Plenty of people quit all the time. By saying they quit or were fired, it makes the missing person sound like a loser. If you say they were laid off, it makes the company the loser. I wish we could have asked who told her that, but she acted spooked. She probably suspects plenty." Nala peered at her watch. "I'm only going to give this fifteen more minutes. Tomorrow is Friday, and we need Chris on his Santa throne. This was a long shot. In some ways, it was more obvious that a competitor would want to wipe out Christmas Land's main draw."

"I agree." Karly wrinkled her nose as her eyes grazed the stacked loungers. "This place won't be in business long. Maybe Chris was threatened by the owners of this place but knew Vacation Land had no future. He may have decided to wait it out by hiding for a while."

It would be just her luck if he popped out of hiding to go back to work on his own, then Selma would refuse to pay. "By the way, have you heard anything about my payment?"

"I've been assured your payment will be forthcoming."

This didn't reassure her at all since Karly already admitted all her relatives tended to lie. The check is in the mail could just be another one.

Max tugged at the leash. No doubt he was bored and eager to get on with it. The path took them along an empty lazy river that had happy fish painted on its bottom. The park *had* potential. Even though they had a long run of hot weather, it might not have been financially feasible to keep the water park open with the children back in school.

A sharp pull on the lead stopped Nala's stroll to see what interested Max. He leaned toward an empty food stand that had shuttered windows, but still had a painted menu displayed with offerings that included cheeseburgers, nachos, and fries. It made her wonder if her dog could smell the cheeseburgers of long-ago.

"The place is closed. No cheeseburgers, buddy."

Max sat down and barked twice.

"I said no cheeseburgers. We'll eat as soon as we get out of here. I promise. There are some promising places in town."

Max gave her a long-suffering look, glanced around, and seeing no one, spoke. "Sitting and barking twice is the signal for drugs."

"You're right. It slipped my mind for a moment. Are there drugs inside the food stand?"

He shot her another aggrieved look. There were, or he wouldn't have barked. "Okay. I'm going to take a photo of the place, then report it. Tyler knows someone." She snapped a photo and texted it to Tyler who would pass it on. "Can you tell me what kind of drugs?"

"Lots of them. I've only been trained for so many. Weed, Cocaine, Meth, and…" he gave a slight sniff, "possibly assorted pills. Those are the hardest since they don't always have a distinct odor."

She tapped out the information and sent it. "All right guys, I think we're going to have to forgo Disco World. It isn't safe here. We need to head out."

"Ahem," Max cleared his throat. "A treat for locating?"

"I've got nothing." Nala patted down her pockets. "Karly?"

She gave her head a slow shake, which caused Max to shoot them both a sullen look. "What a rip-off! I only hope the Frost Empress is paid better for *her* hard work."

The hair on the back of her neck was standing up. Her father remarked on more than one occasion that his instinct saved him even when it appeared nothing was awry. "We got to go, now."

Karly's face puckered up as if she were on the verge of crying. She couldn't be upset because Max didn't get a treat. Her soft-hearted friend wasn't ready for the world of investigation. Even though she might regret it, Nala asked, "What is it?"

"If it isn't safe for us, what about the families that are here?"

Ah, the general public wasn't something she normally had to worry about in her investigations. She placed her hands on the small of her back and looked at the sky. "Most have left. There isn't all that much to do."

An electronic sound penetrated her thoughts. What was it? Her eyes dropped from the gathering clouds to search the nearby area. A mounted security camera had swiveled to pinpoint them, and the lens zoomed out for a better photo. Not good. "Let's hit it."

She grabbed the lead from Karly, knowing that when Max surged into run mode, he could be a powerhouse. They dashed toward another water slide only to find it was a dead end. The three of them looped through the water park and came out where they entered. Despite the hairs on her neck practically marching, she checked to her left and right. It was possible left might be faster, but Staci said there was only one exit. They'd have to go the way they came.

Investigators were limited on what they could do. They couldn't make arrests. Even on the television shows the investigators had to call in the big guys to clean up the mess. Her phone buzzed. Not exactly a good time to answer. They slowed for a corner, Nala withdrew it, and thumbed it on, showing a dexterity which oddly pleased her. It was Tyler calling.

She gasped. "Running! Right now. Leaving park."

Tyler's voice was heard from the cell. "Nala, please hurry but leave the line open."

"I can do that," Nala replied. She moved the phone to her pocket without turning it off.

To her right was a slow-moving family complete with a wagon with toddlers in it. Slowing, she waved at them with her free hand. "Dangerous storm coming. Park is closing."

The mother gave a nod of acknowledgment while the father turned the wagon around, causing an outcry from the children. By that time, they were heading into Jungle Land, which made her aware of how small the sections were if they could jog through them so easily.

Karly gasped, stumbled to a stop, bent over, and held onto her knees. "You go. Don't wait for me."

Nala pulled Max to a halt with a jerk. "I'm not leaving without you. Catch your breath. Maybe running through the park was too dramatic, but we do need to move." She spotted another family and yelled. "Park closing! Dangerous storm coming."

"Ready?" She directed the inquiry to Karly. A hand landed on her shoulder and squeezed hard, surprising her. The lead dropped from her fingers, freeing Max. He pivoted, growled, then barked twice. It didn't take her dog's response to know they were in trouble. Nala tried to stomp on the instep of her attacker and directed an elbow behind her. A grunt let her know the elbow hit, but the foot stomp must have been expected.

Karly yelped in pain, freezing Nala in mid-twist. For a moment, she'd forgotten about her friend. "Let her go!"

Her demand was met with a chuckle. Even though her head was being forced down she could see muscular arms forcing Karly's head down also in a wrestling hold called a half-nelson.

A gruff voice asked, "Whadya think, boss?"

Max had kept his distance, but circled slowly, growling with his hindquarters close to the pavement. He was waiting for an opening to rush in and bite.

Nala's attacker must have suspected as much. "I'm gonna shoot that stupid dog!"

"Run, Max, run!"

She could still hear his low growl. What a time for her dog not to obey her. She tried to twist away, but her attacker had arms like a gorilla and anticipated every move she made. Were people just watching this and doing nothing? What kind of place was this? The very least she could do was get her dog away, then she'd work on Karly. "Max, go get help."

Her dog gave her a last look before lunging away from an employee who tried to grab his lead. With all her twisting, stomping, and elbowing, she forgot to use a woman's most potent weapon. She opened her mouth to scream but before she could let out an eek, a smelly bandana was shoved into it. *Yuck.*

Maybe she couldn't do any actual screaming, but her shoulder shouted plenty as it was used like a rudder to maneuver her. She stumbled in whatever direction he pushed her. Despite the pain, she kept running plans in her head. Max got away, and her phone was still on. Two pluses. All she needed was a believable excuse for their presence in the park. After all, it wasn't illegal to visit the park. Posing as inspectors was the tricky part, but she could spin it.

There weren't any other shoes in the area outside of her own. Her current position didn't allow her to see much more than mangled brochures, abandoned straws, and the occasional wad of gum. *Please don't let this be the last thing I see.*

Stairs met her gaze as she struggled up them. When she stumbled, her arm was wrenched upward. A door opened, and she stepped onto a plush carpet. A slightly accented, but amused voice asked, "Are these our snoops?"

Her goon answered. "They are. The stupid dog ran off. I think she told it to go get help. Like it was going to round up Lassie or something."

She'd settle for Lassie or the local sheriff, but until then, she'd work with what she had. The hold released on her neck, and she was shoved into a chair. As soon as her bottom hit the cushion, she spat out the bandana, sticking out her tongue as she did. "Ugh."

She turned her neck enough to see Karly even though it hurt. Her friend's goon kept a tight grip on her arm and neck keeping her in a standing position. It made her wonder why she earned a chair. Her hand went up to rub the back of her neck as she regarded the decent sized room. An oversized, dark desk and credenza along with leather wing chairs crowded the area. Behind the desk, a middle-aged, balding white guy paid more attention to his cuticles than the drama being enacted a few feet from his face. Next to him, a fit, older man relaxed in a chair. His clothes were tailored and even the roll in his sleeves was pressed. He held a slender knife in his hand and used it to pare his nails. As opposed to ignoring them, his eyes glittered as he gazed at them, and spoke in an accented voice.

"You must forgive my associates. They don't know how to treat a lady."

A loud snort meant someone didn't agree with the label *lady*. Nala held her head up, reminding herself not to be weak and submissive. "I noticed." She gave an aggrieved sniff mimicking her mother's manner.

"Maybe they thought you were somewhere you shouldn't be."

"Where was that? We never went into anywhere that was closed off to the public."

Her questioner gave a slow nod and steepled his fingers, casual, but still taking control of the room. "This much is true. You were questioning guests and taking photographs."

"True, I was" Nala agreed, sticking as close to the truth as possible. "This is the Midwest. We talk to strangers and take photos of everything that we put up on social media later." She managed a shrug that sent a jolt of pain across her back. She breathed in so as not to flinch. It wouldn't serve her to show pain.

Her goon must not have liked her answer because he slammed the back of her head with his open hand, stunning her for a moment.

"Enough!" Knife parer shook his head. "Simon, I don't like your attitude." He waved his hand. "Leave now."

Nala sat up straight, refusing to watch Simon leave. Her goal was to convince her inquisitor of her sincerity. Still, she listened for the door opening and closing before she breathed again. The man who had taken charge of the room pointed to the closed door. "Simon is the type who only has a hammer in his toolbox and everything else looks like a nail. Me, I have many tools, and I'm a reasonable man. I'll ask you again what you were doing."

Karly muttered something that made no sense with the gag. She was probably telling her to say nothing, but she had to say something.

Nala made a show of twisting in her seat, looking down at her hands, and even managed a sob. "No one told me this could be dangerous. I was told to visit. Ask people about how well they liked

Vacation Land and snap photos of things that might be incorporated into Christmas Land."

The man who had been so concerned with his cuticles jerked up his head. Once she could see his face, it was hard to miss that Keith and his Uncle Eb shared the same nose and chin. "They sent you to spy on *me?*" he asked in shock.

Nala managed a weak nod. "They didn't call it spying. It would be more of a game. My friend and I could do whatever we wanted as far as food and rides. It was supposed to be a fun day."

Eb rubbed his hands together. "You hear that, Ramon? The family is worried we might finally provide some real competition. Ha! I told you I could do it."

"Don't forget, Eb. We did it together."

The phone on the desk rang. Both men stared at it, but Ramon said, "Pick it up and put it on speaker."

Eb lifted the receiver and punched two buttons. "Hello?"

Max's rich baritone voice came over the speaker. "I *know* what you did."

"Who is this?"

"Wouldn't *you* like to know?"

"Yes, tell me."

Nala leaned back to catch Karly's attention. Her friend blinked at her, which was supposed to be a sign of something, possibly alerting her that she recognized the dialogue from a teen horror flick. In the actual movie, the girl is killed for accidentally prank calling an actual killer.

"Ha, ah, ha. Ahooo!" Max was never that good at approximating human laughter.

Ramon muted the phone and ordered, "Trace the call."

Eb held up his hands, indicating he had no clue how to do it.

Karly's goon released her. "Here, I'll do it." He booted up a laptop on the desk. "Every land phone in the park is monitored."

His fingers raced over the keyboard, which made Nala wonder why he served as security when he could easily run the IT department.

"Keep him talking," Goon Two advised.

Ramon followed the suggestion, taking the speaker off mute. "What do you know?"

"Everything. I know *everything*."

Typical of Max, but smart, too. It allowed Ramon to imagine the worst. A flush built under his tan.

She caught Karly's attention who gave a nod in acknowledgement and fluttered her free hands. The men were all huddled over the laptop, trying to determine where the call was coming from. Nala would have liked to know how Max dialed the number to begin with and how the two of them could take advantage of their inattention.

Nala slowed pushed up from the chair almost into a squatting position, when Goon Two yelled, "I got it! He's downstairs. Right underneath us. Using the receptionist phone."

"Go get him," Ramon ordered. Nala dropped back into her seat before anyone noticed. Goon Two ran out of the room as Ramon spoke to Eb. "This is a daring fellow. I like to see him caught in the act." Ramon dashed out of the room.

Eb stared at the open door, then back at Nala and Karly. "You look like nice girls. I know you never meant to hurt anyone. I think I'll go see who that fellow is."

Once all three men disappeared, Nala grabbed the knife from the desk and motioned for Karly to follow. They tried the other doors. One was a closet, another a bathroom, but the third was a stairwell that went on forever.

Once on the other side of the door, Nala bent to retrieve her weapon from her ankle holster with a sigh. No wonder most people used shoulder holsters. Having the gun in her hand gave her a slight sense of ease, but she wouldn't relax until they were far, far away from the place, preferably Indianapolis.

Not able to juggle both weapons, she handed the knife to Karly as they made their way down the stairs with its many twists and various landings, with doors that they didn't care to find out what was behind.

EVENTUALLY, THE STEPS bottomed out in a flat area and started climbing again only to come out near a stand of trees close to a small parking lot where two expensive foreign cars were parked. One had a *Vacation Land Rocks* license plate on the front.

Nala stabbed the tires of both cars with the knife. "It's better to be safe than sorry. We need to find Max."

The screech of distant sirens penetrated the heavy air, telling them something was going on. Using the sound to guide them, it still took several tries to find their way to the main parking lot. Meanwhile, the skies had darkened. A rumble of thunder, a flash of lighting, and nature's own water park let loose on them. Her inspector badge wilted under the onslaught.

"I see the parking lot." Karly pointed to an area beyond a chain-link face bathed in the glow of flashing red and blue lights. "Something big must be happening."

"Just another day in Paradise. I hope Max is okay."

Chapter Twenty-Five

THEY HAD TO make it over the fence. "Here, let me give you a boost."

The fence was only about five feet high. Karly stepped into Nala's interlaced fingers and balanced on the top rung before swinging her feet over and dropping to the other side. Nala boosted herself belly up on the top bar, leaned over, and kicked wildly until she flipped to the other side. Not exactly graceful, but it served its purpose.

The rain had stopped a few minutes after it started, leaving the parking lot slick and shining. Motor oil helped create shimmering puddles which both women skirted. A uniformed officer directed the traffic. Most of the visitors' cars had left, but a few gawkers stood under umbrellas, speculating wildly.

"The ticket prices are highway robbery, but I never suspected they'd get arrested for it."

"Oh, I heard it was the Jungle Falls ride. Someone got killed on it."

"Today?"

A trio of barks sounded before Max leapt into action, running to meet them. When he was about three feet away, he jumped and sailed through the air, knocking her down. After everything that had happened so far, she could handle being knocked flat by her pooch. Nala wrapped her fingers in Max's thick fur and rested her face in his ruff. Thank goodness he was okay. There was one thing she had to know. She pulled back from the enthusiastic licks and asked, "The phone call?"

"Hey, come on. I'm Spy Dog. I'm not giving up my secrets." He managed a wide, doggy grin. "You should have seen those men barreling into the office. I barely got off the phone in time to hide under the receptionist's desk. They ran out in the hall yelling *which way did he go*? I crawled out in time to witness law enforcement cornering them. I picked that moment to leave."

She ruffled his fur. "I'm glad you're okay." As for how he used the phone, Max wasn't known for keeping secrets, for exceedingly long, that is. She'd find out later.

Not too far behind her dog, Tyler dashed over. Upon arriving, he held his hand to help her up and inquired in a breathless gasp. "Are you all right?" A slight chuckle sounded. "Especially after Max's greeting."

Nala blinked twice, then shook her head as if to clear it of the image. There was no reason for him to be here and yet he was. Nala pushed up into a seated position, and then stood with Tyler's help. "I think so." Eventually, she'd be sore, but right then she was numb and stunned. "What are you doing here?"

"I drove down when I learned of the possibility of you stumbling across a major drug ring. I was already here when you sent the photo and information about the drugs."

He hadn't told her he was there. Maybe he chose not to because it would be too much like her father, who felt the need to assist even when not asked. Not sure how she felt about it, she was glad when they were interrupted.

Nala focused on the passing cars. A Kentucky State Trooper was followed by an Indiana Trooper and a plain sedan with ATF stenciled above a shield. A Kentucky cop car had Goon One and Two in the back seat. They glared at Nala. One said something she couldn't hear. Just as well. She probably wouldn't like it.

The last cop car featured a glum looking Eb and an oddly serene Ramon. Well, that answered the question if the two had been arrested. Several people who had been watching left once the excitement died down.

"I'm ready to go!" Karly called out, reminding them of her presence. She chafed her arms over her wet polo and shivered. "What time is it anyhow?"

Tyler pulled out his phone and answered, "Close to seven."

"I'd swear we were in those underground passageways forever."

"Wait, what underground passageway?"

Everything had happened so fast that Nala hadn't even taken time to reflect. All they could do was react and keep moving. "Once our kidnappers left the office to investigate who was calling, we started opening all the doors to find an exit."

"You were kidnapped!" Tyler's eyes grew hard and his posture rigid.

Nala nudged him. "Uh, we escaped and went down this underground stairway that went down, down into the ground. There were landings with doors, which we didn't open. We couldn't be sure if there weren't thugs behind them. Finally, we came to a long flat place and another set of stairs that started up. Those stairs led out to a small parking lot hidden by trees. We flattened some tires, hopped over the fence, and here we are."

Karly shuffled from one foot to another. "Umm, guys, I'm freezing here. Could you give me the keys, and I'll start the car?"

"Of course." Guilt enveloped Nala as she patted down her pockets in search of her keys. "I'm so sorry for everything." She located her keys and handed them over.

Karly wrapped her in a damp embrace and whispered into her ear, "This is the most excitement I've had in a long time. Maybe ever. Besides, I'm giving you two some personal time." She dropped her arms and dashed off to the car.

Nala watched her climb into the car, and the reality of everything that had happened came crashing down, causing her to tremble. A wave of warmth settled on her shoulders as Tyler wrapped his windbreaker around her. "You might be going into shock."

He wrapped his arm around her waist and guided her toward the sedan. Shock sounded reasonable, considering the circumstance. It would be nice to dissolve into a puddle of emotions or curl up under a cozy blanket. A deep breath stiffened her backbone that had been on its way to melting only seconds before.

"I don't have time for shock. I have to find Chris." The words gave her a faint boost of energy. She had a mission. Once she was done, then she could rest, but only then.

"I know, sweetie." He pulled her close to his side. "I'll help you find Chris."

If it were only that easy.

"Not sure how. I've spent most of the week looking for him. Still, I have an idea where he is. All I need to do is change clothes and get started." She blew out a breath. "I almost forgot I need to buy cheeseburgers for Hero Dog. I assume you brought your car?"

"You bet."

"All right, you can drive me back, and Karly can drive my car with Max. Let me tell her."

She stepped out of Tyler's half-embrace, immediately feeling chilled. The window powered down and her friend asked, "What's up?"

"Can you find your way back on your own?"

"The car has GPS."

"You're right." Max bumped against her, reminding her to open the back door. "Hope you don't mind being a dog chauffer?"

"Never. It's pretty much my day job."

Nala knelt and gave Max a hug. "You really are Hero Dog. The Frost Empress would be very impressed. I'll make sure to tell her when I see her. Go ahead and go with Karly. We'll bring dinner home. Cheeseburgers for everyone."

Once the door was closed, Nala waved and stepped back to where Tyler was typing in numbers into his cell. A connection was made, and Tyler spoke. "Guess what? My girlfriend figured out how the drugs were being brought into the park."

Girlfriend? Nala's eyebrows went up. It was always a bit of a question as to whether they had a relationship. He *did* rush down here to see if she was okay, which was a huge plus. Maybe they did have a relationship, and he *was* her boyfriend. Her parents would be so pleased. The idea made her chuckle.

Tyler shot her a curious gaze as he listened to whatever was being said at the other end of the phone, then responded. "Yes, secret passage. Come by and I'll show it to you. Better get what you can today because I bet there won't be anything left tomorrow. The cockroaches will all show up and pick the place clean. Right now, they're hiding in the dark, waiting for us to leave."

This sounded like it would delay the trip to the cabin. Her stomach chose that moment to growl, reminding her of its depleted state.

"You want to get in my car. I can turn on the heat, which might help you dry out."

"Sounds good." It sounded more than good. With any luck he might have something to eat, too. They walked over to one of the few remaining cars in the lot. Tyler opened and closed her door before sliding into the car himself. The engine purred to life as he turned the ignition key. He fiddled with the dashboard, turning on the heat and tuning the radio to a soft rock station. Once done, he reached for Nala's hand.

"You can go ahead and be mad at me. I know you don't like my interfering in your cases. Just know, I came because I cared. Dylan, my friend, explained he was close to nailing a major drug lord. This guy has escaped justice many times. Even when he was convicted decades ago, his men broke him out before he was sentenced. I didn't know for sure if Diablo, as he likes to call himself, was even in this area. I wanted to tell you to come home. I didn't because I knew your business was your business. Even though I couldn't help Dylan, I decided to come down anyway. I even joked that you'd flush Diablo out if he was here. I had no clue how right I was."

If she were part of the cheesy holiday movies Karly enjoyed so much, the viewers would go *ahh*. She squeezed his hand and ran the other through her hair. "I probably look horrible."

"You look beautiful to me."

She chuckled. "That's what men say when you look bad when there's nothing you can do about it."

They both leaned forward and kissed, forgetting about everything except the moment until someone hammered on the window. They jumped apart, and she gasped. The last person she expected to see was staring in at them, Mr. Intense, the man who dogged her steps through the park.

"It's him! The creepy guy that kept following me."

Tyler powered down his window to address the man. "Dylan, did you hear? You're a super creepy stalker?"

"I've been called worse." He grinned in Nala's direction. "Sorry to have spooked you, but you've done the county a huge favor. I'd been working with Keith to try to get information, but you knocked it out of the park in a day. Let's go see that secret passageway."

"Okay." She tried for a perky attitude when all she wanted to do was step into a hot shower. "I prefer to be driven to the fence."

By the time they arrived at the fence, the DFA agents had arrived. Tyler boosted her over the fence, and they tramped through the grass, trees, and finally by the cars with the flat tires.

Dylan nodded at the cars. "Whose cars are these?"

"My guess is Eb and *Diablo,* only Eb called him Ramon," Nala stated and moved toward the door they'd exited from. Someone who didn't know could have mistaken the arched door for a portable toilet in the middle of nowhere. Before she could put her hand on the door, Dylan shot forward wearing latex gloves and carefully attempted to move the handle. It wouldn't move. Locked.

"Here, let me help." Nala pulled the stiletto from her pocket, inserted it into the door, and turned the lock. Everyone was staring at her or possibly the knife. "What is it? What's wrong?"

One of the agents pointed to the knife. "Is that Diablo's famous dagger? The one he used to kill anyone who crossed him?"

The knife clatter to the ground from her nerveless fingers. "I hope not. He was using it to clean his fingernails. I picked it up when we left. Feel free to take it. I never want to touch it again. Do I have to stay while you go through the staircase? It was lit when Karly and I used it."

Dylan raised his eyebrows and addressed Tyler. "You need to indulge this woman. She and her team have uncovered evidence we've been looking into for the last six months."

"To think I never even made it to Disco World," she joked. "I'm more than ready to leave."

"At your service." Tyler crooked his arm and led her to the fence, where he boosted her over. On the way to the car, Tyler asked, "Explain to me how you escaped again."

It was a little hard without explaining that Max could converse just as well as any of them. "They got a phone call that upset them, and they rushed downstairs. Eb was the last to leave, and I'm certain he wanted us to escape."

Tyler remained silent for a bit, then shook his head. "Who was it?

"No idea," she lied. No way was she going to claim it had been Max and then try to explain how he did it. "Whoever it was, I'm glad they called."

"Me, too." Tyler helped her into the car.

SOMEWHERE ALONG THE way, she fell asleep between leaving Kentucky and entering Indiana. The car stopping woke her. "Are we here already?"

"Yes." Tyler gave her hand a squeeze. "I even went through the drive-thru to get Max's cheeseburgers, and you were snoring away."

The thought of her having her mouth wide open snoring disturbed her. "Hey, I had a hard day."

"You weren't snoring. I was just teasing. You hold the cheeseburgers, and I'll get the door."

Nala clutched the warm, aromatic bag as Tyler hustled around the car. He'd driven right to the campground. The fact he knew the right cabin did make her wonder. She'd have to ask him about it, but for now, she wanted to eat, shower, and find Santa, hopefully in that order.

The strings of Christmas lights all over the campground were glowing. They might help her find the way on the hunt. Now, if only Max were willing, which he might be if she provided the desired cheeseburgers first. She could hear music or maybe it was television coming from her cabin. Karly's voice carried.

"Then the phone rang, and they picked it up. We knew it was Max." It sounded like she was on the cell.

Then a male voice boomed, "Ho, ho, ho!"

It couldn't be! She flew up the steps and into the cabin, still clutching the burger bag. Sitting by the decorated tree was a bearded man in a reindeer T-shirt and jeans, holding Dasher.

"Chris! Where have you been?"

"Hiding, of course. I was waiting for you to get back so I could tell you all at the same time. First, thank you for rooting out Diablo. It wasn't enough he ruined my date. I heard my house was trashed, too. Have a seat and I'll start my tale."

Tyler came in last and shut the door. He cut his eyes to Nala, who nodded her head to his unspoken question that it was indeed the man she had come down to find.

"Diablo is almost as old as me. However, I may be a bit older.

Back when I was young and stupid and living on the West Coast, I got involved in his organization. Only, I didn't know it at the time. The man has hundreds of legitimate businesses to launder his money. Even then, he was a big deal. I had a dry-cleaning business but had some extra space I rented out for storage. My mistake was I wanted to know what was being stored. One day I picked the lock but got scared and went to the police. It didn't end there."

He patted Dasher as his eyes took a faraway look. "The police were planning on trapping Diablo using my storage facility as bait. I called and told him the place was on fire, which involved burning part of my own store. It worked. They caught him, and then I was asked to testify, which I was not happy about. Since I was already in Diablo's crosshairs, I figured I'd do my best to put him away. Despite my best efforts, he escaped."

It was hard to believe the man had hidden in plain sight for so many years. "You were always out in public view. Weren't you worried?"

"A little. The witness protection staged my funeral. Back then, I was fit with dark hair and a dapper dresser. I put on weight, intentionally, changed my name, and my hair color. Even changed my accent. I was originally placed in New Jersey just because it was dense with people. That's helpful when you want to vanish. However, I started thinking about hiding in plain sight. Even though that chance interaction with a drug lord and later testifying was a major part of my life, I relaxed my guard once I moved to Santa Claus. I started by filling in for the regular Santa occasionally. I hadn't heard about Diablo, thought it was safe, and took the job permanently. Kept quiet about my history, hinting I might be the actual jolly old elf."

"Clever move." Nala applauded his boldness. "Did the Witness Protection Agency call you to let you know Ramon—Diablo—was in town?"

"No. It certainly would have been a help. I was out on a dinner date with a lady I'd met online." He shook his head and a wistful smile appeared. "Pretending to be Santa doesn't attract the ladies. Add to that I have no real back history or family except for my fabricated one. Tends to make females suspicious."

His eyes rolled up as if remembering something. "Close as I came to an almost romance was Estelle." Chris sighed heavily.

An awkward silence stretched throughout the cabin, which Karly pierced with her question. "What happened at the restaurant?"

Chris managed a chuckle and shook his head slowly before answering. "We were at the Chalet having a nice dinner, getting on just fine, when Diablo walked in. My first thought was he'd found me despite the fact I look nothing like I used to, especially with the added years, but I knew who he was. I would have sworn he didn't notice me or at least didn't recognize me despite I knew him immediately. His hair was grayer, but his carriage and voice were the same."

Since Nala had battled her own fears recently, she could imagine his, which had to be honed over the years, constantly worrying about being found. "What did you do?"

"It was the hardest twenty minutes of my life. If I'd bolted out immediately, that would have attracted attention. I finished my meal with Estelle although I'm sure I wasn't much of a conversationalist. We'd arrived in separate cars since it was a first date. I told her how much I enjoyed meeting her, and then left, regretting that I had such an unusual truck. I didn't think he recognized me, but I wasn't taking a chance and he must have at least thought I looked familiar in some way. As soon as I made it home, I staged the house to look like a break-in and took off. Even lit a match for the sulfur smell. It was the agreed upon signal for Bob if I vanished. Because of Diablo, I always had an exit plan in place. Didn't leave a note or anything. My escape went awry when Dasher took off, but I knew Bob would find him and care for him."

Nala prided herself on her investigative skills, but she hadn't found Chris. "Can you tell me where you went?"

"Could but I won't. I may need it in the future." He winked, then laughed. "Ho, ho, ho!"

Yeah, everyone likes a merry old elf except when he wouldn't confirm her suspicion that Chris had been hiding in the RV that had been parked in the square dance parking lot where Max picked up the scent of Dasher. No doubt Bob had been driving the RV around, making it hard to get a firm location on the man.

Tyler, who had been leaning against the door, pushed off and gestured to the bag of cooling food. "You might want to warm those up."

Max, who had been sitting next to Chris, padded over to her and nudged the bag she still held. "Oh yeah, we have cheeseburgers. They might be a little cold, but Max takes his at room temperature anyway."

She pulled a wrapped burger from the bag and passed it to Karly. She took the bag and sauntered off to the kitchen. Guilt settled on Nala's shoulders as she watched her friend putter in the kitchen. Might as well help. She pushed up into a standing position and joined her in the kitchen.

Tyler took her seat and was chatting with Chris in a low voice, possibly asking penetrating questions that would lead to more details about the drug ring. Maybe she should be asking those questions. Nope. Her job was to find Chris, which she did, in a way.

Karly nuked the burgers and portioned them out on plates. Nala put the plates on the counter and pulled condiments out of the fridge. Thank goodness Selma thought of everything. The couple had provided food and lodgings, but it made her wonder if they ever intended to pay her. When everything was said and done, would they shrug their shoulders and say *oops*. On the plus side, Chris was here, and Christmas Land weekends would go on as planned.

Nala played waitress and carried out two plates to Chris and Tyler along with a bottle of ketchup. When she returned to the kitchen, she continued her conversation. "Chris is here. That's a plus."

Karly pointed to a long white envelope. "So is your payment from Chris. He said something about you needed to be paid for your hard work. At least he came through. I had my doubts about Selma."

"Woo-hoo!" She picked up the envelope and peeked inside. "Santa did come early."

There were so many unanswered questions. "If Chris wasn't threatened or harassed, who was trying to get me to leave?"

Karly passed her another plate holding a couple of warmed burgers and fries. "Keith, on Eb's instructions. Eb hadn't wanted to get involved in drug distribution, but he'd accepted the loan for his business without realizing what was involved and couldn't get out of it. He thought you were here to investigate Vacation Land as opposed to photographing the locals. Keith was supposed to make you leave but not be too nasty about it."

It did fit. Nala bit into the warm burger, enjoying the saltiness of the cheese and the charbroiled beef. "Depends on how you judge not too nasty. I've had worse. Not sure how he got my cell number?"

"Your website? Business card? They both have your number on it." Karly pointed out with a smug expression.

"Maybe. Still, how did he know my name? Better yet, how do you know all this?"

"Ah," Karly stalled and reached to stick a tendril of hair behind her ear. "When Keith and I were an item I talked about you a great deal. We may have talked a few times after I left and I mentioned Max, too. He probably put two and two together. Oh, he called me from the station. Keith called me." Her gaze dropped. "He just wanted me to know he never wanted us to get hurt. He used his one phone call to call me." Karly placed her hands over her heart.

"I doubt he was actually arrested. It was all for show so no one in Diablo's group would put together who was feeding the Feds information. If they knew, there'd be a price on his head. Only one cheeseburger remained on her plate. Max must have radar because he padded into the kitchen and leaned against her. "I'm *so* hungry."

"Yeah, I bet you are." She tore the burger into small pieces, popping one in her mouth and throwing another to Max, who snapped it out of the air. "I imagine you had a long talk with Dasher about the private room and the cameras and microphones in the statues."

"Yep." Max agreed, and then caught another thrown morsel.

Just like him to leave her hanging. "Come on, tell me what he said."

"There you go, trying to trick me. You're not going to make me blather secret information. I'll hold it safe until I meet the Frost Empress."

The dog never forgot. She hadn't said Movie Dog would be at the park. She only implied it. Maybe she'd have to live without knowing where Santa had hidden out or how Max had dialed the phone. Santa certainly wasn't talking any more than Max. Still, has an investigator, she'd find out in the end.

THE END

Selma's Famous Ice Box Cake

SERVES: 8-10
PREP TIME: 30 minutes

INGREDIENTS
3 1/2 cups heavy cream
1/2 cup powdered sugar
2 teaspoons vanilla extract
1/4 teaspoon salt
2 pounds fresh fruit, peeled and sliced (about 4 cups)
25 to 30 graham crackers (from about 4 sleeves) regular or chocolate
2/3 cup chopped nuts or additional fruit, for garnish

EQUIPMENT
Stand mixer, hand mixer, or large whisk
Spatula
9x13-inch baking dish
Plastic wrap

INSTRUCTIONS
Beat the cream until it holds stiff peaks. Place the cream, powdered sugar, vanilla, and salt in the bowl of a stand mixer fitted with the whisk attachment. (Alternatively, use a large bowl and electric hand mixer or whisk.) Beat on low speed, then high speed, until the cream holds stiff peaks.

Divide the cream into 4 parts. Use a spatula to evenly divide the cream into 4 quadrants.

Smear a spoonful of cream in the bottom of the baking dish. Smear just a small spoonful of the cream evenly in a 9x13-inch baking dish. This will hold your first layer of graham crackers in place.

Cover the bottom with graham crackers. Place a layer of graham crackers in the dish, breaking them as needed to fit into a single tight, even layer.

Spread whipped cream on top of the crackers. Gently spread 1/4 of the cream (one whole quadrant) evenly on the crackers.

Spread 1/3 of the fruit on the cream. Place 1/3 of the fruit (about 1 1/3 cups) evenly on top of the cream.

Top with a second layer of crackers. Cover the fruit with a second full layer of crackers.

Top with cream and fruit. Top this second layer of crackers with another 1/4 of the cream and another 1/3 (1 1/3 cups) of the fruit.

Top with a third layer of crackers. Cover the fruit with a third full layer of crackers.

Top with cream and fruit. Top with another 1/4 of the cream and the remaining fruit. At this point you'll have 3 layers of graham crackers, 3 layers of cream, and 3 layers of fruit.

Top with a final layer of crackers and cream. Add a fourth layer of crackers and the remaining cream. Spread gently into an even layer or swirl a decorative pattern into the cream.

Garnish the cake. Sprinkle the chopped nuts or fruit on top of the cake.

Cover with plastic wrap and refrigerate. Cover loosely with plastic wrap. Refrigerate at least 2 hours or overnight. The cake is ready when a knife inserted in the center goes in easily and comes out with soft crumbs. Refrigerate any leftovers.

RECIPE NOTES
Storage: Icebox cake is best eaten within 2 days. It does get soggy after more than two or three days in the fridge, especially if very juicy fruit is used.

Fruit choices: Any kind of soft, juicy fruit is very good. Try thinly-sliced banana and strawberries, or kiwi, mango, chopped raspberries and blueberries, or peaches.

Selma likes to use recipes from www.thekitchn.com.

Easy Lasagna

Serves 8 to 10
PREP TIME: 20 minutes to 25 minutes
COOK TIME: 1 hour 10 minutes to 1 hour 30 minutes

INGREDIENTS

1 medium yellow onion

1 tablespoon olive oil

1-pound lean ground beef or bison

1/2 teaspoon kosher salt

1/4 teaspoon freshly ground black pepper

1 (24 to 25-ounce) jar marinara sauce (3 cups), such as Rao's or
    Newman's Own

12 ounces low-moisture mozzarella cheese, shredded (about 3 cups),
    divided

15 dry lasagna noodles (not no-boil, about 2/3 of a 1-pound box),
    divided

15 to 16 ounces whole-milk ricotta cheese (about 2 cups), divided

EQUIPMENT

Chef's knife

Box grater

Cutting board

Measuring cups and spoons

12-inch or larger regular or cast-iron skillet

Wooden spoon

9x13-inch baking dish

Aluminum foil

INSTRUCTIONS

1. **Heat the oven to 400ºF.** Arrange a rack in the middle of the
   oven and heat the oven to 400°F.

2. **Brown the beef and onion.** Finely chop 1 medium yellow onion.
   Heat 1 tablespoon olive oil in a 12-inch or larger regular or cast-

iron skillet over medium-high heat until shimmering. Add the onion, 1-pound lean ground beef, 1/2 teaspoon kosher salt, and 1/4 teaspoon freshly ground black pepper, and cook, breaking the beef up into small pieces with a wooden spoon, until the beef is cooked through, 6 to 8 minutes. Remove from the heat and let cool for 5 minutes.

3. **Prepare the baking dish and assemble the meat sauce.** Open 1 (24 to 25-ounce) jar marinara sauce (3 cups). Spread a thin layer of the sauce in the bottom of a 9x13-inch baking dish. Stir the remaining sauce into the ground beef mixture.

4. **Begin layering the lasagna.** Shred 12 ounces low-moisture mozzarella cheese if needed (3 cups). Place 5 lasagna noodles in the baking dish, breaking them if needed to create a single layer (it's OK if the noodles overlap slightly). Dollop and spread 1 cup of the ricotta cheese over the noodles. Dollop and spread about 1 1/2 cups of the meat sauce on the ricotta, then sprinkle with 1 cup of the mozzarella.

5. **Continue layering the lasagna.** Arrange 5 more noodles over the mozzarella, followed by 1 cup of the ricotta cheese, 1 1/2 cups of the meat sauce, and 1 cup of the mozzarella. Top with a final layer of 5 noodles and the remaining sauce, spreading the sauce thin so that it almost completely covers the noodles. (Reserve the remaining 1 cup mozzarella for the end of baking.) Cover the dish tightly with aluminum foil.

6. **Bake the lasagna for 1 hour.** Bake for 1 hour. Check to make sure the noodles are done by poking the lasagna with a knife; the knife should slide easily through all the layers. If it doesn't, cover and cook for 15 minutes more.

7. **Sprinkle with the remaining mozzarella and finish baking.** Uncover the lasagna and sprinkle with the remaining 1 cup mozzarella. Bake uncovered until the mozzarella is melted and lightly browned, and the sauce is bubbling, 8 to 10 minutes more.

8. **Cool the lasagna for 15 minutes.** Let the lasagna cool on a wire rack for at least 15 minutes before serving.

RECIPE NOTES

Make ahead: The lasagna can be assembled and refrigerated up to 2 days in advance, or frozen for up to 1 month. Thaw the frozen lasagna for 2 days in the refrigerator before baking.

Storage: Leftovers can be stored, tightly wrapped, in the refrigerator for up to 3 days.

Selma likes to use recipes from www.thekitchn.com.

The Late for Love

A Way over The Hill Cozy Mystery
December 2020

THE LATE MORNING sun illuminated the folks below, bringing with it a touch of heat. Indian Summer was the common name for the hot weather that stretched into Autumn. For the residents of Greener Pastures Convalescent and Retirement Center, it was a bonus. Too often, they were trapped inside with the mingled scents of antiseptic cleaner and the lingering aroma of whatever was burnt in the kitchen that day. A gathering of five residents took advantage of the warm weather.

Being bored, the senior sleuths had gathered in the courtyard for a little croquet. Marcy suggested they should take advantage of their leisure time before she made her exit from the facility, taking with her any possibilities of solving more cold cases. A mockingbird perched on the edge of a gutter broke into full-throated song, breaking Jake's concentration as he glared at the painted ball on the patchy grass.

Who invented this game anyhow? What was so great about hitting a wooden ball through wire hoops? He might be old and living in a senior home, but he was still a veteran pilot, which should count for more than a cracked leather jacket and a handful of memories.

His former war buddies, Herman, and Gus, lived at the center along with their sweeties, Lola, and Eunice. Herman and Lola had tied the knot in Vegas *and* North Carolina recently, which in itself was a story. The thought made Jake sigh.

"Come on." Eunice brandished her mallet as if she might use it to encourage Jake. "Quit stalling. None of us want to waste what time we got left watching you trying to remember how to hit a ball."

He glared at Eunice, who smirked back. Even the sharp-tongued harpy had found love, while he had not. What did that say about him? The wooden mallet made a solid thud as it connected with the ball, sending it rolling only to bounce off the wire hoop. Dagnabbit!

Before Eunice could remark on his poor shot, the glass doors leading to the residence wing opened with a distinctive groan. Marcy and Lance, her former partner, stood framed in the opening for a second before exiting. Despite the surgery on her shattered leg and her time spent recovering, Marcy still leaned on Lance. It probably had more to do with affection than her ability to walk.

The senior sleuths didn't need to use their deductive skills to notice the budding romance between the two former partners. It was hard to believe you could work side by side with someone for years and never notice the attraction or possibly never act on it. Although, he wasn't one to talk with one failed marriage and no serious relationships after that. On the good side, their appearance detracted from the tedium of the game.

"Good morning!" Marcy trilled with a cheery smile. The dark-haired detective could be counted on to bring out the best in folks. She took a seat on a nearby bench and glanced around, possibly checking if there might be an extra resident who hadn't been a part of the senior sleuths' organization that might be eavesdropping.

While residing at Greener Pastures, Lance had brought her cold cases to keep her mind active and obviously to visit. Since some of the cases were so old, she came up with the idea of enlisting help from a few select residents who could remember places as they were and old street names, plus knew all the associated rumors.

Solving the cases had been the highlight of his current existence. Jake might even put it up against being an air force pilot because as a pilot, he never saw the direct results of his work and could only speculate if he'd done any good. As a senior sleuth, he could take pride in helping round up criminals who had gone scot-free for so many years.

Everyone abandoned their mallets to crowd around Marcy.

"How you two been?" Gus asked in an overloud voice. Having worked in explosive ordinance, his hearing wasn't the best. It didn't help that he also refused to wear a hearing aid. He said it was something old people wore.

Lance grinned, but Marcy answered as she slipped off the straps of a backpack and pulled it onto her lap. "It's been okay. Getting to know my house again. I'm back at work, but they have me riding a desk."

Even before she left, Marcy made her feelings known about being tied to the desk. All the sleuths managed a sympathetic word or two. Lola, the former showgirl with her elaborate coiffure and acrylic nails, used her walker to ease closer and sit down on the bench. She patted Marcy's hand. "Tough break. At least you have a job. I know you were worried about being forced into early retirement."

"True enough." Marcy forced a laugh, withdrew her hand from under Lola's, and placed it on the backpack in her lap. "I'm not here to whine. Frankly, I miss you guys. It seems like it has been forever since we worked on our last case, as opposed to only being a month."

Herman, a tall, portly man, nodded his silvery head in agreement. "Feels even longer to me. Have you solved any more cold cases on your own?"

A throat clearing drew their notice to Lance. Even though the detective was a few years younger than Marcy's fifty, most people would never guess it with his thinning hair and pot belly. Still, his grin retained a touch of boyishness. "Leave it to you to cut to the chase."

His eyes landed on Herman, then went on to make eye contact with all the sleuths. "I think you might be interested in what Marcy has to say."

This sounded promising. "I'm listening," Jake said, not making the mistake to answer for the others. He'd learn on previous occasions the error of assuming too much.

"Me too!" Herman echoed. Lola and Eunice also agreed, while Gus held a hand up to his ear and asked, "What?" with an impish look. Eunice just elbowed him and didn't bother repeating the question. It was always hard to tell if he hadn't heard or was just jerking their chains.

Instead of replying, Marcy unzipped her backpack with a metallic zing, filling the silence that stretched between them. She removed some manilla folders with typewritten labels and numbers. Jake's shoulders went back and his chin went up as he recognized the cold case files. His day just got better. It made him feel like he should salute and report for a mission.

The files made a shushing sound as Marcy shuffled the files

casually as a person would a deck of cards. "You'd be surprised at the dozens of cold cases we have. At first, I thought Lance was bringing me files to solve because he felt sorry for me."

"Nope." Lance grimaced. "The budget is limited and there are no new hires in sight. Besides, anyone who gets hired will start out on active cases. There's no *manpower*," he cleared his throat when Marcy arched her eyebrows at the last word. "I mean *people power* to deal with the cold cases. We do what we can, but usually move from one active case to the next."

"That's why we're here." Marcy spread out the folders and used them as a fan. "Sure, I missed you guys, but I could use a little help, too. Anyone interested?"

There was a chorus of *yeses* with Herman raising his hand as if still in the classroom. Eunice, even though she was the shortest, worked her way in front of Marcy and plucked a folder at random. "I'll take this one."

Even though they were used to the woman's bossy ways, no one took it lying down. Lola snatched the plump folder from Eunice and opened it. She blinked a couple of times to bring it into focus without any luck, then retrieved her readers that hung on a chain around her neck. "Let's see what we have here before you go volunteering us for a case that is older than we are."

The pages whispered as they were turned, as if sharing their contents. Every now and then, Lola would murmur something inaudible to herself. Her legs were crossed and one foot would vary in its rate of swinging. Whatever it was had to be good. Jake could barely stand it. "Out with it. What is it? A bludgeoned body? A jewelry heist?"

Lola closed the folder and waited. As a former showgirl, she knew how to pick a moment. Satisfied that she was the focus, she tapped the folder with a fuchsia-colored nail. "We have a real live mystery. It was in the papers not so long ago." She flipped the folder open, consulting the file, then addressed the group. "Two years to be exact. A young investigative journalist had the goods on some big rollers. She was supposed to be a prime witness, then she went missing. Not only that, the evidence vanished with her." She gave the file another tap. "Makes me wonder why they gave up so easy with this one."

Lance made a lunge for the folder. "I don't think that would be a good one for you guys. It might be too dangerous."

Instead of handing it over, Lola pulled the folder close to her ample chest.

A loud harrumph came from Gus proving his hearing might be better than most assumed. "Remember when I got trapped by that drug lord? What about when that house was almost demolished with us in it? You think it's worse than that?"

"I don't know," Lance admitted with his shoulders slumping a little. "I just don't want you to get hurt."

"No worries," Jake said, to reassure the well-meaning detective. "I figure all of us must be doing something right since we made it this far. Besides, if we encounter any trouble, even a whiff of danger, we'll call you right away."

Lance sniffed, shot Jake a doubtful look, then nodded. "I guess that could work. Feel free to call us and we'll come by after work to check your progress." He checked his watch. "We have ten more minutes before we need to go."

Wrought iron chairs and a few benches sat in random spots in the courtyard. At one time, there might have been some organization to it, but various residents rearranging them made the area look like an abandoned jacks game played with outdoor furniture. Eunice walked over to a bench and started pulling it closer to Marcy. "Let's circle around and find out more about our newest case."

Even though it galled Jake to take any direction from Eunice, he did because he wanted to find out about the case, too.